P9-CCY-603

THE
TOURNAMENT

Also by Matthew Reilly

THE GREAT ZOO OF CHINA
CONTEST
TEMPLE

The Jack West, Jr. Series
SEVEN DEADLY WONDERS
THE SIX SACRED STONES
THE FIVE GREATEST WARRIORS

The Scarecrow Series
ICE STATION
AREA 7
SCARECROW
HELL ISLAND
SCARECROW RETURNS

Hover Car Racer
CRASH COURSE
FULL THROTTLE
PHOTO FINISH

THE
TOURNAMENT

MATTHEW REILLY

Lakewood Memorial Library
2 Summit Street

Lakewood, NY 14750

G

GALLERY BOOKS
New York   London   Toronto   Sydney   New Delhi

G

Gallery Books
An Imprint of Simon & Schuster, Inc.
1230 Avenue of the Americas
New York, NY 10020

This book is a work of fiction. Any references to historical events, real people,
or real places are used fictitiously. Other names, characters, places, and events are products
of the author's imagination, and any resemblance to actual events or places or persons,
living or dead, is entirely coincidental.

Copyright © 2013 by Karanadon Entertainment Pty. Ltd.

Map illustrations by David Atkinson, Hand Made Maps Ltd.
Internal photograph of the Hagia Sophia by Juanjo González

First published in 2013 in Australia by Pan Macmillan Australia Pty. Ltd.

All rights reserved, including the right to reproduce this book
or portions thereof in any form whatsoever. For information, address
Gallery Books Subsidiary Rights Department,
1230 Avenue of the Americas, New York, NY 10020.

First Gallery Books hardcover edition July 2015

GALLERY BOOKS and colophon are registered trademarks of Simon & Schuster, Inc.

For information about special discounts for bulk purchases, please contact
Simon & Schuster Special Sales at 1-866-506-1949 or business@simonandschuster.com.

The Simon & Schuster Speakers Bureau can bring authors to your live event. For more
information or to book an event, contact the Simon & Schuster Speakers Bureau at
1-866-248-3049 or visit our website at www.simonspeakers.com.

Interior design by Julie Schroeder

Manufactured in the United States of America

10   9   8   7   6   5   4   3   2   1

Library of Congress Cataloging-in-Publication Data is available.

ISBN 978-1-4767-4954-9
ISBN 978-1-4767-4959-4 (ebook)

3201300285799

This book is dedicated to
Cate Paterson, Jane Novak and Tracey Cheetham

AUTHOR'S NOTE

The following is a work of fiction. While it contains characters and organizations that existed, their actions are the product of the author's imagination.

This novel also contains subject matter of an adult nature. The author recommends that it be read by mature readers.

It has long been accepted that the first international chess tournament was the event staged in London in 1851 and won by Adolf Anderssen of Germany. Sixteen men from all over Europe competed to determine the best player in the world. (Prior to that occasion, individual players would play in celebrated one-off matches.)

But a rumor persists in the chess world of a tournament that was held long before the London one, an event that took place in the sixteenth century in the ancient city of Constantinople, now Istanbul.

Sadly, no records of this event remain, and until some kind of documentary proof of its staging arises, it is destined to remain the stuff of legend.

From: *A History of Chess*,
Boris Ivanov (Advantage Press, London, 1972)

—— 1603 ——

PROLOGUE
1603

MY QUEEN IS DEAD. MY FRIEND is dead. The world is not the same. It is darker now.

How she carried herself so well in this chaotic world, I shall never know. In a life lived in a maelstrom of courtiers, bishops and commanders, she always got her way. This she achieved oftentimes through charm, many times through shrewdness, and on rare occasions through the more direct method of executing those who opposed her.

She always knew when people were watching. I have no doubt that when she sent some poor wretch to the Tower, it was as much for the spectacle of it as it was for the crime. Sometimes rulers must set grim examples.

It has been said by many that her extraordinary nimbleness of mind was the result of her education at the hands of the great schoolmaster Roger Ascham. Having personally witnessed some of that education, I can attest that her schooling was of the highest order.

As the child of one of her household's staff and being of a similar age, I was the young princess's principal playmate. Later in life, I would assume the role of chief attendant to her bedchamber, but as a girl, by sheer virtue of proximity, I was allowed to partake in her lessons and thus received a level of instruction that I otherwise would never have known.

By the time Elizabeth was seven, she was fluent in French, capable at Spanish and could speak and read Latin and Greek. When William Grindal—supervised by the great Ascham—took over her education in 1544, she had added Italian and German to that list. While Grindal managed her day-to-day lessons, it was Ascham who always loomed in the background, the grand architect of her overall schooling. He stepped in when major subjects were taught: languages, mathematics, and history, both ancient and recent. A vocal advocate of the benefits of regular outdoor activity, he even taught her archery in the grounds of Hatfield.

He also, it must be said, taught the young Princess Elizabeth chess.

I can still see her as a thirteen-year-old, bent over the board, the wild curls of her carrot-colored hair framing an elfin freckled face, her eyes fixed in a deadly stare at the pieces, trying to deduce the best available move, while across from her, Ascham, utterly careless of the state of the game, watched her think.

As a child Bess lost more games than she won and some in the royal house at Hatfield thought it scandalous that Ascham should continually beat the daughter of the king, often crushingly.

On more than one occasion Bess would fall into my arms in tears after a game. "Oh, Gwinny, Gwinny! He beat me again!"

"He is a cruel monster," I would say soothingly.

"He is, isn't he?" But then she would regather herself. "I shall beat him one day. I most certainly will." And, of course, eventually she did.

For his part, the great teacher made no apologies for his brutal manner of play, not even when Bess's governess wrote a letter to the king complaining about it.

When pressed by an emissary of the king about the matter, Ascham argued that unless one loses, one does not learn. His job, he said, was to ensure that the little princess learned. The king accepted this argument and the beatings at chess were allowed to continue. As an adult, Elizabeth would rarely lose at the game, and on the far more dangerous chessboard of her life—at court in London and on the high seas against the House of Castile—she never lost.

Chess, Ascham claimed, taught many important lessons: to flatter one's opponent, to lay traps and to see them laid, to be bold and to restrain one's tendency to boldness, to appear naive when in truth one is alert, to see the future many moves ahead and to discover that decisions *always* have consequences.

Ascham taught my young mistress well.

But now, to my great shock, I have just learned that Ascham's best lesson might have occurred not in our little schoolroom in Hertfordshire but far from England.

For last week, as her health faded and she lay confined to her bed, my mistress called me to her side and then ordered all the other attendants to leave the chamber.

"Gwinny," she said. "My dearest, dearest Gwinny. As the light dims and the end draws near, there is something I wish to tell you. It is a tale that I have kept to myself for nigh on sixty years."

"Yes, Your Majesty."

"Call me Bess, like you used to, when we were children."

"But, of course. Please go on . . . Bess . . ." I had not called her that for half a century.

Her eyes opened but they stared at nothing. "Many have wondered at the life I have led, Gwinny: a queen who never married or bore heirs; a woman with no military training who fended off Philip's armadas; a Protestant ruler who continually executed Ignatius of Loyola's Catholic missionaries and who on more than one occasion rebuffed proposals of marriage from the Russian tsar Ivan.

"How I came to be such a woman—sexless and aloof with men, wary of courtiers and ambassadors, ruthless when dealing with enemies—was the result of many things, but above all of them rises one experience, one singular experience from my youth, a journey that I took in absolute secrecy. It was an event that I have not dared tell anyone about for fear that they would think me a fabulist. It is this experience that I wish to impart to you now."

———

For the next two days, my queen spoke and I listened.

She recounted to me an event early in her life when, during the autumn of 1546 at a time when Hertfordshire was gripped by a sudden bout of plague, Roger Ascham took her away from Hatfield House for a period of three months.

I remembered the time vividly and for several reasons.

First, the plague of 1546 was a particularly vicious one. Escaping outbursts of the dreaded disease was common for royal children—removing a young heir from the locale of an illness was the best way to avoid a severing of the royal line—and that year many of the residents of Hertfordshire fled the district very promptly.

Second, it was a particularly dangerous time for Elizabeth. Although the passage of the Succession to the Crown Act of 1543 had seen her returned to the line of succession, in 1546, at the age of thirteen, she was still third in line behind her younger half brother, Edward, then nine, and her older half sister, Mary, then thirty. Yet Elizabeth's mere existence still posed a threat to both of their claims and she faced the very real possibility of being taken away in the dead of night and meeting a bloody end in the Tower—an end that could conveniently be blamed on the plague.

The third and last reason perhaps reflects more on me than on my mistress. I remember that particular time well because when she went away to the East, Elizabeth chose not to take me with her.

Instead she took another young member of our household, a spritely older girl named Elsie Fitzgerald who was, I admit, far prettier and more worldly than I was.

I wept for days after they left. And I spent that autumn miserably alone at the home of relatives in Sussex, safe from the plague but missing the company of my friend.

———

When my mistress finished her tale, I was speechless with horror and shock.

In the years following that missing autumn of 1546, she had always maintained that her trip away had been an uneventful one, just another excursion to the Continent with Ascham. Although they had ostensibly gone east to see some chess tournament, upon her return Elizabeth had never talked about chess or any such championship, and her friendship with Elsie was never the same again.

After hearing her account of that time, I now know why.

Her trip had not been uneventful at all.

Ascham had not just taken her far to the east—beyond the borders of Christendom, into the very heart of the lands of the Moslems, the great city of Constantinople—he had also exposed the future queen to many dreadful perils as they became privileged witnesses to the most remarkable event never recorded in history.

When she finished telling me her tale, my queen lay back on her pillow and closed her eyes. "Long have I wondered if I should tell anyone of those days, but now all of the other participants are dead and soon I will be, too. If it pleases you, Gwinny, write down my words, so that others might know how a queen like me is formed."

And so I make this my task, my final task on her behalf, to commit to writing her exact words and recount to you, dear reader, the marvelous things—the terrible things, the terrifying things—she beheld over the course of that secret journey in 1546.

1540

— I —

ROOK

In modern chess, the rooks are presented as castles anchoring the four corners of the board, but it was not always this way.

In fact, the name "rook" derives from *ruhk*, the Persian word for chariot. Pawns were foot soldiers, bishops were elephants, knights were mounted cavalry, and speeding along at the edges of the board were the swift and deadly chariots.

But as times changed and the game spread from Persia to Europe, chess pieces began to reflect the social hierarchy of medieval Western Europe. Thus the chariot became a castle. It was still a powerful piece, able to race down the board in a single move and control entire ranks, but the original reason for its fleetness of foot was lost.

Still, in its own way, the rook-as-castle remains an excellent example of chess pieces reflecting medieval society, for many a king of those times was judged by the strength and grandeur of the castles he kept.

From: *Chess in the Middle Ages,*
Tel Jackson (W. M. Lawry & Co., London, 1992)

I thank God that I am indeed endowed with such qualities
that if I were turned out of the realm in my petticoat,
I were able to live in any place in Christendom.

—QUEEN ELIZABETH I

ENGLAND, SEPTEMBER 1546

I WAS LIVING AT HATFIELD HOUSE in Hertfordshire when the invitation arrived at court in London. It was delivered to Hatfield a day later, accompanied by a typically curt message from my father to Mr. Ascham.

Truly, it was a wondrous thing.

It was printed on the most exquisite paper, a crisp card with gold on its edges. Written on it in shining gold ink (and in English) was the following:

HIS EXALTED MAJESTY
SULEIMAN THE MAGNIFICENT,
CALIPH OF THE SONS AND DAUGHTERS OF ALLAH,
SULTAN OF THE LANDS OF THE OTTOMANS,
LORD OF THE REALMS OF THE ROMANS, THE PERSIANS AND THE ARABS,
HERO OF ALL THAT IS, PRIDE OF THE GLORIFIED KAABA AND ILLUMINED MEDINA,
THE NOBLE JERUSALEM AND THE THRONE OF EGYPT,
LORD AND RULER OF ALL THAT HE SURVEYS,
BIDS YOU MOST WARM GREETING.

AS ESTEEMED KING OF ENGALAND,
YOU ARE INVITED TO SEND YOUR FINEST PLAYER
OF THE GAME KNOWN AS *SHATRANJ, LUDOS SCACORUM, ESCHECS, SCHACHSPIEL,*
SCACCHI, SZACHY OR CHESS, TO COMPETE IN A TOURNAMENT
TO DETERMINE THE CHAMPION OF THE KNOWN WORLD.

I snorted. "For a great sultan who is lord and ruler of all that he surveys, his English is lamentably poor. He can't even spell *England* properly."

Still holding the note, Mr. Ascham looked up at me. "Is that so? Tell me, Bess, do you speak his language? Any Arabic or Turkish-Arabic?"

"You know that I do not."

"Then however lamentable his English may be, he still speaks your language while you cannot speak his. To me, this gives him a considerable advantage over you. Always pause before you criticize, and never unduly criticize one who has made an effort at something you yourself have not even attempted."

I frowned at my teacher, but it was impossible to hate him even when he chastised me so. He had a way about him. In the way he carried himself, in the way he spoke, in the way he chastised me: gentle but firm.

Mr. Roger Ascham was thirty-one then, and in those days—long before he wrote *The Schoolmaster*, the work for which he became rightly famous after his death—he was already one of Cambridge's most celebrated instructors in classical Greek and Latin.

And yet, if I could have wished anything more for him, it would have been that he were more handsome. He was of average build and average height, and in a world of rich young colts with broad shoulders, hard features and the imperiousness of inherited wealth, this made him seem small, soft, harmless. He had a big round nose, hangdog brown eyes and oversize ears that he kept covered with a mop of thick brown hair. I once overheard someone say that at a society ball, not a single one of the young ladies accepted his polite invitations to dance. I cried for him when I heard that. If those silly ladies only knew what they were missing.

But while I shed tears for him over it, he didn't seem to mind. He was more interested in the art of learning and he pursued that passion with a ferocious intensity. In fact, he displayed a deep intensity of concentration in almost *everything* he did, whether it was practicing his beloved archery, debating matters of state, reading a book or teaching me. To learn, as far as Roger Ascham was concerned, was the noblest of all endeavors and it was an *active* one.

He was, quite simply, the most curious man I had ever met.

Mr. Ascham knew all manner of strange arcana, from theories about the ancient stone circles on the Salisbury Plain to the latest scientific methods in medicine and mathematics. And what he didn't know, he sought to find out. Whether it was the visiting astronomer royal, the king's surgeon or a traveling tinker selling a miracle cure, Mr. Ascham would always probe them with pointed questions: asking the astronomer royal if Amerigo Vespucci's claims about using the moon and Mars to determine longitude were valid, asking my father's surgeon why certain plants caused certain kinds of rashes, or asking the tinker if he was aware that he was a quack.

Such was Mr. Ascham's knowledge of so broad a range of subjects, it was not unknown during his time at Cambridge for professors in *other* disciplines to come to his rooms to confer with him on areas of their own supposed expertise.

For in a world where people claimed to find higher wisdom from God or the Bible, my dear tutor prayed at the twin altars of knowledge and logic. "Everything," he once told me, "happens for a logical reason, from the downward flow of streams to illnesses to the actions of men. We just have to find that reason. The acquisition of knowledge, the sheer pleasure of finding things out, is the greatest gift in life."

On one well-known occasion, after a local boy prone to foamy-mouthed fits died suddenly and the local abbot attributed the event to the boy's possession by Satan, Mr. Ascham asked to see the lad's brain. Yes, his brain! The dead boy's skull was cracked open and, sure enough, Mr. Ascham found a white foreign body the size of an apple lodged in his brain. Mr. Ascham later told me in reference to that event, "Before we blame the supernatural, Bess, we should exhaust all the natural explanations first." The abbot didn't speak to him for a year after that. Not everyone shared Mr. Ascham's pleasure in finding things out.

And then, in the prime of his university career, he had come to teach me, a mere child, the third in line to the throne. Even at that tender age, it had struck me that the remarkable Mr. Roger Ascham was wildly overqualified to be tutoring a girl of thirteen, even if she was a princess. I wondered why. What did he see in me that no one else did?

In any case, this exchange between us about the Moslem sultan's use of English was not unusual. I was wrong and he was right—again.

We turned our attention back to the invitation. It added that the chess tournament would take place in one month's time in the sultan's capital, the ancient city of Constantinople.

Accompanying the invitation was a note from my father, addressed to Mr. Ascham.

Ascham,

I understand that your associate Mr. Gilbert Giles was the finest player at Cambridge. Would you please inquire as to whether this is still the case and if it be so, dispatch him to me at once. No less than the reputation of the corpus christianum *requires our best man at this tournament.*

Henry, R

By the way, I appreciated your efforts in the matter of Cumberland's son. They did not go unnoticed.

In those days, it was more than just Christendom's reputation that was at stake: the Moslem sultan was threatening Christendom itself.

His empire spread from Persia in the east to Algiers in the southwest and had recently crossed the Danube. Eight years earlier, in 1538, the sultan's navy, led by the brilliant Barbarossa, had done the previously unthinkable: it had defeated a European fleet—a "Christian alliance" of ships—at Preveza. This Christian alliance, assembled by Pope Paul III himself, lost over forty ships, more than three thousand prisoners, and, after paying three hundred thousand gold ducats in reparations to the Ottoman sultan, a large portion of Europe's pride.

Then Suleiman's land army had taken the city of Buda. Now it was poised at the gates of Vienna. Suleiman's nearest European neighbor, Archduke Ferdinand of Austria, was said to be apoplectic with rage at the sultan's incursions into his territory, but except for sending out ever more spies to report on the movements of the Moslem armies, there was nothing Ferdinand could do. Suleiman's empire was twice the size of *all* of Christendom combined and growing larger by the day.

And that was all before one spoke of Suleiman himself. He was said to be a wise and shrewd ruler, a speaker of no less than five languages. He was a gifted poet and patron of the arts, a cunning strategist and— unlike his bitter enemy, Archduke Ferdinand, and many of Europe's kings and queens—he was utterly beloved by his people.

On more than one occasion my teacher had said to me that while the royal lines of England, France and Spain jockeyed among themselves for preeminence, a great shadow had been rising in the East. If it went unchecked our noble families might one day look up from their squabbles and find themselves paying tribute to a Moslem overlord.

The other unspoken challenge in the gilt invitation was the inevitable contest that this tournament would pose between faiths. Just as he had done at Preveza, Suleiman was pitting his god against ours, and at Preveza his god had won.

"Sir, is this Mr. Giles still the best player in England?" I inquired.

My teacher said, "He most certainly is. I still play him regularly. He beats me nine times out of ten, but on the odd occasion I manage to outwit him."

"That sounds like our record."

Mr. Ascham smiled at me. "Yes, but I have a feeling that our record will soon be reversed. Giles, on the other hand, will always have the upper hand on me. But this"—he held up the invitation—"this is momentous. Giles will be thrilled to answer the king's call."

————

Mr. Giles most certainly was.

Mr. Ascham sent him to meet with my father, who (again, typically) arranged for a test of Mr. Giles's chess abilities: a game against my father himself. Naturally, Mr. Giles lost this game.

Like everyone else in England, Mr. Giles was reluctant to beat a king who, in addition to beheading two of his wives (one of whom had been my mother), had had Thomas Cromwell beheaded for matchmaking for him with one of them. It was not unknown for those who defeated my father at other games to end up with their heads mounted on stakes atop London Bridge.

To my surprise, however, upon winning the game my father reportedly boomed: "Do not play lightly against me, Giles! I do not need a sycophant representing England and the primacy of Christ and the Christian faith at this event. I need a player!"

They played again and Mr. Giles beat my father in nine moves.

Things proceeded swiftly from there.

A small traveling train was assembled, with carts, horses and guardsmen for the journey across Christendom.

But then just as Mr. Giles was about to depart Hertfordshire, a terrible case of plague descended on the district.

My half brother, Edward, the heir to the throne, was whisked away. My sister, Mary, went soon after.

I, apparently, was not so valuable: no one moved with any kind of alacrity to facilitate my removal from Hatfield House, so I simply continued my studies with Elsie and with you, my dear friend Gwinny Stubbes.

Then one day there arose a commotion.

We were sitting in my study reading Livy's account of the mass Jewish suicide at Masada. Elsie, who was several years older than we were, sat in the corner at her mirror, idly brushing her hair. Oh, do you remember her, Gwinny? Lord, I do! At seventeen, Elsie was a genuine beauty, with the willowy figure of the dancer she was. Slender of waist yet pert of bosom, with gorgeous blond hair that cascaded over her shoulders, Elsie drew the eye of every passing gentleman.

With the airy confidence common to beautiful people, she was convinced that her prettiness alone would win her a husband of suitable rank and so did not feel it necessary to study—she spent more time in front of her mirror glass than at her books, and I must confess that in this regard I was a little envious of her. I had to endure many tiresome lessons, and I had royal blood. (I was also, I should add, jealous of her womanliness, given that I was nothing less than awkwardness personified: all knobbly knees and bony arms with a chest as flat as a boy's and a ghastly shock of curly strawberry-red hair that I hated.) That said, most of the time I worshipped Elsie, entranced by her grace, enthralled by her beauty, and awed by her worldly seventeen-year-old's wisdom.

It was while we were thus engaged that I heard the commotion: my governess, Miss Katherine Ashley, raised her voice in the next room.

"You will do no such thing, Mr. Ascham!" It must have been serious. She only called him "Mr. Ascham" when she was upset with him.

"But it will be the learning opportunity of a lifetime—"

"She is *thirteen years old*—"

"She is the brightest thirteen-year-old I have ever taught and mature beyond her years. Grindal agrees."

"She is a child, Roger."

"The king doesn't think so. Why, just last month when he was informed that Bess had started to bleed, King Henry said, 'If she is old enough to bleed then she is old enough to be married off for the benefit of England. Daughters have to be good for something.'" That sounded like my father.

"I don't know," Miss Katherine said, "the kingdom of the Moslems could be a very dangerous place for her . . ."

Mr. Ascham lowered his voice, but I could still hear him.

"*London* is a very dangerous place for her, Kat. These are pivotal times. The king grows sicker and more erratic every day, and the court is divided in its loyalties to Edward and Mary. Our Elizabeth has the weakest claim to the throne, yet her very presence in England threatens each of their claims. You know how often rival heirs die mysteriously during plagues . . ."

Listening from behind the door frame, I gasped softly.

Miss Katherine was silent for a long moment.

Mr. Ascham said, "She will be well guarded on the journey. The king is providing six of his finest troops to escort us."

"It is not just her physical safety that concerns me. I want her morals protected, too. She will need a chaperone," Miss Katherine said haughtily. "It is scandalous enough that she should be traveling with two bachelors in yourself and Mr. Giles, but soldiers, too."

"What about you and John, then?"

"Oh, don't be silly. I am far too old and far too fat to undertake such a journey." Miss Katherine was, it must be said, a rather large woman. She had married the kindly John Ashley only the previous year at the advanced age of forty (although she still liked me to address her as "Miss" because, she said, it made her feel young).

"All right, then—" Mr. Ascham rallied.

"A *responsible* chaperone, Roger, married or at least betrothed. One who will be a moral example to Elizabeth. Not some silly strumpet who will be tempted to stray in an exotic land or liaise with the guards on the journey there—wait, I know! Primrose Ponsonby and her husband, Llewellyn."

My teacher groaned at the suggestion. "The Ponsonbys . . ."

Miss Katherine said, "They are model Christians, tragically childless, yet ever keen to be of service to the king. If they go with you, Roger, my fears will be somewhat assuaged."

"Very well. Agreed."

A moment later the two of them entered our study.

Mr. Ascham nodded at me. "What say you, Bess, since we have to leave this place anyway, would you like to go on an adventure?"

"To where, sir?" I asked, feigning ignorance.

"You know exactly where, young miss. You have been listening from behind the door." He smiled. "You need to gasp more quietly if you are to become a master spy, little one. To the chess tournament in Constantinople. To watch Mr. Giles compete."

I leaped up, smiling broadly. "What a splendid idea! Can Gwinny and Elsie come, too? Can they? Please?"

Mr. Ascham frowned, glanced at Miss Kate. "I fear I am already bending far too many rules just by taking you, my young princess," he said. "It is too much to ask of your chaperones to govern three of you, but two would be manageable. You may bring one friend along."

I hesitated, glancing at my two friends. There you were, Gwinny, shy and sweet, a wallflower if ever there was one, looking at me with quiet hope, while Elsie's entire being blazed with excitement; her eyes wide, her fists clenched in desperate anticipation. She adored romantic tales about dashing princes in glittering palaces. A trip to an exotic city in the East was her dream come true. I had her undivided attention and I liked it.

"I shall take Elsie!" I cried, and Elsie squealed and threw her arms around me in utter delight. As I struggled in her embrace, I confess I did notice how you bowed your head in dismay.

The young make mistakes. This is what they do. And given the awful things that occurred in Byzantium, perhaps this choice was a mistake.

But having said that, given the true and lasting friendship that we have forged over the course of our lives, Gwinny—and mark my words, queens need true friends—there is a part of me that is glad for that error, for in choosing Elsie, I spared you the trauma of witnessing firsthand the events I beheld in the Moslem sultan's court.

THE JOURNEY, OCTOBER 1546

WE LEFT HERTFORDSHIRE ON THE FIRST of October in the year of our Lord 1546, with a small caravan of two wagons and six guardsmen to protect us on our way.

Mr. Ascham rode out in front astride his beloved courser, a big mare that had failed woefully as a jouster. My teacher didn't care; he had bought her for her gentle temperament. He rode with his longbow slung over his shoulder. He had written a book on the subject of archery in which he argued that every male of adult age in England should be compelled to become expert in the use of the bow. Indeed, whenever he traveled, he always wore his leather archer's ring on his right thumb and a bracer on his left forearm should ever he be required to notch an arrow at short notice.

Riding in the main wagon with Elsie and me was Mrs. Primrose Ponsonby, who even in that bouncing cart sat with perfect poise, her back erect, her hands placed neatly in her lap. She was twenty-six years old, married but childless, and was more pious than a nun. The hood of her sky-blue traveling cape was perfectly pressed (its pale blue color brought to my mind images of the Virgin Mary and I wondered if this was her intention); the powder on her face was flawlessly applied; and her lips were, as always, pursed in a scowl of disapproval. Everything offended her: the low neckline of Elsie's stomacher (a sign of the loose morals of the day), the mud-spattered armor of our escorts (lack of discipline), and, of course, Moslems ("Godless heathens who will burn in hell"). At times I thought Mrs. Ponsonby actually *liked* being offended.

Elsie couldn't stand her. "Sanctimonious prude," she muttered when

Mrs. Ponsonby yet again told Elsie to cover her décolletage with a shawl. "We'd have more fun with Pope Paul himself as our chaperone."

Mrs. Ponsonby's husband, Llewellyn—a short, ruddy-faced man, as pious as his wife but from what I saw, more her servant than her equal—rode on a donkey beside our wagon. He was ever scurrying about doing her bidding, tripping over himself in his haste to effect commands that always began with the shrill call of: "Llewellyn Ponsonby!"

I sighed. They were not exactly a winning example of the benefits of marriage, and as chaperones, well, I feared that Elsie was right.

We had to pass through London on our way to Dover. There Mr. Ascham and Mr. Giles stopped briefly at Whitehall to collect something from my father: a gorgeous scarlet envelope with gilt edges similar to those of the sultan's original invitation. This envelope was sealed with a dollop of wax that bore the imprint of my father's ring in its center. A private note from king to king. My teacher would carry this envelope on his person for the duration of our journey.

I did not know what message or messages it contained. As I would discover later, neither did my teacher.

———

While I would have liked to, I did not accompany my teacher into the palace at Whitehall. I rarely saw my father and never in the harsh light of court. He loomed at the fringes of my world, a godlike figure whom I glimpsed occasionally but rarely saw in full.

Of course, he was spoken about every day. He was loved and feared, admired and feared, respected and feared. It was said by many that my father had executed more people than any English monarch before him. But he was also known for his keen, educated mind; his prowess at any kind of sport; his ability to write music; and his fondness for any pretty thing in a skirt, even if she was married to another.

His interactions with me were usually perfunctory, businesslike affairs. I was a by-product of kinghood and a bothersome one at that: a daughter. He had been tender toward me on perhaps three occasions and on each of those occasions I'd adored him. His recent observation about me being "old enough to bleed" was more the rule: my ability to marry and breed for England suddenly made me useful.

Elsie and I lingered outside the palace under the watchful gaze of our two chaperones, our six guardsmen and seven recently beheaded traitors mounted on spikes above the gates.

The angry roars of a bear being baited rose from a nearby alley, followed by the cheers of a crowd. I peered into the alley and saw the poor animal: it was a mighty beast chained by the neck to a stake lodged in the ground and it bellowed with impotent rage as two mastiffs attacked it, drawing chunks from its hide. The bear managed to hit one of the dogs with a lusty swipe, and the dog went flying with a yelp into a wall, where it collapsed in a heap, mortally wounded. As it lay dying, another mastiff was released to take its place. The crowd cheered even more loudly.

Mrs. Ponsonby was predictably appalled. "I thought Englishmen were made of better stuff than this. Come, girls. Avert your eyes."

On this rare occasion, I found myself agreeing with her.

———

After our short stop at Whitehall, we proceeded apace to Dover and thence across the Channel to Calais.

From there, at Mr. Ascham's suggestion, we all changed into garments that were decidedly less colorful than the attire we had worn across southern England. Elsie and I wore plain cassocks and skirts without farthingales (which I must say made movement considerably easier). With her graceful neck, blond hair and nubile body, Elsie still managed to look angelic even in that crude smock.

Mrs. Ponsonby puckered her lips in outrage when Mr. Ascham made her don a plain brown traveling cloak. Her blue one, he said, was not appropriate for an overland journey across the Continent—dressing so would almost certainly attract the attention of bandits. Elsie could barely contain her delight at this exchange.

Mr. Ascham dressed for our journey in a fashion that I feel warrants further description.

In Hertfordshire he always wore the stiff formal attire of a gentleman: ruff, gown, bulging breeches and stockinged feet. But now he donned an outfit that was decidedly different: full-length brown trousers of a sturdy weave, knee-high brown riding boots and a brown jerkin made of tough Spanish leather. Over this he draped a long coat of oiled black canvas that reached all the way to his ankles. On his head he placed a broad-brimmed brown hat that seemed impervious to rain.

All this gave my beloved schoolmaster a far more rugged appearance than that to which I was accustomed. He looked more like an explorer or an adventurer than a little girl's teacher from Hertfordshire.

He looked harder, rougher, and perhaps even a little dashing.

———

We made good progress through France.

Although nominally my father was the king of France, such an appellation seemed a sore point to the local inhabitants, so we traveled through the lands of the Franks incognito, disguising our status to the extent that we did not even stay overnight in the homes of royal relatives.

Instead we lodged at taverns and public houses that were usually foul-smelling and rancid places not suitable for dogs let alone human beings. On a handful of occasions—yes, it's true!—we even slept in our wagons by the side of the road while our guards stood watch in the firelight.

While I'd been somewhat saddened at Whitehall by the entertainments of my fellow Englishmen, I was shocked by the ways of the French country folk: at their wanton drinking and reveling, and their appalling personal hygiene. A man would piss into the gutter and then immediately use his unwashed hands to grasp a chicken leg and eat it.

I mentioned this to my teacher, asking what such sights could possibly add to my royal education.

Lakewood Memorial Library
12 W. Summit Street
Lakewood, NY 14750

"Bess," he said. "The majority at court may not think that you will ever sit on the throne of England, but in matters of succession one should never discount even the most remote heir. Should Edward catch smallpox and Mary, with her zealous faith, put the court offside, then you will find yourself Queen of England, Ireland and France. And if you do, then the education you receive from me will be decisive in whether or not you are a *good* queen of England. This journey will be the easiest lesson I shall ever give you, for all you have to do is watch. Watch and observe the customs, activities and proclivities of real people, for it is real people over whom a king or queen rules."

Although not entirely convinced, I said that I would do so.

———

Each evening, wherever we happened to be staying, Mr. Ascham and Mr. Giles would play chess. Usually Mr. Giles won, but not before the game had lasted some time and only a few pawns and the kings remained on the board. I would often retire before they finished.

One day I asked my teacher why, if Mr. Giles was such a highly regarded chess player, he needed to play every evening.

Mr. Ascham said, "It is especially important that Mr. Giles keep his mind fresh and alert. Playing chess is no different from any other sport. As with jousting or archery, one must keep one's muscles practiced and prepared."

"Sport? You call chess a sport?"

"Why, of course!" Mr. Ascham seemed shocked. "It is the greatest of all sports, for it pits the player against his foe on an absolutely equal footing. Size is no advantage in chess. Nor is age or even—young miss—gender. Both players have the same pieces, which all move in accordance with the same rules. Chess is the sport of sports."

"But a sport is a physical activity. Must not the definition of a sport be that a player is made weary from the exertions involved in its play or at least perspires while engaging in it? Chess is but a parlor game which fails on both counts."

"A parlor game! A *parlor* game!" Mr. Ascham exclaimed indignantly. But instead of arguing the matter further with me, he simply nodded in acquiescence. "All right. Let us accept your definition for now, and from our observations of the upcoming tournament, let us see if chess qualifies as a sport in accordance with it."

While they played their nightly matches, Mr. Ascham and Mr. Giles would converse casually—discussing that day's journey or the rise of Martin Luther or any other matter that took their interest.

I admired the easy way they chatted. They were, quite simply, good friends, so comfortable with each other that they could talk about anything, from honest advice to criticism. One day, as I rode on Mr. Ascham's horse with him, I asked him how and when he and Mr. Giles had become friends.

My teacher laughed softly. "We were both hopelessly in love with the same girl."

"You were rivals and now you are the best of friends? I don't understand."

"She was a local debutante and the most beautiful girl in all of Cambridge." Mr. Ascham shook his head. "Beautiful but also willful. Giles and I were students, brash and young. We competed shamelessly for her affections—I with awful love poems, he with flowers and wit—and she happily accepted *both* of our advances before she ran off and married the heir to a vast estate who turned out to be a drunk and a fool and who eventually lost all his lands to a moneylender. I don't know what became of her, but out of our combined failure Giles and I became firm friends."

"And now he teaches at Cambridge?"

"Yes. Secular philosophy. William of Occam, Aquinas, Duns Scotus, that sort of thing."

"And he is a bachelor like you, is he not?" I asked, trying my best to sound innocent. Elsie was particularly curious about this. She thought Mr. Giles quite fetching, "in an intellectual kind of way."

"Indeed he is," Mr. Ascham said, "but unlike me, not by choice.

Giles was married once—to the daughter of his philosophy professor, a brilliant and delightful girl named Charlotte Page. Charlotte's father allowed her to sit in on his lectures, hiding at the back of the room, and thus she learned everything the boys did. She was a match for any of them and Giles simply adored her. They married, but a year after they were wed, she took ill with the plague and died at the age of twenty-one. Giles has shown no interest in courting since."

I looked over at Mr. Giles riding on his horse nearby, staring idly at the landscape, lost in thought, and I wondered if he was thinking about her. "Poor Mr. Giles."

Mr. Ascham smiled grimly. "Yes. But then, is it better to love deeply and truly for a short while than to never love at all?"

I didn't know. At that stage in my life, boys were an oddity. Whereas only a year before I had found them annoying, now I found them intriguing. The idea of actually loving one, however, was a vague notion at best.

"Is this why you are a bachelor?" I asked. "Are you waiting for a similar all-abiding love?"

"I may well be," my teacher said. "But the real reason is that I have certain projects I wish to complete before I settle down."

"Such as?"

"Well, for one thing, you."

THE HABSBURG LANDS

AT LENGTH WE VENTURED ACROSS BURGUNDY, through the Rhine Valley, and into the lands of the Habsburgs.

Moving in a wide arc around the mountains that guard the Swiss Confederation, we passed through thick forests and spectacular valleys and beheld the soaring castles of the Germanic nobility.

I imagine that I traveled with a permanent expression of wonder on my face—every day of our journey brought new sights, new peoples, new cultures.

In the Habsburg lands, our lodgings improved. Through a labyrinthine network of intermarriage that not even the astronomer royal could calculate, my father's family had many distant relatives in these parts and it was their hospitality that we enjoyed. (It did not escape my notice that in France, where my father was supposedly king, we had moved with stealth and caution, while in the Germanic regions, where he held no such title, we traveled openly and freely.)

We stayed in grand country houses and sometimes in castles perched on hilltops, and we ate according to our station once again: roasted venison, manchet, red deer pasties and some of the most delightful gingerbreads. To the evident disapproval of our chaperones, on one occasion Mr. Ascham and Mr. Giles partook of Rhenish, a strong German wine (and I know that Elsie managed to quickly quaff a glass of the stuff, too). All three of them complained of stinging headaches the next morning. The pious Ponsonbys drank only pear cider and suffered no such ills.

The farther eastward we traveled, however, the more we stayed at the taverns and *Bierhallen* found in the mining towns of Bavaria. Here Mr. Giles would play chess against talented locals while we observed or ate.

I watched these games keenly, utterly enthralled, while Mrs. Ponsonby knitted calmly by my side, outwardly uninterested but in truth, ever watchful.

Elsie, on the other hand—and it must be said, she was quite easily bored—would sometimes watch, but more often she would disappear to our rooms or to some other place I knew not where. And just as Elsie didn't care for Mrs. Ponsonby, Mrs. Ponsonby didn't care about Elsie: "My job is to watch over you and you alone, Elizabeth," she said to me once. "I leave it to our good Lord to save the soul of that little slut."

In any case, I thoroughly enjoyed watching Mr. Giles play. He was a most inventive and clever player.

Some evenings, he would give me lessons in chess. Like many inexperienced players, I was always using my queen to carve great swathes through his pieces, but then he would invariably take my rampaging lady with a knight I had not seen coming. Many times he would take her after checking my king with that same knight, a move he called a "*fork*."

"The knight is the queen's greatest enemy," he told me at one tavern, "for while the queen can replicate every other piece's moves, she cannot mimic the knight's leaps. Thus, whenever you move your queen, always keep an eye out for a knight's fork. Never let her land on a square that will allow an enemy knight to take her and your king at once. It is the amateur player's greatest mistake."

After watching him play many games, I began to notice that Mr. Giles used two kinds of openings, rarely deviating from them. When I asked my teacher why this was so, he explained that Mr. Giles was "controlling the center of the board" and "providing a foundation for later attacks." I just liked taking pieces.

When he played with me, Mr. Giles would often say, "Now, Bess, in chess, never play the pieces, play your opponent. Watch his eyes, watch for the moments when he blinks excessively, or when he holds his breath, for those are the times when your foe is planning something. Likewise, control your own expressions, because in life as in chess, your face can betray your intentions." As he said this, he gave me a meaningful look: "This is especially important for queens and princesses."

He smiled. I smiled back. I liked Mr. Giles.

Mr. Giles also laid fiendish traps for his opponents and, again, after watching him play many times, I began to see when he laid them. On those occasions, I would wait tensely for him to spring his trap (and true to his own dictum, he never let his facial expression give away his intentions).

His chief trap occurred when his opponent castled. On seeing this, Mr. Giles would casually position his queen in front of one of his bishops and wait for his moment.

Then just when his opponent thought the game was moving on to a new phase, Mr. Giles would strike like a cobra. His queen would rush diagonally across the length of the board until she stood nose to nose with her rival king and, protected by her trusty bishop far behind her, Mr. Giles would quietly say, "Checkmate."

At one tavern, Mr. Giles did exactly this move and it enraged his opponent, a local salt miner who fancied himself at the game and was reputedly unbeaten in that town. Upon being mated, the miner kicked back his chair, rose and shoved Mr. Giles harshly backward.

Mr. Ascham, standing nearby, moved with surprising speed and caught Mr. Giles before he hit the ground.

The miner loomed above them, a stout fellow with a face enfilthed by his day's labor underground.

"You cheated!" he growled.

"I apologize for beating you, sir, but I did not cheat," Mr. Giles said in a conciliatory way.

"We will play again!" the Goliath boomed.

Mr. Ascham stepped forward. "I think we are done for the evening. Perhaps we can buy you a drink as thanks for a game well played."

"Or maybe I will break you both in two, rut your little girl here, and then buy myself a drink!" the miner said. A few of his friends chuckled ominously.

"That will not happen," Mr. Ascham said, his voice even.

The big miner stiffened. The entire bar went quiet. I gazed around at the crowd who were now taking a keen interest in the confrontation.

The miner locked eyes with my teacher. "I know you travel with guardsmen, foreigner, but your guards are outside now. I will have beaten you to a pulp before they get through that door."

Then, with a suddenness that shocked me, the miner lunged at my teacher, swinging a massive fist at his face.

Mr. Ascham moved with a speed I had not thought him capable of.

He ducked the behemoth's lusty blow and then bobbed up and loosed a brief but powerful punch to the big man's throat, striking him squarely in the Adam's apple.

The enormous miner stopped dead in his tracks. His eyes bulged red and he gasped for breath as if he was choking. His hands clutched at his throat as he dropped to his knees.

My teacher, calmer than calm, his eyes steady and unblinking, stood over him. The miner was at his mercy.

"My friend played a fair game, sir, and he meant no offense. Nor do I. I do not desire to hurt you any more." Mr. Ascham's eyes scanned the hall for any who might wish to avenge their choking friend. "But I will defend my traveling party if you make me."

He pushed Mr. and Mrs. Ponsonby and me toward the door. Mr. Giles followed, walking backward. Elsie appeared then from somewhere—a side door, I believe; she must have heard the ruckus—and joined us at the exit.

Mr. Ascham threw a couple of silver coins to the floor in front of the kneeling man. "We bid you all good night and shall forthwith take our leave."

We left that mining town immediately and made camp in some woods far to the east much later that evening. But as we rode away from that town, I saw my teacher's hands on his reins.

They were shaking.

————

The following day, as I rode in the cart alongside Mr. Ascham on his horse, I said, "Mr. Ascham, I was unaware you were so, well, capable in a fight. Have you always been so?"

My teacher shook his head. "I'm no great fighter, Bess. In fact, had that fight gone on any longer, that miner would probably have knocked me senseless. But I did enough to get us all out of there safely, which was all I wanted to do." He smiled sadly. "Bess, despite all of humanity's many advances in medicine, the sciences, architecture and the arts, we live in a brutish world, one in which force is still the ultimate arbiter."

"But what about England? Is it not a nation of laws?" I argued, just as my teacher had taught me. "The rule of law is what makes ours a civilized nation."

Mr. Ascham snuffed a laugh. "We are not so civilized."

"But I can walk down any street in Hertfordshire without fear of any bodily harm."

"This is true. But do you know why that is the case?"

"Because of the rule of law." I thought some more. "Because the average Englishman knows that it is better for all if all obey the law."

"Bess, if someone were to harm a hair on your head, your father would have that man's head cut off and placed above Aldgate. Your safety is guaranteed by the violence at your father's disposal. If you were to walk a street in the north, in a town where your identity as the king's daughter was unknown, you would not be so safe."

"So what are you saying?" I asked. "Might is right?"

"That is exactly what I am saying, and it was why as a young man I made sure I learned some incapacitating fighting moves such as you witnessed last night. It is also why I am an advocate of proficiency with the bow. Now that I think of it, it might be wise to add some basic defensive techniques to your curriculum."

"You intend to teach me to *fight*?"

"*Mister* Ascham!" Mrs. Ponsonby said indignantly from the seat beside me. She had been eavesdropping and not so subtly. "I must protest! A lady, much less a princess, needs no such skills. I pray that you will reconsider this rash idea."

"Thank you for your concern and for your prayers, Mrs. Ponsonby, but I feel this could be a worthwhile lesson for—"

"I might have to inform the king of this upon our return," Mrs. Ponsonby interrupted.

"Please do so," Mr. Ascham replied reasonably. "I have always welcomed his views on my teaching methods. Until then, such decisions are mine, not yours, so I fear I must overrule you on this matter." He was always courteous with her despite her breathtaking pomposity. I barely contained my smile.

He turned to face me. "Bess, perhaps I have not adequately informed you of my ultimate intention in your education. I intend to make you *formidable*. By the time I am done with you, I would hope that if you were turned out of England in nothing but your petticoat, you would be able to live capably anywhere in Christendom."

I liked the sound of that education.

———

At lunch the next day Mr. Ascham began my new curriculum in personal defense with a question: "All right, Bess, what do you think is the first strategy you should employ in a fight?"

I raised my fists. "This?"

"No. Wrong. You should run. If you are not there to be hit, you cannot *be* hit."

My brow furrowed. "That sounds very cowardly. And not very English."

"The world is not very English. Be it a stupid tavern brawl or a naval battle, a scrap avoided is the best result for everyone concerned."

"But last night you did not avoid the scrap."

"Last night I had a responsibility that I could not run from, namely, your safety. I had to end that confrontation as quickly as I could and then get us all out of there."

"So what if I cannot run?"

"Then you do this." He held up his right hand, palm vertical with every finger extended forward—and then suddenly he thrust that hand toward my eyes. I flinched as his fingers gently jabbed my face, two of them touching my eyelids.

Nearby, Mrs. Ponsonby snorted in disgust. She glanced at her husband and he dutifully echoed the noise.

Mr. Ascham ignored them.

"Given your age, Bess, most assailants will be larger and stronger than you, so you will need to use guile instead of muscle. Extend your fingers like so and poke him in the eyes. Blind him. Everyone's eyes are vulnerable, even those of the biggest thugs. And not even thugs can fight without sight. But make sure you keep your fingers bent, otherwise you will injure them in the jabbing. Now try it."

I did so and was surprised by how easy it was to strike my teacher in the eyes with at least one finger or the thumb.

"Now," he said, "what do you do after you poke your opponent in the eye?"

"Punch him in the throat. Like you did."

"No. Wrong. You run."

"*Again?*"

"A scrap avoided is the best result for everyone concerned," he repeated like a mantra. "You are only trying to disable him long enough for you to get away."

"But what if he is not so disabled?"

Mr. Ascham then taught me to punch someone in the throat as he had done the night before. "Some men strike at the jawbone, but this is foolish because punching a bone is like punching a wall. Hitting the throat, however, will stop your attacker from breathing and if he can't breathe, he can't fight. Now, what do you do after you have struck him in the throat and made him gasp for air?"

I grinned. "I run."

He smiled. "You, my princess, are such a quick learner."

We journeyed on.

INTO WALLACHIA

A FEW DAYS LATER, WE LEFT the lands of the Habsburgs and entered the eastern half of the Continent.

The landscape changed immediately. Gone were the rust-and-gold leaves of autumn in the West. Here everything was darker. The mountains were black and threatening, the trees thin and skeletal, the roads muddy and boggy.

The language also changed: on the western side of Europe, the common language between foreigners was Latin, but in the East it was determinedly Greek. For over a thousand years, from their base in Constantinople, eastern Roman emperors had held Latin in contempt, a crude tongue that was not "sacred" like Greek. This had not changed with the accession of the Moslem sultans.

As we approached the Black Sea, we passed through the land known to some as Romany and to others as Wallachia. It was a grim place inhabited by gypsies and peasants who all bore the haunted looks of the permanently oppressed. Their villages are hardly even worthy of the title "village." A Romany hamlet is little more than a collection of hovels flanking a central boggy track.

"Did you know, Bessie," Elsie whispered to me one night as we lay in our covered wagon by the side of one such track, "that a hundred years ago the ruler of Wallachia was a madman named Vlad the Third? His unspeakable acts of torture and murder defy belief: his preferred method of execution was impalement on a stake. The victim would be impaled up through the anus and out through the mouth—all while still alive—and then be left to slide down the stake and die slowly."

"How horrid . . ." I said.

"According to the local stories, this Vlad would have whole villages impaled. So murderous was his reign that rumors began to circulate that he drank the blood of the dead at his table. He became known as Vlad the Impaler. Apparently, he was a devoted Catholic—"

"Elsie," Mr. Ascham said sternly, poking his head inside our wagon. "Stop scaring Bess with your silly campfire tales."

Even so, the next day, as we passed through another hamlet he rode a little closer to my wagon than usual.

Sullen-looking gypsies watched us as our caravan went by. On some occasions, the gypsies would follow us beyond the borders of their hamlets, trailing us at a distance. One time, a group of them shadowed us for three whole days and nights. During that time, Mr. Ascham posted an extra guard to keep watch over the wagon in which I slept.

On one of those nights I asked, "Sir, is it true that gypsies kidnap children? Is that why you've allocated an extra man to watch over me?"

Mr. Ascham looked out at the moonlit landscape. A jagged ridgeline of pine trees stabbed the sky, framing the valley.

"Unfortunately, young Bess, the frightening bedtime stories we tell about gypsies back in England do indeed have some basis in fact," he said, not taking his eyes off the hills.

In the distance, a wolf howled. At least, I thought it was a wolf. It might have been a human.

"And what exactly do these gypsies do with the children they take in the night?" I asked. In the stories back home, one never actually found out what happened to children who were so kidnapped.

Ascham turned to look at me. He said seriously, "That is something I do not wish to burden your young mind with at this stage of your development."

I rolled my eyes. "Surely it couldn't be worse than impalement?"

"Yes, it could," he said, and he would speak no more on the matter.

———

Mr. Giles continued to play chess when he could, but there were fewer large villages in Wallachia and so fewer opportunities. When he did play in a small tavern one evening, I noticed an odd-looking fellow watching the match closely from the back of the room. He was a small man with a dark Persian complexion and a long ratlike nose.

I started. I had seen this man before: at the last tavern, two days previously. I mentioned it to Mr. Ascham.

"Well spotted, Bess. That gentleman has been following us for a week now," my teacher said calmly, not turning to look at the rat-faced man. "He always lurks at the back of the room and he watches Mr. Giles's matches very closely. No, Bess. Don't turn around."

"Who is he?" I asked in a hushed whisper.

"My guess is that he is an agent of the sultan's, sent to observe and report on Mr. Giles. Perhaps to gauge his ability before his arrival at the tournament. Perhaps to see who travels with him. We are in Ottoman lands now, Bess, and it should come as no surprise that the sultan's eyes watch over us."

On another occasion in Wallachia, we stayed at a large and very rowdy tavern.

Our rooms were upstairs, while at ground level there was a beer hall filled with dirty locals who played cards, smoked pipes and drank a potent foul-smelling local brew. Naturally, Mrs. Ponsonby was appalled and fanned herself vigorously and ostentatiously, as if to fan away the very vice in the air. At a table in the corner, two men were playing chess for money.

I should mention that on every occasion he played chess on our journey, Mr. Giles had played it solely for the sake of playing. On some occasions, local players wanted to play him for money, but Mr. Giles always demurred. He would play, but for enjoyment only.

At first I thought this odd as he stood a good chance of beating them. One day I asked him why.

"When one travels in foreign lands, Miss Bess," he said, "one is essentially a guest in someone's home. And it is not polite to take your host's coin. Beat them, sure, but do not play for money. No one likes an outsider who arrives in their house, wins and then walks jauntily away with their host's hard-earned silver. If you do that, you are liable to be chased out of town, thrown out of town, or worst of all carried out of town to a pauper's grave after someone has stabbed you in the back."

"Goodness."

In that tavern in Wallachia, however, the local chess champion would *only* play for coin.

And since it was his board, one could not play him without taking his wager. Mr. Giles resolved not to play that night, but of course when word got around the establishment that one of the recently arrived guests was on his way to Constantinople to play in the chess tournament, the local champion loudly and coarsely challenged Mr. Giles to a game.

And so Mr. Giles played him and the whole tavern gathered round the corner table to watch.

As the game began, I surreptitiously scanned the room and sure enough, there he was in the far corner: our rat-faced shadower. His eyes were fixed on Mr. Giles.

It turned out to be a gripping game. While the local champion might have been boorish and crude, he was a fine player and the game lasted far longer than any of the others Mr. Giles had played on our journey.

For the duration of the game, I sat with Mr. Ascham, watching intently. Elsie, thrilled to be at a place that in some way resembled civilization, flitted excitedly from one spot to another: she variously sat with us and watched the game, flirted with the younger men at the bar who had no interest in chess, or disappeared to our rooms to emerge a short while later wearing a different dress that flattered her breasts more.

At one stage, I went to the nearby bar to get a drink for Mr. Ascham and myself. (My teacher said, "It will be good for you to actually pay for something at least once in your life. Perhaps you should go and ask Mr. Giles if he would like something to drink as well.") Aghast at the prospect of me doing something so unroyal as ordering some drinks, both Mr. and Mrs. Ponsonby accompanied me.

At the bar, I (quite proudly) ordered our drinks: my teacher wanted to try the local ale, while Mr. Giles and Mrs. Ponsonby—in an effort to choose something a little less potent—ordered perry. Mr. Ponsonby asked for watered-down spice wine and I had milk.

The tavern's owner had an enormous belly and unshaven jowls but he was a friendly fellow who could speak Greek. "Heading to Constantinople for the chess tournament, eh?" he said as he opened a bottle of ale. Behind him, his boy prepared the other drinks.

"Yes."

"Keep an eye out for the representative of Wallachia, a very strong player from Brasov named Dragan," the owner said.

"His name is Dragan?" I said. "As in *dragon*, the mythical creature?"

"Yes, and he breathes a unique fire of his own. Trust me, if you meet Dragan of Brasov, you will most certainly remember the encounter!"

"Thank you. I shall keep that in mind," I said.

"One other thing, little one," the owner said more softly. "Watch yourself in Byzantium. Stay close to your companions. There be strange tales coming out of that city of late. Word is, there's a fiend on the loose there, the devil's spawn, they say. Prowls the slums outside the palace late at night, kills men, women *and* children, stabbing them hundreds of times. Then he tears the skin off the bottom half of their faces before he vanishes into the night."

"He tears the skin off their faces?" I said.

"Around the mouth and jawbone. Flays 'em like a hunter skinning a wolf, exposing the flesh and bone undernea—"

"I say, that's enough, sir," Mrs. Ponsonby interjected. "You've no right to scare a child so."

But I was enthralled, a little terrified, but enthralled nonetheless. "Why would anyone do such a thing?"

"Who knows?" the tavern owner said. "Who *can* know what drives the mind of a madman?"

"How many people has this fiend killed?"

"At last count, eleven. The peasants of Constantinople are living in fear. You watch yourself."

"I most certainly will."

I returned to our table with Mr. Ponsonby and handed a drink to my teacher, while Mrs. Ponsonby took a mug of perry over to Mr. Giles at the playing table.

I asked my teacher hesitantly: "Sir, have you heard about some murderous fiend at work in Constantinople?"

"I've heard rumors, yes."

"Do they concern you?" They very much concerned me.

"Until I verify them with someone who actually lives in Constantinople, no. Till then, they are just ghost stories, like the one Elsie told you about the blood-drinking Wallachian tyrant, designed to frighten the young and impressionable."

Mrs. Ponsonby rejoined us then, sipping daintily from her own mug of the local pear cider.

We continued to watch the game. At one point, Mr. Ascham nodded at Mr. Giles's opponent. "You know, Bess, I was just observing something."

"What?"

"Whether they gather in a king's court or a tavern in Wallachia, everyone wants to be somebody."

"What do you mean?"

"Exactly what I said." He gave me a look. "Some things, Bess, I cannot teach you. Some things you must learn for yourself."

I frowned, nonplussed. I didn't like those lessons.

At that moment, Mrs. Ponsonby coughed uncomfortably. She touched her stomach and winced.

"Are you all right, Mrs. Ponsonby?" I asked.

"I suddenly feel . . . quite unwell," she said. She was going pale before my eyes. "If you will excuse me a moment . . ."

She darted up the stairs to our rooms, chased by her concerned husband. Mr. Ascham jerked his chin, indicating that I should go, too, so I dashed up the stairs and arrived in our rooms to find her on her knees, bent over a chamber pot, retching most violently, her husband standing helplessly over her.

"It must have been . . . the perry . . ." she groaned. "Bad cider . . ."

Insufferable as she was, I ended up helping her, holding her hair away from her face as she vomited up the contents of her stomach. Then, with Mr. Ponsonby, I helped her into her nightgown and put her to bed. She was asleep within minutes, her effete but loving husband mopping the perspiration on her brow.

I returned to Mr. Ascham's side downstairs, delightfully unchaperoned. The game was still going. I looked around and saw that Elsie had disappeared once again.

Relieved for once of the presence of my moral guardians, I decided to go in search of Elsie. I knew she wasn't up in our rooms, so I checked the road out in front of the tavern. She wasn't there. I inspected the outhouse in the rear yard, but did not find her there either.

Returning to the tavern, I heard a noise coming from around the corner of the building.

It was a peculiar grunting, followed by a strange feminine gasping.

I peered around the corner—

—and threw my hand to my mouth.

There, just around the corner of the building, in a small alley between it and the next house, were Elsie and two male youths.

Elsie stood bent forward over a barrel with her dress hitched up around her waist, while one of the men, a thin boy of perhaps seventeen, stood behind her with his breeches around his ankles, thrusting his manhood into her with vigorous energy.

I could see Elsie's face. She was clearly enjoying herself, making a short, gasping squeal of delight every time the young fellow thrust himself into her. For his part, the young man grunted each time he pumped her.

I watched, shocked beyond measure but also entranced and curious.

Of course, I had heard about this. The other girls of Elsie's age talked incessantly about the act of consummation, copulation, or being "occupied" by a man, especially as they approached marriageable age. When they spoke to me about it, they put on airs of experience and worldliness but when I overheard them talking amongst themselves, they spoke of it with considerable trepidation. It was a Great Unknown. And possessing skill at it was something they viewed as critical to keeping a husband happy. Elsie was an active participant in those conversations.

I stared with wide eyes as Elsie experienced something akin to ecstasy, jolting with the young fellow's every thrust, her squeals becoming faster.

Then, after a time, the young man reached some sort of climax himself, for he shouted as he gave one final thrust. He then pulled himself away from Elsie. (I confess at this point I tried to glimpse his manhood—I was more curious than anything else—but he pulled up his breeches too quickly for me to get a look at it.)

At this stage, Elsie nodded to the second youth, who quickly yanked down his own breeches, stepped up behind her, and assuming the place of the first lad, penetrated her with his engorged organ (which I saw clearly this time; it was stiff and long like a baton and surrounded by dense black hair; not small, hairless and shriveled like my half brother's willy-winky).

And so it began again.

The thrusting was more vigorous this time, Elsie's panting more intense, more obviously pleasurable. After a short period of this rutting, she extricated herself from him, turned herself around and sat on top of the barrel so that she was facing him. Then she pulled her cassock over her head, throwing it off completely, so that she sat there in the nighttime air, naked as the day she was born. She spread her legs wide, inviting the youth to enter her again, which he did without hesitation.

His penetrations were faster now and as he gripped Elsie's waist, he seemed to enrapture her. In between panting gasps, she started to say, "Harder, man . . . harder . . ."

He pumped her with even greater energy, desperate to please. Her breasts jiggled with his every shunt and her eyes closed in sheer delight.

Then the second youth yelped as he reached his own climax. Elsie moaned sensually, her entire body relaxing as she leaned back on the barrel.

The youth then hurriedly yanked up his pants and the two young men disappeared down the alleyway, whispering animatedly, clearly happy with the event.

As for Elsie, I watched her sigh with tremendous satisfaction before she retrieved her cassock and casually put it back on. It was at this point that I hurried back inside so as not to be seen by her—much shocked, definitely titillated, but most of all, fascinated by the actions of my older friend.

Contrary to those discussions with the girls back home, Elsie had not shown any trepidation at all. Nor had the scene I had just witnessed had anything to do with pleasing the two men involved, let alone marrying them. What I had just seen Elsie do had been done, it seemed, for one reason and one reason only: the pursuit *by Elsie* of her own pleasure. I didn't know what to think of my friend. I was very confused.

I reentered the tavern just as Mr. Giles checkmated the local champion and reluctantly took the man's silver coins.

THE OTTOMAN CAPITAL

EMERGING FROM THE GRIM DARKNESS of Wallachia, we entered the homelands of the Ottoman Turks. The landscape became drier, more dusty, and the odd clump of snow could be found by the side of the road. Winter was not far away.

I traveled in the first wagon, seated beside Elsie, while Mrs. Ponsonby now traveled in the second, lying covered in a blanket, her husband gripping her hand. Her condition had not improved in the two days since we had left that tavern in Wallachia. She had a terrible fever that caused her to perspire greatly and shiver uncontrollably. Neither Elsie, I, nor any of our guardsmen dared give voice to the thought we all shared: that Mrs. Ponsonby's malady could be plague.

"What do you think about Mrs. Ponsonby?" I asked Mr. Ascham. "Is it . . . ?"

"It is not plague," he said simply.

"She thought it might have been bad perry," I said.

"It was not bad perry. Apply logic, Bess. If the perry had been off, wouldn't Mr. Giles also be ill? He drank the same drink."

I frowned. This was true.

"But what if," my teacher said, "there was something *else* that was wrong with that perry?"

"I don't understand," I said.

"The poor woman drank the wrong cider," Mr. Ascham said, staring resolutely forward. "Back at that tavern, both she and Giles ordered perry. But she must have inadvertently switched her mug of cider for that of Giles. It was laced with something, a poison of some sort, something that was intended to make *him* fall ill, not her. Do not forget the sultan's man who has been following us—it would have been easy for him to pay the barkeep's boy to add something to Giles's drink."

I spun where I sat, glancing from Mrs. Ponsonby's shuddering body to Mr. Giles on his horse nearby. "But . . . why? Why invite Mr. Giles to play in the tournament and then poison him on the way?"

"Ah, the sultan did not invite Giles. He invited our king to send a player. The sultan did not know who Henry would send. But evidently the sultan's man has been watching and evaluating Mr. Giles's play and has found Giles to be a threat worthy of hobbling." Mr. Ascham shook his head grimly. "I have not even met this sultan yet and already I do not like the rules by which he plays."

———

The lands of the Ottoman Turks were, I must admit, far more impressive than I had anticipated.

Their roads, some of them dating back to Roman times, were paved and clean and kept in excellent condition with few ruts or potholes. Their houses were sturdy and well built, and the Turkish people—unlike their surly Wallachian neighbors—were bathed and clean, wore brightly colored clothing and were friendly. Many smiled at us as we passed by on our way to their capital.

"I had expected the lands of the Ottomans to be, well, more backward," I said to my teacher.

Mr. Ascham said, "Every nation thinks their own culture is the pinnacle of civilization and that all other cultures are primitive and barbarous. It is a sad but natural prejudice of the human mind. This is why one must travel as much as one can. Travel is the finest form of education."

Soon after arriving in those lands, I beheld for the first time a Moslem place of worship: the peculiar style of domed church that the Moslems call a mosque. I would see many more and they all followed the same basic architecture: each had a slender tower rising from it called a minaret and at prayer times, a male singer would mount this tower and from its summit call the faithful to prayer with a most unsettling elongated wail.

I was now truly in a foreign land.

Although I would never have admitted it to my teacher, I must confess that he was right: travel *was* the finest form of education and I was experiencing a tremendous thrill from our journey. Traveling abroad, and so very far from England, had shown me how cloistered my life back home was. Later in my life, a life during which I would encounter many kings and dignitaries, I often wondered if the difference between great rulers and poor ones was the amount of travel they had done before their coronation.

And then one morning, after four weeks of overland travel, we crested a rise and my breath caught in my throat. I was looking at the great city of Constantinople.

———

It was a stunning metropolis—a rolling sea of cream-colored buildings and white-painted mosques, all interspersed with tall trees and the odd taller Roman structure. Bathed in the dusty light of the Turkish sun and framed by the glittering golden waters of the Bosphorus Strait, the pale buildings of the city took on an almost heavenly appearance. My first glimpse of Constantinople was literally a breathtaking experience.

The core of the city was nestled on a sharp peninsula that lanced eastward into the Sea of Marmara—into which the Bosphorus flowed—and it was protected by a massive eighty-foot-high defensive wall that had been built by Roman Emperor Theodosius a thousand years before.

The mighty wall—it looked like one wall, but it was, in fact, actually two walls—ran from north to south, cutting the peninsula off from the mainland. At each extremity, the great barrier extended all the way to the water's edge. There were several fortified gates spaced at regular intervals along the wall, but the primary one was an immense portal known as the Golden Gate even though its thick, studded doors were made of bronze (the original golden ones were long lost to history).

In the far distance, obscured by the hazy air peculiar to the lands of the East, I observed a great hulk of a building that made Theodosius's wall look puny: it had a colossal dome and a towering minaret that soared into the sky and was easily the largest structure in the city.

We left our guardsmen at the Golden Gate: foreign troops were forbidden to enter the city. Once inside, as distinguished guests, we would be escorted by the sultan's crimson-robed palace guards.

But the city's guards stopped short at the sight of Primrose Ponsonby.

Concerned that she might be bringing plague into their city, they refused outright to admit her. No argument or exhortation could sway them. In the end, Mr. Ascham decided that Mrs. Ponsonby would lodge with our soldiers at an inn in the ramshackle market village that had attached itself to the outer side of the massive gate. Her doting husband, clearly distraught, would remain with her until she recovered.

Yet even in her feverish state, Mrs. Ponsonby found the energy to ask Mr. Ascham: "But who will watch over Miss Elizabeth?"

"I will," Mr. Ascham said.

I had to turn away so that none of them could see the smile that had arisen unbidden on my face.

Inside the walls of Byzantium, my teacher would be my chaperone.

— II —

PAWN

In chess, queens, knights, rooks and bishops can make powerful sweeping moves, but the humble pawn cannot.

This is because the pawn represents the ordinary infantryman. Lacking a horse or any other source of power, he can only move a single square at a time (except for his opening move) and then only forward or diagonally. Even the emasculated king can move backwards.

Pawns are weak. They are small. They are often exchanged for little or no tactical gain.

But we love them. We love their nerveless obstinacy in the face of attack, their modest aspirations in life and their unswerving loyalty to their king.

Is it not passing strange how often, in the latter stages of a game, the king finds himself abandoned by his queen, his religious advisors, his castles and his mounted lords, yet defended by a few loyal pawns?

Forgotten, mistreated and regularly sacrificed in pursuit of strategies of which they may not have even been aware, pawns somehow always manage to be there at the end.

From: *Chess in the Middle Ages,*
TEL JACKSON (W. M. Lawry & Co., London, 1992)

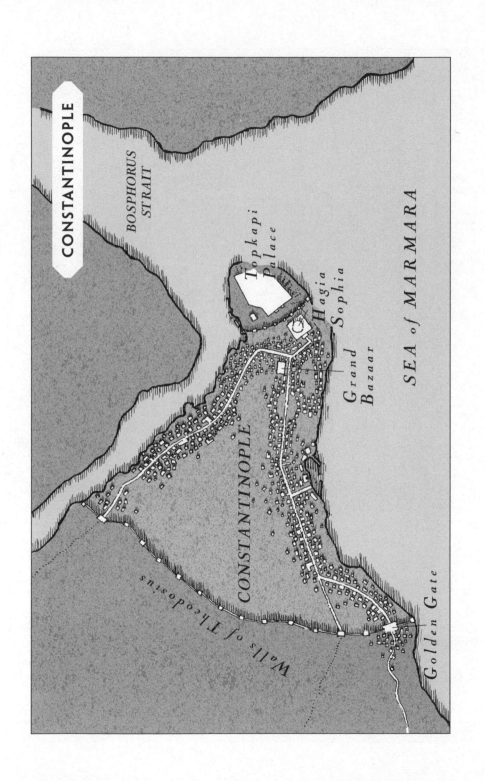

CONSTANTINOPLE

BOSPHORUS STRAIT

Topkapi Palace

Hagia Sophia

Grand Bazaar

SEA of MARMARA

CONSTANTINOPLE

Walls of Theodosius

Golden Gate

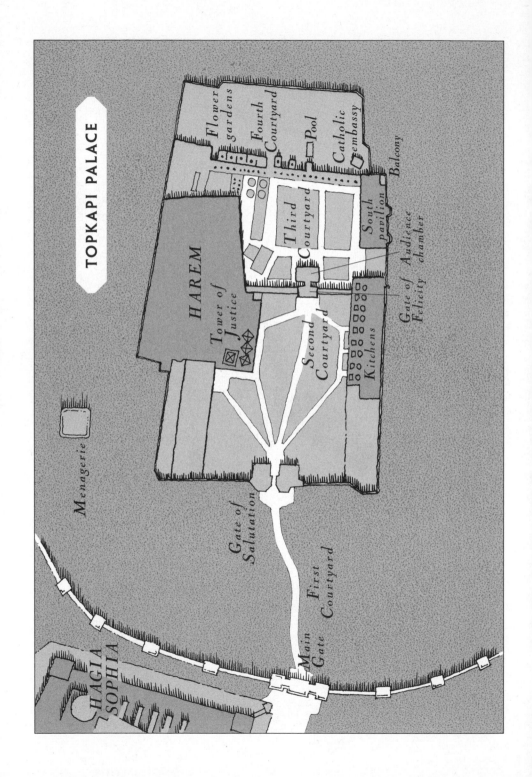

THE HAGIA SOPHIA

I was one day present when she [Elizabeth] replied at the same time to three ambassadors, the Imperial, French, and Swedish, in three languages: Italian to one, French to the other, Latin to the third, easily, without hesitation, clearly, and without being confused.

—ROGER ASCHAM

INTO BYZANTIUM

WE WERE CONVEYED THROUGH CONSTANTINOPLE in glorious gold-rimmed carriages reserved for visiting players and their companions.

While traveling across the Continent, I must confess to the sins of vanity and pride: despite my teacher's comment about the natural prejudices of all people, I felt I could honestly say that England surpassed the other lands of Europe in both complexity and cultural sophistication. But as we passed through the Golden Gate and rolled out onto the streets of Constantinople in our splendid carriages, I could not in good conscience come to the same conclusion about my homeland when compared to the Ottoman capital.

Put simply, Byzantium made England's greatest city, my beloved London, look like a Wallachian hamlet.

Grand boulevards swept past bustling bazaars and sleek marble buildings. Many-arched aqueducts shot across valleys, bringing water to the million-strong population, while bathhouses still bearing Roman paint opened onto fountain-filled plazas. We passed some commercial docks on the southern side of the peninsula; they were packed with ships, loading and unloading cargo.

People went about their business on cobblestone streets, trading, shouting, conversing, smoking. Children played in alleys; men walked about in loose-fitting robes, obviously unarmed. Many women, however, wore cloaks that covered every inch of their bodies, including their faces. They looked out at the world through gauze meshes and walked with their heads bowed subserviently a few paces behind their husbands.

Upon entering the city, Mr. Ascham had suggested that Elsie and I don similar attire, scarves that covered our heads and cloaks that extended all the way to our wrists and ankles. I obeyed, but not before asking why this was necessary.

"Some Moslem holy men believe that an unveiled woman will stir a man's loins and provoke him to unseemly acts," he said. "So they demand women cover themselves in public."

"But that's absurd! Why should the woman change her dress when it is the man's urges that are at issue? Why not call upon the men of Islam to control themselves?"

Mr. Ascham shrugged sadly. "I have found that it is rarely useful to question people on the practices of their faiths. What people do in the name of religion is not necessarily religious. It often has baser reasons behind it."

At this point we rounded a bend and emerged on a wide square, and there before us sat the immense domed building I had glimpsed earlier through the haze.

It lorded over all before it like a king on his throne: the great cathedral to holy wisdom. Known to the Turks as the Ayasofya, in Latin as the Sancta Sophia, and to Europeans as the Hagia Sophia, it was Isidore of Miletus's masterpiece.

From a squat, square, fortresslike base, the stupendous building soared heavenward in a sequence of ever-rising domes buttressed by gargantuan pillars and supports, until it reached the largest hemisphere of them all, the breathtaking main dome that surmounted the structure.

This main dome—my teacher informed me with even more than his usual enthusiasm—was nothing less than the greatest feat of engineering in the whole world, all the more so for having been built in the sixth century. The dome itself was fully one hundred feet across, spanning the Hagia's vast nave in one giant leap, soaring an incredible two hundred feet above the basilica's floor.

"Until recently, no other cathedral in Christendom has come close to it in size and ingenuity of design," Mr. Ascham said. "It is as if the knowledge that built it was lost for a millennium and has only recently been rediscovered. Originally it was built as a Christian church, but with the taking of Constantinople by the Moslems in 1453, it was converted to a mosque. Note the minaret alongside it is built with more modern bricks." He indicated the slim redbrick spire constructed beside the main structure. "Having said that, despite its colossal size and ingenious construction, because of its Christian origins, many Moslems of this city feel indifferent toward the Hagia Sophia and refuse to worship in it."

I did not feel indifferent toward it. I gazed up at it in absolute wonder, humbled by its history, majesty and immensity.

We pressed on, moving around the Hagia Sophia toward the sultan's palace, which occupied the very tip of the peninsula.

I felt like I was walking into a fabulous and exotic world. England, with its gray skies, muddy streets, feuding dukes and disputed successions, seemed completely and wholly backward compared to this.

Upon seeing Constantinople, I could see why my teacher had brought me here.

THE PALACE OF THE SULTAN

PASSING THE MIGHTY HAGIA SOPHIA, we arrived at the sultan's palace.

Mounted on a high promontory overlooking the Sea of Marmara to the south and the Bosphorus Strait to the east, it claimed the most strategic and commanding position in the city. A striking tower rose from within its own set of high stone walls.

"That tower is the Adalet Kulesi, the Tower of Justice," Mr. Ascham said. "The Moslems pride themselves on being a just and fair people."

"Are they?"

Mr. Ascham cocked his head. "Some say they are *overly* zealous in their pursuit of justice. Thieves have their hands cut off. Adulterers are stoned. Do *you* think this is just?"

I pondered this. "Crimes must be punished so that order is maintained."

"True. But shouldn't a punishment be commensurate with the crime?" my teacher said. "If we executed every adulterer in England, the population would be reduced by half."

"We hang thieves in England," I said. "Here they only lose a hand. Harsh, swift punishments make for secure streets."

"They certainly do," Mr. Ascham said, just as we passed a young man with a stump for a right hand. "The question every society must ask itself is: how much force are people willing to accept in exchange for the safety of their persons and possessions?"

I frowned. "I don't think I know the answer to that."

Mr. Ascham smiled. "I'm pleased to hear it. For the answer to that question is a balancing act for every king and queen. Tyrannical rulers get deposed and beheaded. Weak ones find themselves manipulated by cunning lords and duplicitous advisors. Successful rulers find the balance that suits their time."

I nodded at the palace ahead of us. "And in your opinion is this Sultan Suleiman a successful ruler?"

"The Moslem people follow the edicts of a great prophet named Muhammad who instilled in them a respect for a higher law. This is the mark of every great society in history: the realization that all folk, rich and poor alike, are better off abiding by accepted laws rather than the sword. For only once laws are in place can a society truly flourish: the protection of the law gives a population safety and security, and once people have that, they happily contribute to their society. Farmers farm, warriors train for war, artists paint, playwrights write. People become experts in trades and occupations and so society advances at an even greater rate. All because the people accepted basic laws."

"What happens in societies that don't accept such laws?"

"They end up marching on the spot," Mr. Ascham said sadly. "Look at Africa. There the native tribes still fight each other with spears and sticks, engaging in raids for food and women. Every time a new tribe wins a battle, society has to start all over again, so there is no progress."

"With respect, didn't you tell me only recently that, ultimately, force prevails?" I said, not a little cheekily.

My teacher half-smiled at me. "I'm pleased to see you were paying attention. And you are right, you've found a paradox in my argument. The only answer I can give you is this: a society of laws is the best we have come up with, but unfortunately not every society chooses to go down that path."

———

We came to the sultan's palace, and truly it was a wonder of the world.

We passed through an immense and well-guarded outer gate and stepped out into a wide grassy courtyard shaded by many trees. Through this courtyard stretched a broad, curving path that brought us to a second gate in a smaller but still sizeable wall.

This inner gate was called the Gate of Salutation and it was surmounted by two triangular spires that looked to me more European than Ottoman. Our guards explained that the gateway had been designed and built recently by Hungarian architects brought to Constantinople by the sultan. To my eyes, it looked very Hungarian: overdone and dandyish.

After passing through this gate, we were met by an official party of ministers dressed in red silk robes and high white turbans. Some black African eunuchs stood behind them.

Leading the official party was the *sadrazam*, the grand vizier or chief minister to the sultan. While the others all wore turbans, the *sadrazam* alone wore one with a beautiful snow-white heron plume rising from its linen coils. He was an exceedingly tall and thin fellow and he bowed low as our player, Mr. Giles, was introduced by a herald.

The herald spoke first in Turkish and then in Greek, which, we were told, would be used as a common language at the tournament: "Mr. Gilbert Giles! Representative of King Henry the Eighth, king of England, Ireland and France!"

The *sadrazam* shook Mr. Giles's hand.

"Gentlemen. Welcome to the city of Constantine," he said in English. Forgetting myself, I gasped in surprise at his command of my mother tongue.

This caught the *sadrazam*'s attention and he spied me. "Why, hello, little girl." He moved toward me. "I am Mustafa. What is your name?"

"Elizabeth, sir," I said, bowing.

"Are you an enthusiast of chess, Miss Elizabeth?"

"Yes, sir."

"You play?"

"Yes, sir."

"Ah, the English." He turned to his own group, switching to an archaic form of Latin that I could actually understand. "A most bizarre people. Imagine it, girls playing chess. I have even heard that girls go to school there. And they once had a ruling queen."

His retinue all recoiled as one in shock.

"You do not have queens in the Moslem world?" I inquired politely, also in Latin.

The *sadrazam* whirled at the sound of my voice, his eyes wide at the realization that I had understood him perfectly.

"But of course we do," he said in Greek, recovering, his eyes cold. "Only they do not rule. They are merely vessels for the sultan's seed, wombs on legs, useful only for the production of heirs and troublesome the rest of the time." He turned from me, our conversation over, and with a tight smile addressed Mr. Giles and Mr. Ascham.

"Gentlemen, you must be tired from your journey. These eunuchs will escort you to your quarters in the south pavilion. Tomorrow evening, His Majesty the sultan will host a banquet in honor of the players. It will begin at sunset. Good day to you."

THE CITY OF CONSTANTINE

WE SETTLED INTO OUR QUARTERS—three small but well-appointed rooms gathered around a central entry vestibule. Mr. Ascham and Mr. Giles had a room each while Elsie and I shared. That evening I delighted in a wonderful night's sleep in a comfortable bed under a solid roof.

The following day we ventured out into the city.

Up close, it was even busier than I had at first perceived.

One immense bazaar, known as the Grand Bazaar, was simply the greatest marketplace I had ever seen and it was all contained under a single gigantic roof. Stalls stretched as far as the eye could see. Chaos reigned. It seemed that everywhere there was movement and noise: carpet sellers mixed with root farmers who traded with spice merchants who yelled at shepherd boys whose lambs strayed among their sacks. If the Bosphorus Strait marked the dividing line between Europe and the Orient, this was the spot where European and Oriental commerce collided.

The aromas of the spices almost colored the air—cinnamon, cassia, saffron, turmeric (which we call "Indian saffron")—and everywhere I saw the notoriously potent yellow-and-orange Persian spice mixture known as *adwiya*.

Oriental silk dealers displayed their wares on vast racks: silks of every conceivable color, divinely smooth to the touch, delightful to the eye and of the highest quality, for the artisans of the Orient have long been experts in the harvesting of silkworms. Elsie and I were in heaven, and Elsie purchased two multicolored skirts and one translucent silk veil of the kind worn by belly dancers to cover their faces but not their eyes.

She also, I should add, helped me choose a new dress, dissuading me from buying a purple robelike thing ("Oh, no, Bess, that won't do! You need something that complements your gorgeous hair!"). She convinced me instead to purchase a shimmering golden dress that did indeed go very well with my curly orange locks ("Remember, Bess: match the dress with your hair and the jewels with your eyes. Oh, look at you. You won't be able to keep the boys away from you!"). I loved such times with Elsie.

Signs in the local language were everywhere. I had always considered myself rather adept at the acquisition of foreign tongues but the language of the Turks in Constantinople baffled me. Not only was it a strange guttural form of speech but it was also written in a script that was entirely unlike the Roman script I was used to in England. Rather, it was a series of curves, slashes and dots that made no apparent sense whatsoever. My teacher told me that while the script was Arabic, the language it conveyed was actually Turkish, confusing me even further.

I viewed all the signs of the bazaar with squinting eyes, trying to detect some kind of pattern in them. After a time, I found that one phrase seemed to be repeated in several stalls:

سلطانك كنديسينك ده قوللاندغى كيبى

I asked a trader who spoke Greek what it meant and he said that the phrase translated as: "As used by the Sultan himself."

"Oh! It's an endorsement . . ." I said to my teacher. "Just like at home." When my father wore a certain boot maker's boots or ordered a play to be performed at Whitehall, that variety of shoe would then be made, or the play in question would then be performed, "at royal command." That the king might use a certain product was a big selling point for its trader and increased his sales immeasurably.

There were also, it should be said, other indications of the sultan's overriding power.

Twelve rotting bodies hung by their necks from a great tree in a square outside the Grand Bazaar. A nearby sign (we were informed) identified them as resistance fighters from the city of Buda, Habsburg holdouts who refused to accept the sultan's rule of that city. The corpses rocked awkwardly on the ropes as ravens pecked out their eyes.

We returned to the palace around lunchtime, not wanting to stay out too long and overexert ourselves, for that evening we had a formal occasion to attend: the sultan's opening banquet.

———

After a restful afternoon in the much quieter world of the palace, that night, dressed in our finest evening attire, we left our rooms to go to the banquet.

Mr. Giles was nervous, Mr. Ascham was curious, and I was just excited to be wearing my new gold dress.

Elsie, however, was beyond excited. It took her all afternoon to get ready. She fussed over everything: her hair, her powder, her shoes, her bosom, her hair again, the set of the hoops under her skirt and her bosom again.

I inquired as to why she was so flustered. She had been to many banquets before.

"Bessie, Bessie," she said. "Don't you know? Beneath their veils, Moslem women are the most beautiful in the world, and tonight, within the confines of the sultan's palace, the women of the palace have been granted leave by the sultan to dress as they please and show off their beauty to his esteemed visitors. They will be on full display, as will we, representing the womanhood of England. In closed settings such as this, Moslem women are renowned for dressing fabulously, painting their faces with the most artful skill, and wearing around their necks and wrists marvelous and exotic jewelry. In such company and as a representative of Mother England, I must look my very, very best!"

I wasn't convinced that her desire to look her finest was done entirely for England. I knew enough to realize that her efforts may also have been intended to enhance her chances of snaring a visiting European prince—or, given what I had witnessed her doing in that back alley during our journey, some other kind of gentleman—but in the end, as always, her enthusiasm won me over and I helped her prepare anyway.

By the time we left our rooms, she looked radiant: she wore a sky-blue dress with a very slim waist, a white lace hem and, of course, a plunging bust line. Her gorgeous blond tresses were raised off her bare shoulders, exposing her long neck. A few escaping curls—carefully crafted to appear so—cascaded to her décolletage, as if pointing the way. A silver pendant and matching bracelet on her left wrist completed the dazzling ensemble. Elsie was a goddess.

———

The sultan's banquet was to be held in what was called the Third Court-yard, but to get to that place, all guests had to pass through the bot-tleneck that was the imperial audience chamber. There they would be formally introduced to the sultan himself before moving on to the ban-quet.

Our party arrived at the entrance to the audience chamber to find a short line of guests already waiting at its archway, men and women of various nationalities, all wearing outfits peculiar to their regions: Ital-ians with their ruffled cuffs, Castilians in their stiff-collared Spanish outer jackets, Austrians in their broad-shouldered ermine coats and, of course, churchmen from Rome in their flowing robes.

I noticed that the lead person of each delegation carried a scarlet envelope just like the one Mr. Ascham bore on behalf of my father. In addition to this, it became clear to me that each delegation had also brought a gift of some kind for the sultan: every party carried a large chest filled with treasure. They had each then added some extra touch peculiar to their culture: furs, paintings, and in one case a glimmering sword with a hilt embedded with rubies. Every delegation had done this; every one except ours.

Our delegation, I noted with dismay, bore no gift at all.

No chest, no collateral trinket, just the scarlet envelope. I wasn't certain if this was evidence of my father's stinginess, or of an ignorance of protocol on his part, or just his renowned intolerance of useless token gestures.

We took our place in the line behind a group bearing the coat of arms of Ferdinand, the archduke of Austria. Mr. Giles went over and spoke with the Austrian player, a square-jawed young man named Maximilian of Vienna, while I was delighted to see a girl of about seventeen standing in the midst of that delegation wearing a pretty white dress with a cerise sash.

I took Elsie by the hand and approached her. "Hello," I said in my best German. "My name is Bess and this is my friend Elsie. We are from England. What is your name and are you excited to be here for the chess tournament?"

The girl bowed her head shyly. "My name is Helena, but I will not be seeing any chess. I am to go immediately to that part of the palace known as the harem, where the sultan's wife, children and concubines live. I am Archduke Ferdinand's gift to the sultan."

I blinked back my shock, thunderstruck. This seventeen-year-old girl was a *gift*, a prize of no greater value than a sword or a fur.

But Elsie wasn't perturbed at all. "You are to become a concubine of the sultan? How exciting for you! Consort to a king . . . !"

I returned to my teacher's side, indignant. "Do you know that that girl over there is an offering from Archduke Ferdinand to the sultan?"

My teacher sighed. "No matter how distasteful we may find the practice of slave giving, sadly it does still happen in these parts. I must say, however, I am rather surprised that the archduke of Austria would even send a *player* to the sultan's tournament, let alone such a gift: a virgin concubine is seen as a most valuable and deferential thing to give. I am surprised because the sultan and the archduke have long been bitter enemies: over the last twenty years, Suleiman has seized much of Hungary from Ferdinand, saddled him with a weighty annual tribute and twice laid siege to Ferdinand's beloved Vienna. Who knows, perhaps it is a sign of more peaceable relations."

A short while later, Mr. Ascham spotted a group of cardinals and priests joining the queue. He elbowed Mr. Giles, drawing his attention to a tall gray-haired priest wearing a long black cassock, a tuftless biretta and a large wooden crucifix around his neck.

"Giles, look. That's Ignatius of Loyola."

Mr. Giles nodded. "I had wondered if he would come."

"Who is he?" I inquired.

"Only one of the most famous teachers in the world," my teacher replied. "Ignatius of Loyola is a Jesuit priest from Spain and a staunch advocate of the power of knowledge."

"And also a renowned enthusiast of chess," Mr. Giles replied. "That young monk with him is Brother Raul of Seville, Spain's finest player. Both Ignatius and Raul are devotees of the *Repetición*."

"Ah, but does Brother Raul come here representing Spain or the Papal States?" Mr. Ascham asked.

"A very good question, Roger, and according to Maximilian of Vienna the cause of much gossip and scandal. Maximilian just told me that Brother Raul is here representing the Papal States. Advised by Ignatius, the Church moved faster than the Spanish and claimed Raul as *their* player in his capacity as a Jesuit monk. It was most impertinent, invoking the name of God against that of the Holy Roman Emperor himself. It means that King Charles is represented here by a capable but lesser player by the name of Pablo Montoya."

"These Jesuits dress very plainly," I observed, "for an audience with a king." Their ankle-length black cassocks were of a simple coarse fabric. To me they looked like beggars.

"Jesuits own no property," Mr. Ascham said, "not even the clothes on their backs. They are devout servants of the Church, foot soldiers of Christ. But they fight their holy war through education and evangelism, sending missionaries to the farthest corners of the world. The Jesuits are a curious group, for they prize science and learning while the very Church they serve decries such things; yet the Jesuits are at the vanguard of the pope's fight against Luther and the Protestant movement."

"And my father."

"And your father. Mark that man, young Bess, for should you ever become a Protestant queen, you will find yourself dueling with Loyola's missionaries for your people's souls."

I nodded at the cardinal leading the delegation from the Papal States. "Their cardinal has no such qualms about wealth." Unlike Ignatius and their player, the head cardinal wore scarlet robes made of the finest silk and many gold chains.

"Ah, yes," my teacher said with some distaste. "Cardinal Farnese."

Cardinal Farnese was enormously fat and the loose skin around his neck folded to form many chins: he was clearly a man who ate well and often. He had hair of a deep, shiny black with gray tips above the ears, and he held his Roman nose haughtily high. He also carried his hands in an unusual, almost feminine, way: he held his pudgy fingers—bedecked with many glittering rings—aloft, above things, as if touching the grit of the world pained him.

Mr. Ascham said, "When it comes to material matters and the Roman Catholic Church, Ignatius is the exception rather than the rule. The Church and most of its senior clergymen enjoy the trappings of their wealth and power. This is part of Luther's problem with them. And the likes of Cardinal Farnese do not help their image—he is the pope's brother, most trusted advisor, and, many believe, his likely successor. Pope Paul favors his family; he made his grandsons cardinals before their seventeenth birthdays." My teacher frowned. "But it is a curious thing for Farnese to be here leading the delegation from the Papal States."

"Why do you say that?"

"Because Cardinal Farnese is particularly harsh in his anti-Moslem rhetoric. He despises the Islamic faith and he doesn't mind saying so. Last year, he practically called for another crusade on Jerusalem. He once likened a polygamous Moslem marriage to a male ape keeping a harem of she apes. For their part, the Moslems hate him for his views; the most senior cleric here in Constantinople, the Imam Ali, has publicly called for a fatwa against Farnese—essentially, a death warrant that any Moslem may carry out—but as yet the other clerics have not agreed to such an extreme move. Sending Farnese to this tournament is a most provocative act on the part of the Church. They are almost daring the imam to act."

"Is that so—" I said before I was interrupted by, of all things, a loud animal roar.

I turned to see a new delegation moving through the courtyard outside the audience chamber: a group of burly rough-faced men wearing fur-lined hats and leading behind them a wagon on which was mounted a cage with thick black bars. Inside the sturdy cage, hunched to fit into it, was an enormous bear.

At the head of this delegation was a short boy of perhaps sixteen.

He strode casually past the entire line and made to shove past me but I stood my ground.

The boy snorted as he stopped. He wore many gold neck chains, a green felt jacket and a hat lined with black sable, the most expensive fur in all of Europe. But he was short, while I was tall for my age, so I stood half a head above his angry little eyes.

"Let us pass, girl," he said in Greek. "I am here to see the sultan and present to him the most wondrous gift he shall receive today, a Russian bear to add to his famed animal collection."

"Then you will wait your turn like everyone else," I said primly. "Take your place in the line, with your bear."

"Do you know who I am!" he demanded.

"Should I?"

"I am Ivan, grand prince of the Duchy of Muscovy, which means I do not wait in *lines*, least of all behind someone like you."

"*Grand* prince?" I said. "Little boy, everyone here is in some way royal or representing royalty. And Muscovy is not exactly a leading kingdom of the world."

"It will be when I am done," he said.

That was quite enough for my little-girl mind. Like many a young girl confronted by a bratty young lad, I adopted a posture of high superciliousness.

"My, my, such grand designs. And given that you are already such a pushy lad, Lord help the rest of Europe when you grow to adulthood and lead armies. Ivan, was it? I shall call you Ivan the *enfant terrible*, or maybe just Ivan the Terrible for short. Join the line, Ivan."

The boy's face went beetroot red and he was boiling up to reply when a commotion arose behind us in the line.

A large party had arrived, and like the Red Sea for Moses, the line parted for it. Whispers and murmurs shot through the line and I heard voices saying, "It's Buonarroti . . . Signor Buonarroti himself . . . They say the sultan commissioned two chess services from him just for this event . . ."

I peered down the line and saw that the party happily overtaking it was dressed in fine Italian raiment. A pair of cardinals led the group, but the central figure at whom all were gazing was an older fellow with a broad face, sad eyes, a long white beard and a pug nose. His two servants carried in their hands a pair of flat wooden boxes carved from the finest oak and sealed with gold clasps.

This was too much for young Ivan. "Who is this fellow to push past the queues?" he cried, suddenly won over to the theory of orderly lines.

"Shh, Your Highness," his chief aide whispered. "It is the great artist

Signor Michelangelo di Lodovico Buonarroti Simoni. He has crafted the chess sets on which the tournament is to be played and he has brought them himself."

At the mention of the man's name, my teacher's head snapped up and his eyes found the old long-bearded Italian.

"Michelangelo . . ." he said.

"Who is Michelan—" I began.

My teacher was still peering out over the crowd, so Mr. Giles answered me.

"A genius of world renown," Mr. Giles said. "Artist, painter, sculptor, architect. Some say he is more brilliant even than Leonardo. Once, Mr. Ascham took me to see his *Pietà* in Rome. It brought tears to my eyes. Word is, he has just finished a painting on the ceiling of the pope's chapel in Rome that has no equal anywhere in the world."

As the line parted deferentially for it, Michelangelo's party strode directly into the sultan's audience chamber, led by the master artist himself.

Cries of delight were heard from within the chamber moments later.

I looked at my teacher and he looked at me.

"This event," he said, "is momentous."

THE SULTAN

AT LENGTH OUR TURN CAME to enter the audience chamber.

"Just stay behind me," Mr. Ascham said, "and let Mr. Giles do the talking. And if you can, please stifle any gasps of shock this time."

I nodded vigorously and we stepped inside.

A golden room greeted me—gold thread in the carpet, gold brocade on the walls, every mighty pillar was painted gold, and mounted on a golden podium in the exact center of the chamber stood a magnificent golden throne shaded by a golden awning.

Seated on that throne, dressed in a dazzling high-collared golden gown studded with rubies, was Suleiman the Magnificent, the lawgiver, caliph and all high sultan of the Ottoman Empire. It was said that the sultan usually only appeared to his own councilors as a shadow behind a gauze screen, but clearly that was not his intention today. Now, in front of the world, he was going to appear in all his formidable glory.

He sat in a commanding pose, legs apart, fists on his armrests, glaring down at us imperiously as a herald called in Turkish and then in Greek:

"Sire, from England, representing that land's most esteemed majesty, King Henry the Eighth, Mr. Gilbert Giles and escorts."

The men bowed. Elsie and I curtsied.

The sultan cocked his wrist an inch, bidding us rise.

He had an incredibly severe face: downturned eyebrows, high pronounced cheekbones, a sharply hooked nose and a sizeable black mustache that framed his mouth like an inverted *U*. His dark eyes blazed with intelligence. He wore on his head a white turban with a jewel-encrusted brooch. The high collar of his golden gown glinted in the light of the oil lamps: veins of gold cord ran through its fabric like intertwining snakes.

Flanking the sultan were a dozen men—the kind found in royal courts everywhere—ministers, advisors, clerics, plus a handful of esteemed European ambassadors based in Constantinople (one of whom was a silver-maned cardinal dressed in the scarlet robes of the Holy See, the local ambassador of Pope Paul III himself). The *sadrazam* stood at the sultan's right hand, while beside him stood a long-bearded Moslem mullah wearing the simple black turban of the Shiite sect: he was the Imam Ali, the senior cleric who I had been told despised the visiting Catholic cardinal.

And among all these men, there was one woman.

The queen.

Oddly, she was not of Persian appearance, but rather possessed the pale porcelain skin of a European. This was the famous *hürrem* sultan or, as she was known in Europe, Roxelana. Her rise from slave girl to concubine to first wife of the sultan was the stuff of legend, a fairy tale come true. She was originally from Ruthenia, but as a girl she had been captured by Tartar raiders and sold into the sultan's harem. Through beauty, wiles and a fearsome intellect, she now shared the bed and held the ear of one of the most powerful men in the world.

Upon the mention of Mr. Giles's name, the sultan's severe countenance transformed into a delighted smile.

"Ah, so this is the famous Mr. Giles!" he said in Greek. "I have heard of you. A formidable player from the University of Cambridge. It is a pleasure to welcome you to my tournament."

"The honor is mine, Your Majesty," Mr. Giles said.

As he said this, I suddenly saw an individual among the men gathered around the sultan whom I recognized. I started, almost gasping out loud again, but this time I managed to stifle my astonishment.

It was the rat-faced fellow who had followed us from tavern to tavern in Wallachia. I saw him whisper into the ear of the *sadrazam* before he melted away into the background. Mr. Ascham had been right: our shadow had been an agent of the sultan.

It did not escape me that someone in the sultan's employ—perhaps someone in that very chamber—had most likely tried to poison Mr. Giles on the way to Constantinople, and here was the sultan delightedly welcoming him to his tournament. My thoughts, however, were cut off when the herald said loudly and formally: "Mr. Giles! You warrant that you are here to compete in the sultan's tournament!"

"I do," Mr. Giles answered equally formally.

"And you warrant that you are here freely and of your own volition!"

"I do."

"And do you come here with an answer to the sultan's demand!"

"I have that." Mr. Giles stepped forward and handed the mysterious red envelope to the grand vizier.

While all this was going on, the sultan's gaze passed idly over the rest of our party—past me and Elsie (although I think he glanced at her a second time), before coming to rest on Mr. Ascham.

"You, sir," he said. "I am informed that you are Mr. Roger Ascham, the famous English schoolteacher."

Mr. Ascham bowed low. "Your Majesty. I am. And I am humbled that you might know of me."

"A sultan must know many things," the sultan said as his eyes turned suddenly and locked on to mine.

"For if you are Ascham, then this young lady with the charming red curls must be your charge, Elizabeth, second daughter of Henry, born of Anne Boleyn, his second wife and the cause of Henry's most unpleasant schism with the Roman Catholic Church." The sultan threw a knowing glance at the nearby cardinal. "A schism, I might add, which I have followed with considerable amusement."

He turned back to me. "But since then, this little one has been shunted down the line of succession by a half brother born of Henry's third wife. Welcome to my kingdom, Princess Elizabeth."

I curtseyed.

"It is an honor and a privilege to be here, Your Majesty," I said in Greek, trying to disguise my surprise that the sultan knew so much about me.

I was thus doubly shocked when he proceeded to address me in German—a language that few others in that room, even the religious men, would know.

"I have spies everywhere, young Bess," he said, utilizing the short-ened form of my name that only those at Hatfield knew and used. "It is a necessary evil of being a great king. Should you ever rule England, I recommend you avail yourself of a competent master of spies. Real knowledge of the state of the world is the greatest treasure any ruler can possess." He reverted to Greek, and with an oily smile said, "I hope you enjoy the chess."

And with a nod of dismissal, our audience was over.

Speechless, I was nudged by my teacher out of the golden room.

THE OPENING BANQUET

EMERGING FROM THE SULTAN'S AUDIENCE CHAMBER—and have no doubt, I emerged quite unnerved—we stepped out into the third of the palace's courtyards. This courtyard featured several wide rectangular lawns and was bounded by the Gate of Felicity—which led back to the Second Courtyard—and the south pavilion, where our quarters could be found, a lattice-walled arcade that led to a fourth and final courtyard, and on the final side, the harem, the sultan's private wing.

For the evening's welcoming banquet, this Third Courtyard had been transformed into a fantasyland of light.

A thousand lanterns suspended from crisscrossing ropes bathed the courtyard in a brilliant yellow glow, turning night into day. Twenty banquet tables stood in perfect rows open to the Turkish sky. Every utensil was fashioned from silver. Place cards marked every space with the guest's name written in their native tongue.

The dinner that followed was like no other I had ever experienced. It was opulent, extravagant and everything in between: cheeses from Lisbon, olives from Florence, wines from France and Spain, grapes from Arcadia, but also delicacies of Moslem origin: the most mouth-watering spices from Morocco, the Indus River valley and Egypt, plus figs and delicious fruits I could not name but which I was informed came from the Bedouin Arabs who inhabit the harsh deserts to the south of Constantinople.

A hundred guests were waited on by as many servants, who hurried to and fro between the tables and the vast kitchens, the entrance to which was situated at the southwest corner of the courtyard. Musicians played, magicians performed, and there was even a stage on which huge muscle-bound wrestlers—their bodies glistening with oil—grappled with each other in exhibition matches. Many of the women in attendance at the dinner, Elsie among them, watched these giants with considerable interest. The largest of the wrestlers, the local champion who went by the name of Darius, had utterly enormous muscles, a very handsome olive-colored face and long straight black hair that flowed down to his shoulders. Most of the women, Elsie included, eyed him longingly as they unconsciously bit their lips.

Speaking of Elsie, as the banquet progressed, she once again disappeared into the crowd, leaving me essentially alone, since Mr. Ascham and Mr. Giles were making conversation with some of our neighbors.

And so from our (very distant) table I gazed at the assembled guests: chess players from around the world, accompanied by ambassadors and dignitaries and, in some cases, their royal patrons themselves. There were not many children; only a handful who, I guessed, were royal ones like Ivan of Muscovy and myself.

I watched Michelangelo as he held court at his table. There was not a moment when someone did not arrive at the famous artist's side to pay their respects.

It came as a great surprise to me then, when, just before the main course was served, Michelangelo abruptly stood, waved away the latest supplicant, gazed around the illuminated courtyard, spotted our table and walked directly over to us.

He arrived at our remote spot, smiled kindly at me, and then to my even greater surprise, sat down beside my teacher and said most casually, "Roger, it is so nice to see you again."

"And you, Michel," my teacher said easily. "You have many admirers these days."

"I know, I know," the great man groaned. "Fame, let me tell you, is most overrated. I spend so much time accepting praise from these people that I have less time to create the works they love. Oh, to have the splendid anonymity of my youth again."

"It is the curse of the brilliant," Mr. Ascham said. "And you have always been brilliant. You were commissioned to create the chess set for this tournament?"

"Two sets. And the sultan pays handsomely. More handsomely than the pope and more promptly, too."

"Are you pleased with your work?"

"Oh, Roger, you know I am never completely pleased with any of my works," Michelangelo said. "I still look upon my *David* and sigh at his hands. And I wish I'd had more time on the *Doni Tondo*. The chess sets, however, are adequate."

My teacher laughed. "Adequate for you means superlative for the rest of us, Michel. I cannot wait to see them."

The great artist leaned close to my teacher. "I heard about that business with the Earl of Cumberland's son at Cambridge. A most distasteful affair by the sound of it, but by all accounts you excelled yourself."

Mr. Ascham glanced at me, as if deciding whether or not I should hear about this matter. "Whatever the status of his father, that boy was disturbed, and even common prostitutes deserve justice."

"You'll get a reputation." Michelangelo grinned. "I recall that time in Rome when you resolved the matter of those stolen chalices from the church of Santa Maria di Loreto. You proved that the local priest, far from being the victim of the crime, had sold the chalices to pay off his gambling debts. For a long time after you left, it was quite the scandal."

Mr. Ascham shrugged. "When all the facts were ascertained, the conclusion was inevitable. Something was done and it was done for a reason. Logic."

"That no one else was able to see."

"All crimes are committed for a reason," my teacher said firmly. "I just uncovered the reason behind that particular crime—"

"Oh, admit it, Roger, you simply couldn't abide an unresolved event," Michelangelo said gently and with a grin. "You *enjoyed* unraveling it and you investigated it as an intellectual exercise, as a tribute to Averroes himself."

"I think Averroes would have been proud of me. Aristotle, too."

Michelangelo laughed. "Roger Ascham! You have not changed one bit! Although I do fear that one day your curiosity will be the death of you. It is wonderful to see you again." The great artist then glanced at me. "And who is this beautiful young lady?"

"This is Elizabeth. My finest student."

"Roger's finest student?" Michelangelo's old eyes shone. "This is no small compliment coming from Roger Ascham. A 'fine' student in his estimation is likely to change the course of history. I shall have to keep an eye on you."

I bowed my head, blushing.

Michelangelo glanced sideways at my teacher. "A royal student, Roger?"

My teacher nodded with his eyes.

"Oh, Roger! You truly are a unique educator! Only you would bring a royal heir halfway across the world in the name of her education! How wonderful!"

My teacher then introduced Mr. Giles, before asking Michelangelo, "Where are you staying while you are here?"

Michelangelo said, "I have been granted special permission to stay in the sultan's private area, the harem. It gives me some blessed peace. Since I arrived at the palace a week ago—I made the journey with the delegation from the Papal States—I have been *constantly* pestered by Rome's ambassador here, a man who must be Italy's most self-aggrandizing and insufferable—oh no, here he comes."

"Il Magnifico! There you are!"

Both my teacher and Michelangelo turned.

A cardinal of Rome stood before us in all his glory: red robes, staff, gold chains, decorated miter. He had a flowing mane of silver hair, perfectly coiffed, and I recognized him as the cardinal who had been in the sultan's audience chamber, one of the privileged local ambassadors. Behind him, like a shadow, loomed a tall blank-faced manservant, a personal guard of some sort.

The cardinal extended his ring toward Michelangelo's face. I distinctly saw the great artist pause momentarily before he dutifully leaned forward and kissed it.

"Cardinal Cardoza," Michelangelo said evenly. "So . . . nice . . . to see you again." He gestured at us. "Cardinal, this is Mr. Roger Ascham from England, and his party: Mr. Gilbert Giles, their player in the tournament, and his student, Elizabeth. Cardinal Cardoza is the Holy See's ambassador-in-residence here at the sultan's court."

The cardinal was an older man of about sixty years, with pale blue eyes and silver brows that matched his flowing hair. He was also a large fellow, big but not fat, broad in the chest, a man who had perhaps been a capable athlete in his younger days.

He gripped his shepherd's crook in one hand and in the other he held an unusual device: it looked like a horse's tail, a small whiplike thing with multicolored lengths of hair that the cardinal used to flick away any insect that dared approach his face.

Despite Michelangelo's courteous introduction, Cardinal Cardoza completely ignored us. He struck me as the kind of fellow who always gravitates to the most important person in a room and clings to that person like a leech. I had seen many such people in my father's presence back home.

The cardinal said to Michelangelo, "I was just speaking to Cardinal Farnese. Farnese tells me that His Holiness is *delighted* that you have accepted his invitation to take over as the architect of his grand basilica."

"Your Grace is most kind," Michelangelo said. "I am an old man. I had actually thought my time for building grand edifices had passed."

Cardoza said, "Not at all! The pope grew weary of Sangallo's moods and you have *infinitely* more experience and skill anyway. You know, I became close with His Holiness during our days together in Ostia. I know him very well. In fact, in a more private environment, I could inform you of some of his personal preferences so that your designs might please him."

"You are too kind."

"It is nothing."

"I'm sure I shall see you later," Michelangelo said.

Cardinal Cardoza smiled. "Enjoy the dinner. I have partaken in far too many banquets like this, so I am going to enjoy a private meal in my rooms. Magnifico." He swept away, trailed by his silent manservant.

Michelangelo watched him go, then turned to my teacher. "Be wary of that man, Roger. He is a cunning one. Slippery. It is said that Queen Roxelana cannot abide him and simply leaves the chamber when he arrives for an audience with the sultan. And I have it on good authority that the citizens of Ostia were happy to see the back of him; there were allegations of . . . impropriety . . . with some boys of the district."

My teacher watched Cardinal Cardoza cross the courtyard and arrive at his table, where he collected the visiting cardinal, Cardinal Farnese, and the two of them headed off together.

Mr. Ascham said, "What about the other cardinal, the pope's brother, Cardinal Farnese? I was most surprised to see him here, given his statements about the Moslem faith."

The artist sighed. "God, give me patience. I had to ride in a carriage with him all the way from Rome. Cardinal Farnese is a pig, with his snout buried deep in many troughs. He is also a fool who offends more out of ignorance than intent. Archduke Ferdinand of Austria has despised Farnese ever since he discovered that Farnese sold him indulgences at ten times the price paid by the Polish king, Sigismund. The Jesuits find him embarrassing. The imam has told his Moslem followers to ignore him, yet four times on our way through the city, crowds of young Moslem men held up the soles of their sandals as Farnese rode by."

"Excuse me, sir, but I don't understand," I interrupted politely. "What is the significance of that act?"

My teacher answered: "To Arabs and Moslems, it is a most insulting gesture to point the sole of one's shoe at someone. Those young Moslem men were protesting against Cardinal Farnese's views." Mr. Ascham turned to Michelangelo: "Which begs the question: why would Pope Paul send Farnese here?"

Michelangelo said, "My view is that the pontiff wanted to be provocative, to stick a thorn in the sultan's side during his great international event. The sultan would not dare allow a visiting cardinal of Rome, even one as offensive as Farnese, to be harmed at his tournament. It would be an embarrassment in front of the very world the sultan is seeking to impress."

"I did not know the pope engaged in such petty schemes."

Michelangelo shook his head. "It has been my life's joy to create works for the greater glory of our Lord and His Church. Only sometimes I wish our Lord employed better people."

———

As he made to depart from our table, Michelangelo told us that we should accompany him to the palace's kitchen, where he wanted to call on the assistant chef, one Brunello of Borgia.

"Brunello was the finest chef in Florence," Michelangelo told us as we headed toward the kitchen area in the corner of the courtyard. Ten enormous chimneys rose above it, each one venting a gigantic oven. "The sultan brought him to Constantinople specifically for this occasion. He has been here for three months, teaching the local cooks how to prepare dishes that the sultan's European guests will enjoy. I am keen to see the kitchens here. I have heard they are larger than any in Italy."

The great artist marched ahead of us at a spritely pace.

"How did you come to be so intimately acquainted with Michelangelo?" I whispered to my teacher as we hurried along behind him.

Mr. Ascham gave me a sideways look. "This surprises you?"

"A little, yes."

"I must confess I quite enjoy surprising you. Some years ago, Michelangelo read a treatise I wrote as a student about education and he invited me to Rome to meet with him. Of course, I leaped at the invitation. I ended up instructing his beloved grandnephew for six months and in so doing we became friends. I watched him paint some of *The Last Judgment*, one of the greatest privileges of my life."

I had never actually contemplated my teacher having a life before he began teaching me, let alone one of exotic travel and of meeting great artists.

And there was another thing. "And what happened with the Earl of Cumberland's son at Cambridge? My father also mentioned this in his note to you."

Mr. Ascham's face darkened. "It was a most unpleasant affair involving the son of a powerful man and his . . . distasteful . . . proclivities. It is not a story for young ears."

"Was it to do with passion?" I said in a voice that I hoped sounded mature and experienced. "Fornication even?"

My teacher gave me a long look before he answered. "It did indeed have something to do with the young man's urges. He would hire prostitutes from other towns and . . . do things . . . to them before killing the poor women. But you do not need to know the whole sordid tale. I was brought in to act as an impartial judge on the matter, but due to my, well, overzealous curiosity, I discovered more than anyone wanted to know. Now, please, let us engage in more pleasant topics and enjoy this marvelous evening."

As he said this, we passed through a large doorway in the very corner of the courtyard and entered the kitchens.

I beheld a bustling madhouse of activity: hurrying slave girls, shouting cooks, blazing fires, smoking ovens, turning roasts, squawking chickens, quacking ducks, thudding cleavers and the most delightful mix of aromas I had ever smelled in my short life.

Shouting above the din was the head chef, a fat Moslem wearing a blood-smeared apron and an enormous turban.

Standing near him at a long blocklike table, commanding his own small army of Turkish cooks, was a squat bearded man of Italian appearance wearing a small crucifix around his neck: Brunello of Borgia.

"Why did the sultan feel the need to bring a European chef to

Constantinople?" I had quite enjoyed the local fare. "When one travels, shouldn't one taste the unfamiliar local dishes on offer?"

"Yes, I agree, one should, but the bellies of old men are not as accommodating of new foods as are the stomachs of the young," Mr. Ascham said with a gentle smile. "It is not uncommon for visitors to these lands to fall terribly ill after eating the local spices and meats. The sultan is most wise to provide an alternative for his esteemed guests."

Amid all the mayhem, Brunello saw Michelangelo and he quickly wiped his hands on his apron and hurried over to us.

He was joined by a woman as wide as she was tall, and a gangly boy of about fifteen.

"Signor Buonarroti," Brunello bowed, "welcome to my kitchen. It is an honor."

"Brunello," Michelangelo said, "the honor is mine. You are an artist yourself. The only difference between us is that your art is literally consumed by its audience and so sadly does not remain afterward for later edification. Its joy is in the moment."

"You are too kind," Brunello said. "Signor, my wife, Marianna, and my son, Pietro."

Michelangelo bowed to Brunello's family.

I have to say, the way the great artist interacted with his social inferiors had a profound effect on me. He would have been well within his station to treat everyone from the cook to the cardinal with disdain and even outright condescension. But he did not. Quite the contrary: he treated the chef's skinny son with the same gentle courtesy with which I had seen him treat everyone else.

My father, on the contrary, treated every inferior—from his wife to the noble whose wife he took to his bedchamber—with open contempt. I assumed my father thought this kind of behavior reinforced his status, but upon seeing Michelangelo's courteous decency to all, I realized that the truly powerful do not need to put their power on display at all times.

Michelangelo shook the boy's hand. The boy lowered his head

meekly and I wondered if he was shy or just overawed by the great man. I couldn't tell.

Michelangelo then introduced my teacher to Brunello and a pleasant but brief conversation was had.

As they spoke, I noticed that Brunello's wife wore a rosary around her own neck. Attached to the rosary's crucifix was a small black ribbon tied in a bow.

"Are there many Christians in Constantinople?" I asked her politely in Italian.

When she spoke, her voice was flat, uninterested. "Owing to its long history, there are many Jews and Christians in the city as well as Moslems."

"What does the Moslem sultan have to say about these rival faiths worshipping in his capital?" I thought this was a most astute and adult question, but her response was still completely devoid of interest.

"He does not seem to care," she answered blandly.

I was saved from further efforts to engage her when Brunello excused himself, saying that the main course was about to be served. This was also the time at which the players in the tournament would be introduced, so we took our leave from the kitchens and returned to our table out in the courtyard.

THE PLAYERS

WE ARRIVED BACK AT OUR TABLE just as Elsie returned from the other side of the courtyard leading a striking young Persian girl by the hand.

The girl was an Arab beauty. Perhaps sixteen, she had a tiny waist yet full breasts and high curving hips which she wore tantalizingly exposed between gaps in the gorgeous silver sari that entwined her body. She had a deep olive complexion and the most perfect almond-shaped eyes I had ever seen.

"Bessie, Bessie," Elsie said breathlessly. "You must meet Zubaida here. She is an acquaintance of the crown prince, the sultan's firstborn son and heir." Elsie threw a look over to the elevated table at which the sultan ate. A very handsome young Turk sat beside him looking profoundly bored: the crown prince.

Elsie's voice softened to a whisper. "Zubaida says that the prince will be holding an unofficial gathering later tonight in his rooms inside the harem."

The girl, Zubaida, leaned in close. "The prince is known for his Dionysian gatherings. There will be music and wine and dancing and ganja and I am told that some of the wrestlers have been invited!"

She and Elsie tittered excitedly at that news.

By virtue of my classical education, I knew that Dionysus was the Greek god of wine and winemaking, and also ecstasy and a certain kind of free-spiritedness. But I was unsure what a Dionysian *gathering* was. I guessed it was a reference to the wine. There was also something else Zubaida had mentioned that I did not understand.

"What is ganja?" I asked.

"It is the strange weed that many smoke here," Elsie said. "They say it relaxes the mind and calms the soul, and sometimes gives wondrous visions. Oh, Bessie, we simply must go to this private party!"

I glanced at Mr. Ascham. "I don't know, Elsie. I don't think Mr. Ascham would approve—"

"Oh, goodness gracious me, aren't you the goody-goody," Elsie said quickly and a little nastily. "Do you always do only what your teacher approves? You're starting to sound like Primrose Ponsonby. And there I thought you were old enough to understand . . ."

"I'm old enough—"

"We shall see. Later tonight, when your teacher is asleep, I plan to slip out of our rooms and go to this party. We will see if you are brave enough to join me."

I hesitated, uncertain and uncomfortable.

Zubaida said, "The gathering will be held in the prince's private quarters inside the harem. Tell the guards at the entrance that you are *a privileged friend of the crown prince* and you will be granted entrance."

At that moment, some horns blared and Zubaida hurried away. The official ceremony was about to begin.

————

The official opening ceremony of the All High Sultan's Invitational Chess Championship of 1546 began with a speech from the sultan himself, first in Turkish, then in common Greek. In his speech, he welcomed the various champions to his kingdom and wished them well in the tournament.

Then the sultan returned to his throne and the grand vizier stood and in a loud voice proclaimed: "Ladies and gentlemen! It is my pleasure and privilege to introduce to you . . . the players!"

One by one, the sixteen players were introduced and brought onto the stage.

There was the talented Spanish monk I had seen earlier, Brother

Raul of Seville, playing on behalf of the Papal States. Rumor had it that he had not lost a match in six years.

Then there was the other Spaniard representing King Charles, Pablo Montoya of Castile. The nephew of the famed chess master Luis Ramirez de Lucena, it was said that Montoya had read his uncle's book, the *Repetición de Amores y Arte de Ajedrez con ci Iuegos de Partido,* over a dozen times.

Maximilian of Vienna represented the archduke of Austria and the Habsburgs, while a young man named Wilhelm of Königsberg ascended the stage on behalf of the new Protestant duchy of Prussia.

And, of course, there was our man, Mr. Gilbert Giles, who the *sadrazam* very diplomatically announced to be representing "the Christian kingdom of England." A few other Western players were introduced and the crowd clapped politely.

Then came the Eastern players.

A brutish Wallachian fellow named Dragan of Brasov—the same Dragan the tavern owner in Wallachia had mentioned.

An Oriental named Lao from the Chin lands at the end of the Silk Road.

The champion of Muscovy: a grim fellow with a hard, wrinkled face and a perpetually downturned mouth. As he ascended the stage, the little prince Ivan clapped loudly and vigorously.

A handsome prince from the Moghul Empire named Nasiruddin Akbar. He had deep brown skin and a slight build and was reputed to have played chess since he had been an infant.

There was an old and gnarled librarian from the House of Wisdom in Baghdad named Talib. He was the oldest player in the tournament but a most respected one. He had long been an *aliyat,* the title given to the highest rank of players, those who could see a dozen moves ahead in a given game.

And last of all, there were the local Moslem heroes, two of them.

The first of these was the palace champion, a handsome young man of royal birth named Zaman. He was a cousin of the sultan's and had only recently attained the rank of *aliyat*, the youngest ever to achieve the title.

The second was Ibrahim of Constantinople, and when his name was uttered a great roar went up from the kitchen staff watching the announcement ceremony from the wings. Ibrahim was the people's champion, the winner of a chess tournament that had been held in Constantinople the previous year. He was about the same age as his compatriot Zaman, perhaps in his midtwenties, but there the similarities ended. Where Zaman was dashing, well dressed and regal, Ibrahim was emaciated, dirty and hunched, a peasant. He had no formal chess ranking.

When it was all over, sixteen men stood on the stage facing the assembled crowd, accepting its applause and adulation: men from every corner of the civilized world, representing their kings, their faiths, their nations.

Over the din, the *sadrazam* called, "Tomorrow morning, a draw will be held to determine the first-round matches! Each match will consist of seven games, the winner being the first player to win four of the seven games. All matches will be played in the Ayasofya with the spectacular chess sets created by the renowned artist Michelangelo Buonarroti. The winner of the tournament will take home one of those chess sets as a trophy for his king. Play well, gentlemen, for your people's pride depends on you! Ladies and gentlemen, honor the champions, and may the best man win!"

The crowd's applause was deafening.

————

As the cheering reached its height, I felt a tug on my sleeve. It was Elsie. Her new friend Zubaida had returned and was at her side.

"Bessie!" Elsie said. "Come on! Zubaida says there are fireworks to be set off shortly above the Fourth Courtyard! Let's sneak out there and get a good spot."

My teacher heard this exchange and at my beseeching look said, "Oh, go on."

We scurried away from the banquet area, heading for the rearmost courtyard. We dashed through the lattice-walled arcade that separated the Third Courtyard from the Fourth and slipped through one of its ornate gates and beheld the rear courtyard: some stairs led down to a broad lawn overlooking the Bosphorus. A striking oblong reflecting pool lay at the base of the stairs and off to the right stood a lone white building (which I would later learn was the Catholic embassy).

All of a sudden, with a shrill whistling noise, the first firework rocketed into the sky, fired from a position atop the latticed arcade. It burst in a dazzling starlike shape and we heard the crowd in the other courtyard ooh and ahh with delight. This, it appeared, was the signal to bring all the guests into the Fourth Courtyard for the fireworks show, for at that moment some ushers pushed three other gates open.

And at that exact moment, I saw something in the shallow pool, and with a start, I caught my breath—

Suddenly there came shouts.

They were followed by a rush of movement at the gate behind us.

A phalanx of palace guards rushed to the gate. More guards dashed toward our position on the stairs, yelling, "Get back! Get back!" before pushing us through the gate, back into the Third Courtyard and slamming the latticed doors shut behind us.

But my eyes had already glimpsed the dreadful image that the guards had not wished anyone to see.

By the dying light of that first firework, I had seen the hideous corpse of a man—enormously fat, naked and bearing many stab wounds—lying motionless beneath the surface of the shallow reflecting pool at the base of the stairs.

Even in that brief instant, I could tell who it was.

With its broad face, its many chins, its distinctive black hair with silver tips above the ears and its bloated, obese belly, the corpse was that of the visiting cardinal from Rome, none other than the pope's brother, Cardinal Farnese.

And even when seen through the rippling water of the shallow pool, I could see that the lower half of Farnese's face had been monstrously mutilated, the skin wrenched away so as to expose the flesh under his cheeks, the white curve of his jawbone and every single one of his teeth.

— III —

BISHOP

In the earliest forms of chess, the piece that we know as the bishop was actually an elephant.

It was only when chess swept across Europe between the 10th and 12th centuries that the elephants became men of faith, reflecting the powerful role played by the Catholic Church in medieval politics.

As a chess piece, the bishop is unique: it can only move diagonally and is thus restricted to squares of a single color. Some have suggested this reflects the wiles of medieval churchmen who, lacking military power, could only ever act circuitously, never directly.

Interestingly, in France, the elephant piece was transformed into *le fou*, the jester or the fool.

From: *Chess in the Middle Ages,*
TEL JACKSON (W. M. Lawry & Co., London, 1992)

I have no desire to make windows into men's souls.

—Queen Elizabeth I

THE HOURS
AFTER THE BANQUET

ELSIE, ZUBAIDA AND I RETURNED TO the Third Courtyard, silent and stunned.

"You're back?" Mr. Ascham remarked. "So soon?"

I tried to answer him but found myself unable to speak. I was in a state of considerable dismay. It was not so much the sight of the dead body—I had seen hangings and beheadings on numerous occasions in England—but rather the cruel display of it.

The hideous image of the cardinal's submerged and spread-eagled corpse—and the grotesque skinning of the lower half of his face—was seared into my mind's eye. Clearly, the killer had wanted the sultan's guests to see his grim handiwork, but the palace guards had acted quickly and it seemed that only Elsie, Zubaida and I had been witness to the foul sight.

At last, I found my tongue. "Sir . . . I . . . I mean, we . . . we saw—"

A loud bang made me jump, startled. More fireworks were launched from other places around our courtyard, lighting up the sky and making further conversation impossible. The banquet crowd, unaware that their vantage point should be any different, clapped in delight at the spectacle.

As the rockets exploded and the crowd clapped, I glanced at the sultan's stage and saw a guard appear there and whisper in the ear of the grand vizier, who—after a brief look of shock—whispered in the ear of the sultan.

The sultan cocked his head ever so slightly before resuming his happy observation of the fireworks display, giving away nothing.

Soon after, he left the stage, and with the departure of the sovereign, the banquet ended and gradually the Third Courtyard cleared as all the guests retired to their rooms for the night, greatly impressed by the dinner, the entertainment and the fireworks the sultan had put on.

———

We returned to our quarters in the south pavilion. Mr. Giles and Mr. Ascham talked animatedly while I walked behind in silence. When we arrived at our lodgings, Mr. Giles retired to his room while Elsie disappeared into the little room we shared.

Still troubled, I stopped my teacher as he made for his room.

"Sir, a moment?" I said softly.

"Yes, Bess—" He cut himself off. "By God, you look like you've seen a ghost. What's wrong?"

"I saw . . . I mean, Elsie and I . . . we saw something, in the Fourth Courtyard, something horrible—"

"What did you see?"

I swallowed deeply. "We saw—"

"Make way for the sultan!" a voice boomed from the hallway outside our rooms before the vestibule door was thrown open and four palace guards rushed inside. Striding in after them were, first, the grand vizier, and then, Sultan Suleiman himself.

Mr. Ascham and I stood with straight backs, as though we were soldiers on parade. Mr. Giles and Elsie emerged from their rooms, startled.

The sultan spoke simply and directly.

"There has been a murder in my palace. The visiting Cardinal Farnese. His body has been desecrated. The palace gates have been locked and patrolled since the banquet began, so the killer remains within these walls. I want him found.

"You"—the sultan stepped in front of my teacher—"Mr. Roger Ascham. I am advised by Michelangelo that you have distinguished yourself on several occasions in the unraveling of unusual crimes: a theft in Rome and a series of foul murders in England."

"I have, Your Majesty."

"You use logic as a tool, Michelangelo says."

"I did on those occasions."

"Does logic apply to the acts of madmen?"

"It did in the Cumberland matter. A certain kind of woman harmed the killer as a child and so as an adult he attacked women of a similar kind."

The sultan gazed at Mr. Ascham for a long moment, appraising him, taking this in.

"A riddle for you, then," he said. "A test of your logical approach. A murderer is on the loose. The city lives in fear. The peasants in the slums think he kills men, women and children indiscriminately, but in truth he has killed two old mullahs, six young boys and three girls in their teens. His victims are always stabbed many times, and once dead, the killer flays their cheeks and jawbones. Who is he and why does he do these things?"

My teacher returned the sultan's gaze. He thought for a good while before answering, and when at last he spoke, he did so slowly and in a most measured tone.

"I would guess—from these very few facts you have given me—that your killer is a young man, perhaps sixteen years of age or thereabouts, and he has a facial deformity of some kind, a harelip or a tic. I would further posit that he is an idiot or of feeble mind or perhaps simply insane, but at the least he is a person of considerably low intellect."

I listened in amazed silence. I couldn't fathom how my teacher could deduce such specific things from so brief a postulation.

But he wasn't finished.

He went on: "I draw these conclusions largely from the descriptions of the victims you have given me, for in purely logical terms, the nature of the victim can tell us something about the nature of the killer. Your killer sought solace from the two mullahs, but they told him he was an abomination, the spawn of Satan, that his deformity was an outward sign of inner impurity. In a frustrated rage, he killed them, stabbing them many times."

"Interesting. How do you know he is a *young* man?" the sultan asked.

"Because of his other victims. You say he killed six boys," Mr. Ascham said, "which means he killed more boys than he did any other group. I'm guessing the dead boys teased him about his disfigurement. Boys are cowards: they do not taunt full-grown adults or youths a lot older than they are, hence my guess that he is about sixteen. Similarly, the girls probably rejected his advances or tittered at his ugliness, and again, in an idiot's rage, he slaughtered them."

"This is all based on *your* premise that he has a deformity," the sultan said. "How do you know for certain that this is the case?"

"The skinning of the faces of the victims," my teacher said. "He imposes on them in death the same disfigurement he bears in life. The final revenge."

The sultan pondered my teacher for a long time, taking in his conclusions. I myself was still somewhat stunned that my courteous and unassuming teacher could apply his logical mind so skillfully to so gruesome a riddle.

Mr. Ascham asked, "This murder that occurred inside your palace tonight, does it bear any similarities to the ones you have just described to me?"

"It does. And I find your deductions most intriguing, most intriguing. You will come with me. Now."

———

My teacher was whisked away by the sultan and his men.

I did not go with him. I returned to the room I shared with Elsie to find Elsie whipping off her evening gown and putting on a different dress, the light silk thing that she had bought in the Grand Bazaar.

"What are you doing?" I whispered.

"I am going to the crown prince's gathering, of course," she said. "Now that your boring old schoolmaster is occupied elsewhere, this is the perfect chance to slip away. I thought you said you might come, too."

"Oh, no," I said quickly. "No." I found boys interesting, yes, but a gathering—with wine and dancing and young men—was not something I felt at all confident attending. Nor did I like the idea of venturing out into the night on an evening when a man had been murdered. But most of all, I was simply worried about Mr. Ascham and I wanted to be here when he returned. I didn't like Elsie calling him boring.

"Have it your way," Elsie said before sweeping out of the room lightly on her toes, carrying her sandals in her hands, leaving me standing there in our room alone.

———

An hour later, I heard the outer door to our rooms open and close. My teacher had returned.

I hadn't slept. I couldn't. I had just sat on my bed and waited tensely, waited for the sound of that door opening. I sagged with relief when I heard Mr. Giles greet my teacher. "Roger, what the devil is going on?"

Sitting with my ear to the curtain that separated my room from the vestibule, I listened in on the subsequent conversation between them.

Mr. Ascham said, "The sultan took me to a special dungeon, separate from the main dungeons beneath the Tower of Justice, deep within the palace. It is a series of cages built into the bones of some old Roman ruins. You won't believe what he showed me."

"What?" Mr. Giles asked.

"In one of the cages of this dungeon was a mute boy of about sixteen with a ghastly harelip and the deep brown skin of a tannery worker. He scurried around the cell more like an ape than a man, grunting like an animal. He had the mind of a small child."

"You were right . . ."

"I was. But then the sultan said: 'My men caught this lad six days ago, standing over the body of his latest victim. We have not told anyone that the killer has been caught. And now, tonight, I have a high-ranking cardinal from Rome, the pope's brother, killed in an identical manner. Can you explain *this* with your logic, Mr. Roger Ascham?'

" 'Did the boy escape from his cell during the banquet?' I asked the sultan.

" 'No,' he said. 'He was here the whole time. Which means I have a problem.'

" 'You do,' I said. 'You have another killer on the loose, one who is shrewd enough to impersonate the insane boy in an attempt to conceal his own crime.'

" 'Yes,' the sultan said darkly. 'Like many royal courts, mine is a den of ambition and intrigue, deception and flattery, of men and women who would curry my favor to enhance their stature or get into my bed. Add to that the foreign ambassadors who report my every move to their masters and one will see that it is a tangled web of enmities, alliances and outright scheming. I trust no one.

" 'But you, Roger Ascham, you come here with no agenda and a reputation for acumen which you have just proved to me: with but a few facts, you were able to describe this deranged boy whom you had never seen before almost to the last detail.'

"The sultan said, 'The cardinal's body has been removed from view, but word of his death will get out. Keeping rumors at bay in a palace is impossible. And so I will allow the fiction that Cardinal Farnese was killed by the insane fiend to continue, but in the meantime, *I want his killer found.*

" 'I need an outsider, someone with no connection to this palace, to investigate this crime and find the murderer. And I need that investigation performed without compromising my tournament. The criminal behind this wanted to embarrass me in front of the world and he almost succeeded.

" 'My tournament will thus go ahead as planned, but as it does, I want you to find this killer and bring him before me. Will you accept this task?'

"What could I say?" my teacher said to Mr. Giles. "I did not come here to meddle in palace intrigues or investigate murders. Indeed, I found the whole Cumberland affair for which I am now apparently famous to be wholly unpleasant. Plus, I have to watch over young Bess. Bringing her to Byzantium was already a bold thing to do. I didn't expect something like *this* to be added to it. But he is the sultan. What option did I have? So I just said, 'Your Majesty, I will do my best to find your killer.' "

VENTURING OUT
INTO THE NIGHT

SHORTLY AFTERWARD, MR. ASCHAM AND MR. GILES retired, and so did I.

But still I couldn't sleep. Myriad images swirled inside my mind: of the cardinal's fat naked body in the rippling pool, of his grotesque half-skinned face, of fireworks exploding, guards running and gates slamming shut.

Beside me, Elsie's bed lay glaringly empty.

I stared at it a little jealously. I envied Elsie's ability to think only of herself at such a time. I couldn't help but put myself in the minds of others. I imagined the dead man's no doubt horrifying final moments. I imagined the sultan's fury. I thought of my teacher and this great new obligation foisted upon him: to be personally commissioned by a sovereign often reduced the most resolute gentleman to a quivering wreck; my father had executed men for failing him in matters far less important than this. And lastly, I thought of Mr. Ascham's consideration of me in the whole affair: he still worried about me. Perhaps Elsie was better off living life the way she did.

Evidently, my teacher also couldn't sleep. Sometime after midnight, I heard him pad out into our vestibule. He was pacing, thinking. Then he apparently came to a decision because he ducked back into his room and returned a few moments later wearing his boots and long coat. He was heading out.

I pushed through the curtains.

"Sir, where are you going at this hour?"

"Bess?" He looked at me askance, realizing. "You heard my conversation with Giles, didn't you? About the cardinal's murder and the deranged boy in the dungeon?"

I nodded.

"Then you know of my newfound commission."

I nodded again.

Mr. Ascham sighed. "I cannot sleep. I have too many thoughts running around in my head. The sultan has given me complete freedom of movement and action inside the palace, so I thought I might go downstairs and examine the body of the slain cardinal."

"May I come with you?" I asked. "I, too, cannot sleep."

Mr. Ascham suddenly looked at me very closely. "Wait a moment. *This* was what ailed you earlier, when you wanted to speak with me, wasn't it? But then we were interrupted by the arrival of the sultan. Do you know something about this matter, Bess?"

"I saw the cardinal's body. It was horrible, just lying there in the shallow pool—"

"Wait, wait, wait. You saw the body *as the murderer left it*?"

"Yes, sir, I did. But I didn't mean to . . ."

Mr. Ascham held up his hand, digesting this revelation. "Don't apologize, you did nothing wrong. In fact, you may be of some use. Can you show me where you saw it?"

"Why, yes, of course."

My teacher frowned in thought. Clearly, he was weighing his options: the help I could provide him versus the dangers of exposing a young princess of England to further gruesome sights.

"You have a stronger constitution and a sharper mind than many adults I know, Bess. But there is a fiend on the loose here and your father will have my head if anything happens to you. Although"—a strange look passed over his face—"it *could* actually be good for you. What better lesson for a potential future queen: to peer through a window into the hearts of men's souls."

He crouched in front of me so that we faced each other nose to nose. "Can you promise me three things, Bess? Can you promise me that you will stay close by my side during whatever follows?"

"I promise."

"Can you promise me that you will do exactly as I say during whatever follows?"

"I promise," I said eagerly. "And the third thing?"

"Can you promise me that you will never *ever* tell Mrs. Ponsonby about your participation in this affair?"

My face broke into a broad grin. I nodded vigorously. "I absolutely promise."

"Excellent," he said. "Come then, put on a cloak, and stay close to me."

———

We stepped into the corridor outside our rooms.

An armed man stood there and I stopped short.

Bald and muscular, he had the deep black skin of an Abyssinian and he wore a white tunic and a bronze collar around his neck: a pre-eminent slave. His cheekbones were etched with raised dots and tribal scarring.

Mr. Ascham didn't even miss a step.

"Elizabeth, this is Latif, one of the sultan's most trusted eunuchs," he said. "In addition to the local languages, he speaks Latin and Greek and a little bit of English. The sultan has assigned him to be my escort throughout the investigation. Latif, this is my student, Elizabeth."

The big eunuch bowed to me but said nothing. He carried an ornate bronze bow and matching quiver on his back, and two gold-hilted cutlasses on his belt.

"Latif," Mr. Ascham said. "I would like to see the exact place where the cardinal's body was found and then I would like to see the body itself."

THE POOL AND THE DUNGEON

IT WAS WELL AFTER MIDNIGHT WHEN Mr. Ascham, Latif and I arrived at the latticed arcade that separated the Third Courtyard from the Fourth.

The palace was silent in the moonlight. The many tables from the banquet had long since been packed away. Four stern-faced palace guards bearing scimitars and spears guarded the lattice gate leading to the reflecting pool in the Fourth Courtyard, but at a word from Latif they stepped aside and let us pass.

As we stepped through the gate and came to the stairs beyond it, I recalled the grim sight of Cardinal Farnese's corpse lying faceup and spread-eagled in the shallow rectangular pool.

We beheld that same pool now.

No corpse lay in it.

A few small smears of blood on the pool's right rim were the only evidence of anything untoward happening there. They wouldn't remain for long: at that very moment, a slave girl was on her knees scrubbing them away.

"He was in that pool?" Mr. Ascham asked.

"Yes, he was lying on his back with his arms spread wide, Christlike. His eyes were open and the skin around his jaw had been . . . torn away . . ."

I guided my teacher to the edge of the pool. "He lay this way, with his feet pointed toward the Third Courtyard."

Mr. Ascham surveyed the scene in silence.

Then he turned to me and said, "Bess, was there much blood? On the stones surrounding the pool? On the rim, perhaps?"

I thought about this. "No. Just those small smears that are being cleaned off now."

"What about the water in the pool: was it clear or was it reddened by the blood of the dead man?"

"It was clear," I said. Despite his many wounds, I had been able to see the cardinal's body clearly under the water's surface.

"I see." Mr. Ascham turned to Latif. "Who ordered the body to be taken away?"

"His Majesty the sultan did," our escort said curtly. "He did not wish any of his guests to see it."

"Who specifically took it away, then?"

Latif spoke briefly in Turkish with the slave girl scrubbing the rim of the pool. "Captain Faad, the head of the Palace Guard, took the body away."

"Where is it now? I would like to see it."

"Why?" Latif said with a frown. "The man is dead. He cannot tell you anything."

"We shall see about that."

Latif shrugged and another quick conversation with the scrubbing girl was had. "The body was taken to the sultan's main dungeon," he reported.

Mr. Ascham nodded. "Please take us there, then, so that I may see this corpse for myself."

———

For as I long as I could remember, the most frightening structure in all of London was the Tower.

It stood like a dark behemoth at the eastern extremity of the city, at the point where the Thames left the walls of London and headed for the sea. When one passed by the Tower in a boat, one could hear the wails and cries of the traitors inside being tortured. A few days later, their heads would be on display atop London Bridge. As a young girl, I prayed to the Lord that I would never find myself in the Tower of London.

But judging from the accounts I had read of English soldiers who had been captured during the Crusades to the Holy Land, the dungeons of the Moslems were an even greater hell.

They were the stuff of grim legend. Those Englishmen who had been captured during the various holy wars in Jerusalem had returned with tales of the most frightening barbarism. Beheadings, brandings, severed tongues and hands. And this was all before one heard of the Moslems' instruments of torture: spiked head cages, neck vises and heated tanks of scalding water into which naked men were plunged.

Curiously, in the centuries after those ill-fated Crusades, all of those contraptions of torture found their way into the dungeons of Europe. Europe received much knowledge from the Moslems—astronomy, mathematics, the works of the ancient Greeks, chess and, evidently, many methods of breaking a human body slowly and in great agony.

It was with these thoughts flitting through my mind that I descended a long flight of stone stairs beneath the Tower of Justice and entered the dungeons of the sultan.

———

After passing through several tunnels we came to a guard station where Latif spoke briefly with a hard-eyed guard who bore a hideous Y-shaped scar on his right cheek. The guard let us pass and we entered a wide stone-walled chamber lit by torches and ringed by barred cells.

An iron cage hung above a pit of hot coals; manacles dangled in front of a bloodstained wall; dry hay lined the floor. The place smelled of urine, blood and shit. Dull moans could be heard from within the cells but the guards had long ago grown deaf to them.

Lying on a wide stone slab in the center of the dungeon was the body of Cardinal Farnese. I imagined that the slab was usually used for beheadings or, perhaps, for amputating the hands of thieves.

It lay naked and faceup, the cardinal's immense paunch bulging over his genitals. His skin was pale and gray. Dozens of bloody stab wounds pierced it. And the exposed bones of his jaws and teeth pointed up at the stone ceiling.

My teacher circumnavigated the slab, peering at the body curiously without the slightest appearance of discomfort. He glanced over at me. "Are you all right?"

I nodded even though I was utterly horrified.

Mr. Ascham touched one of the stab wounds, as if checking to make sure it was real. Then he casually picked up one of the dead cardinal's hands and looked at both sides of it with no more care or enthusiasm than a woman at a fruit stall assessing a bruised apple. He let the hand fall back onto the stone slab with a dull slap before he checked the other one. Both hands were pudgy and pale, wet and gray, and as far as I could tell, completely unremarkable.

Now my teacher came to the corpse's mutilated head.

He bent over the cardinal's exposed jawbone and looked at it closely. I couldn't imagine how he could get so close to something so foul and yet still be so calm. I half-expected the corpse to leap up and bite him.

He peered inside the cardinal's skinless mouth—and here my teacher emitted a grunt of discovery.

"What is it?" I asked.

"The cardinal's gums and tongue are covered in a rash, a rather aggressive rash. The tongue is greatly swollen, too." At this point, to my great disgust and horror, Mr. Ascham reached *into* the dead man's ghastly mouth with his index finger and poked around inside it.

"How very interesting," he said casually. "The entire underside of his tongue is covered in a black residue. The good cardinal, it appears, indulged in regular opium use."

Then my teacher did something even more peculiar: he pushed down sharply and firmly on the corpse's chest, peering intently at the dead cardinal's mouth as he did so.

"What are you—?" I began.

He held up a finger, and pumped the chest a few more times.

When at last he stopped, he said thoughtfully, "No water."

"What do you mean?"

"No water in his lungs," he said. "Which means he was not breathing when he was thrown into the pool. He was dead already."

Mr. Ascham pursed his lips. Then he straightened. "Come, Bess, we're done here. It was beneficial to see the body so close to the time of the murder but we will learn no more tonight. Let us return to our lodgings and get some sleep, for tomorrow promises to be a busy day."

AFTER DARK IN
THE SULTAN'S PALACE

WE RETURNED TO OUR QUARTERS. There my teacher bade me good night and retired to his room. He closed the heavy curtain that served as a door but I could see the light of a candle in there and heard the scratching of a quill for some time thereafter—he was writing down his thoughts while they were fresh in his mind.

I myself was both fatigued and invigorated by the evening's events. I went into the room I shared with Elsie and hurried to her bed to wake her and tell her about the awful things I had seen.

Her bed was still empty. I had forgotten about the late-night gathering hosted by the crown prince that she had crept away to attend earlier.

I didn't pause to think about Elsie for long. My weariness was suddenly quite profound. I folded into my bed and was asleep within a minute.

———

I was shaken awake by a most excited Elsie.

"Oh, Bessie, Bessie, you won't believe the wonders I have seen!"

I sat up. I didn't know how long I had been asleep. It was still dark outside, but judging by the soft glow on the horizon I gathered it was closer to dawn than to midnight. Elsie had been out a very long time.

"What? Where?" I whispered weakly.

"Why, at the party in the crown prince's quarters, silly," she said. "Oh, Bessie, how could I possibly sleep—this place is so wondrous. Sultans, princes, artists, champion chess players, wrestlers, fireworks and now a scandalous murder. After I slipped out of here, I went directly over to the harem, where I told the guards the password—that I was a privileged friend of the crown prince's—and thus I was granted entry and escorted to his rooms.

"Oh, my . . ." she sighed dramatically. "You cannot *imagine* what I beheld there. *Dionysian* does not even begin to describe it. The crown prince's quarters were simply lavish: a broad chamber composed of cushioned lounges and cozy side booths. And the whole place was veiled in a haze of incense and smoke from ganja-weed pipes. Somewhere a lyre played. Olive-oil lamps illuminated the chamber in a dim golden glow that allowed for fleeting glimpses of what was taking place."

"What was taking place there?" I asked.

"The first thing I saw was the silhouette of a couple, a woman kneeling astride a man, the two of them moving to a slow rhythm that caused the man to throw his head back in pleasure and the woman to grip his shoulders to contain her own delight. It was fornication, Bessie, right there out in the open!"

"Goodness me," I said.

"I ventured farther into the dim chamber," Elsie said. "There was subtle movement all around me, half-seen shadows in the golden mist: caressing and kissing, heaving and sliding. It wasn't the rushed rutting I have seen back in England, designed for quick and base pleasure—it was smooth and gentle, mutual pleasure, happily given and willingly received.

"The sweet smoke all around me meant that I could see only one or two pairings at a time, but as I penetrated deeper into the chamber, I realized that there were couplings everywhere: young people, perhaps twenty of them, all naked, all frolicking in some way or another. In one corner, I glimpsed a chess player kissing the breasts of a young woman; in another, a great oiled wrestler occupied a tiny servant girl, making her pant pleasurably; in a third, two young Turkish men kissed each other tenderly."

"Two *men* kissing?" I gasped. I had heard the occasional comment back in England about men who enjoyed the company of other men, but it had never made much sense to me. It seemed very peculiar. My father would sometimes insult two men by saying they were in love with each other and everyone present would laugh. And he would often call one earl a "dirty sodomite." But I had never actually imagined two men kissing tenderly.

Elsie went on. "Then the haze parted and I spotted our new friend Zubaida lying on a lounge, half naked, smoking an opium pipe as she surveyed the delightful scene. After she took an inhalation of the pipe, she caressed herself, drawing a finger from the tip of one of her nipples down the length of her stomach until it ended inside her, and with her senses heightened by the magic of the poppy seed, she pleasured herself. My!"

My eyes almost popped out of my head as I listened.

Elsie said, "Not far from Zubaida, above that theater of hedonism, up on the largest chaise of all, was Crown Prince Selim who was himself being pleasured by a slave girl while he casually smoked an opium pipe.

"I went over to Zubaida.

"'Ah, Lady Elsie . . .' she said languidly. 'You came! Find a—mmm—partner and—enjoy yourself.'

"I gazed around this chamber of pleasure and threw off my gown, joining them in their nakedness. I won't lie to you, Bessie, I have enjoyed congress with men before and it is just the most *sublime* thing, intoxicating, almost addictive, really. I confess I have mounted quite a few gentlemen back in England, even some married ones. Indeed, the married ones seem to exert themselves with the most vigor of all."

I listened in stunned silence, completely absorbed. Elsie had never spoken to me about such topics. At the time I felt she was confiding in me, but now I believe she just needed *someone* to tell about her nocturnal adventure, and in faraway Constantinople I was the closest thing Elsie had to a confidante.

She went on. "So I strolled around that hazy chamber, completely nude, like a woman in a market, assessing the wares on offer. And I was not the only such observer. At one point, I found myself standing on a small balcony beside the young Austrian girl, Helena, the virgin who was to be presented as a gift to the sultan: she was flanked by two stern-looking eunuchs, watching the scene. I guessed that as a virgin who would one day pleasure the sultan, she'd been sent to observe the gathering—chaperoned by the sexless eunuchs—and thus learn the various techniques of pleasuring a man.

"Oh, it was just divine, Bessie! The smell of the incense, the shadows writhing in the candlelit mist. I assessed the delicious prospects on offer and settled on a cluster of three wrestlers, glistening with oil from their earlier exhibition matches, who sat in a booth in a corner, chatting with two girls and sipping wine.

"One of these wrestlers caught my eye. He was a gorgeous man, with a square jaw, huge chest and bulging arms. He looked me up and down, then nodded approvingly."

"My goodness, Elsie, what did you do?" I leaned forward.

"What do you think I did?" Elsie said tartly. "I winked at him, then guided him over to an empty bed of cushions and let him occupy me beautifully for the next two hours. He took me in every way, Bessie, every way, but his massive body always moved with a gentleness, a *slowness* that was designed to heighten the extraordinary pleasure of our copulation. My body just thrilled at his ministrations."

I gasped again. Till then, I'd not heard sexual congress described so openly or sensually. Back home in England, such talk was repressed; it was just *not done*. But Elsie, quite clearly, found the act of copulation—and the memory of it—exhilarating.

"Oh, how he could teach the men of England a thing or two about lovemaking," she continued. "And the Persian girls, too, Bessie, you won't believe what they do! They shave the hair around their pudenda into neat little triangles or, in some cases, they shave it all off, making them completely hairless down there!"

"My Lord . . ." I breathed. What a bizarre thing to do.

"I must admit," Elsie said, "it looked very sophisticated and alluring, especially with their narrow waists and curving hips. Perhaps I shall try it. In any case, at length the night drew on and the oil lamps dimmed and the crowd slowly dispersed, I among them. I left my stallion with a dainty kiss of thanks and made my way back here, but on the way, I saw something most scandalous.

"As I was leaving the harem, I caught sight of a robed figure—a woman, I was sure—darting down a side corridor and slipping into a curtained room. Thinking it might be a second exclusive gathering, I followed her and cautiously drew aside the curtain.

"Oh my Lord, Bessie, inside the little room I saw the largest of all the wrestlers—the huge broad-shouldered fellow with long dark hair named Darius—making love to a woman with genuine unbridled passion. I noticed immediately that the woman was not Persian but rather had the fair skin of a European. They kissed forcefully and he held her up against the wall, her robe bunched up over her naked hips, her legs wrapped around his waist. He gripped her slim body with giant hands and I truly thought that if he wanted to, he could have snapped her in two.

"Then she climaxed and threw her head back and I glimpsed her face, and I ducked back behind the curtains. Bessie, it was the queen! The sultan's wife! Coupling with the most celebrated wrestler in the realm!"

"Goodness me . . ."

"Needless to say, I scurried away from there and hurried back here to our rooms. Oh, Bessie, I can't tell you how magical it all was. Magical, delightful, delicious and decadent. I'm so thrilled you brought me here! Zubaida says the crown prince will be hosting more gatherings during the tournament. I can't wait to go again! Who knows, maybe I will catch the eye of Crown Prince Selim himself."

Elsie threw herself back onto her pillow, sighing dramatically.

I did not know what to say.

I just said, "Elsie, are you not frightened by the murder of the cardinal last night? Do you think it wise to be venturing out into the palace after midnight?"

"You may not understand it now, Bessie, but trust me, the pleasure I experienced tonight was worth venturing out for."

THE TOURNAMENT BEGINS

A GLORIOUS DAY REPLACED THAT GRIM night. After we partook of a sumptuous breakfast delivered to our rooms by Pietro, the chef's teenage son, our little party gathered in the vestibule.

"The tournament draw is to be held in an hour," my teacher said. "Giles, your plans before then?"

"Just to keep my mind at ease, in case I am drawn to play in the first match."

"Right. Elsie, please stay here with Mr. Giles and give him any help or attendance he might require; we need our man to be in top form when he is called on to play. As for you, Bess, you can come with me."

"Where are we going?"

"We are going to commence our investigation and we will begin by retracing the dead Cardinal Farnese's steps last night. Which means, first of all, we shall visit his host, the pope's ambassador here at the sultan's court, Cardinal Cardoza."

———

Cardinal Cardoza's embassy was not far from our lodgings. One of only a few ambassadors granted the privilege of living inside the palace walls, he and his staff resided in the stand alone structure I had seen the previous evening out on the wide lawn of the Fourth Courtyard. A white two-story marble building, it was one of the oldest structures in the palace and looked out over the Sea of Marmara to the south. It was also very close to the shallow pool in which Cardinal Farnese's body had been found.

As we approached the embassy with Latif, Mr. Ascham moved away from my side, peering oddly at the grass. Then, instead of going straight to the structure's front entrance, he walked in a full circle around the building, his head bent the whole time, looking intently at the ground.

Only when he had conducted a complete circuit of the embassy did he allow Latif to take us to the main entrance. Latif knocked loudly on the ornate door.

Cardinal Cardoza's manservant answered it. "Latif, good morning," he said. His voice was as emotionless and blank as his face. He was taller up close and I saw that he had the rough brown complexion of a Sicilian or a Sardinian. His eyes were dead.

"Sinon," Latif said. "I have an investigator from the sultan to see Cardinal Cardoza."

The manservant—Sinon—threw a neutral glance at Mr. Ascham and me. He pulled open the door and allowed us in. "Come inside, please."

He guided us into the embassy. We entered a beautifully decorated atrium furnished with a large oak desk, some chairs and many Catholic icons mounted on the walls: crucifixes, chalices, candlesticks, all made of gold.

To our left, I saw a small chapel with rows of pews and an altar. Near its doorway, a set of stairs ascended to the building's upper level. To my right were a couple of curtained-off guest nooks and some windows overlooking the sea: every one of them bore thick velvet drapes. The whole place exuded ecclesiastical wealth, the kind my father despised. A priest nodded to us as he left his nook and disappeared into the chapel to pray.

Fetched by Sinon, Cardinal Cardoza appeared on the stairs. "Hello, Latif. I was wondering if I might receive an emissary from the sultan this morning."

Latif said, "Cardinal Cardoza, this is Mr. Roger Ascham from Cambridge. At the sultan's command, he is investigating Cardinal Farnese's death."

"An English inquisitor?" Cardoza said. "Intriguing." His eyes fell on me. "Tell me, do all Englishmen bring children along when they investigate hideous crimes?"

"This is my student, Elizabeth," Mr. Ascham said evenly. "When I brought her to Constantinople, I did not anticipate that I would be charged with finding a killer. She is in my charge and so must accompany me wherever I go. I hope you do not mind."

"Not at all." The cardinal's eyes lingered on me longer than I liked before returning to face my teacher.

Mr. Ascham said, "I would like to ask you some questions about Cardinal Farnese."

Cardinal Cardoza nodded sadly. "But of course. I have hardly slept. I am still appalled and aggrieved that my visiting brother from Rome should fall afoul of this beast prowling the streets of Byzantium."

He had deep red bags under his eyes. It *looked* like he had hardly slept.

My teacher said, "Your Grace, I am not so sure that is what happened, which is why I am trying to reconstruct the cardinal's movements last night."

At this, Cardinal Cardoza cocked his head. He looked at Mr. Ascham with extra interest.

Mr. Ascham said, "You and Cardinal Farnese left the banquet together, did you not?"

"Yes, we did."

"And you returned here?"

"Yes. I had arranged for separate meals to be brought here. We were planning to discuss some correspondence he had brought from Rome over dinner. But I was detained on our way out of the courtyard by some other Christian guests, Brother Raul from Spain and his patron, the famous Ignatius of Loyola, so Cardinal Farnese went ahead of me. My discussion went overlong and I was delayed by almost half an hour. When I arrived here, Cardinal Farnese was nowhere to be found."

"I see. Can you tell me if the cardinal was in any known danger prior to coming to Constantinople?"

"Nothing beyond the obvious. His writings on Islam have provoked angry comments from the sultan's religious advisors and other Moslems, but nothing that I would call dangerous."

"You wouldn't call a fatwa dangerous?"

"That was mere posturing on the part of the imam. None of the other Islamic scholars agreed with him, so the fatwa was never issued."

"Did the cardinal receive any threats of violence after his arrival here?"

"None that I know of, beyond locals showing him the soles of their shoes."

"Cardinal Farnese would have informed you if he was in danger?"

"We have been friends for many years, Mr. Ascham. Since long before we were cardinals. He would have told me, yes."

"May I see his room?"

The cardinal's eyes darted sideways.

"Why would you want to do that? See his room?"

"You say he returned here to dine with you in private but then departed—or was abducted—before you arrived. It is conceivable that he did not make it back here at all. An examination of his room might give us some clue as to his actions when he returned, if indeed he did."

Cardinal Cardoza seemed to consider this.

"All right," he said slowly.

The cardinal ushered us up the stairs. His manservant, Sinon, followed behind us, an eerie shadow.

Cardoza said, "Cardinal Farnese was sleeping in my personal bedchamber, as his rank required. I am sleeping in a common monk's nook for the first time in years."

We came to the top of the stairs and entered the cardinal's bedchamber.

A breathtaking room greeted us. It featured an enormous bed dressed in gorgeous blue satin sheets. White gauze curtains swayed with the breeze coming off the sea, veiling the windows in the same way a bride's veil covers her face. It was clear that Cardinal Cardoza usually slept in great luxury. My teacher surveyed the room, and even if the others could not sense it, I could feel his disapproval. It was *too* well appointed, too luxurious for his practical mind.

A leather trunk sat at the foot of the bed; it bore a small golden crucifix on its lid.

"Cardinal Farnese's traveling trunk?" my teacher inquired.

"Yes."

Watched by Cardinal Cardoza, Mr. Ascham opened the trunk. Inside it were the dead cardinal's things: traveling clothes, some books, a satchel, and a flyswatter just like Cardinal Cardoza's with a multicolored horsehair tail, only this one was smaller, with fewer tails.

My teacher picked up two of the books: Dante's *Commedia* and the Bible. He glanced around the room. "Everything appears to be in perfect order . . ."

"As one would expect," the cardinal said tersely. "Which would make coming to see the dead man's sleeping quarters altogether unnecessary, sir."

"Quite the contrary, it was very necessary. Indeed, it has been very helpful," my teacher said.

"How so?"

"Because it tells us that the visiting cardinal did not disturb any assassin when he returned here. There are no signs of a scuffle or fight. If someone waylaid the cardinal, then they disturbed absolutely nothing in the doing."

Cardinal Cardoza took a second glance around the room, now seeing my teacher's conclusion. "Oh . . ."

"I have seen all I need to see," Mr. Ascham said. We all returned to the atrium downstairs, where Mr. Ascham stopped suddenly. "His meal," he said, looking around.

"I beg your pardon?"

"Cardinal Farnese's meal. The one that had been delivered here. Was it touched? Had he eaten any of it?" My teacher looked about the atrium as if the meal might still be here, but it had long since been taken away.

Cardinal Cardoza shrugged. "Why, yes. As I recall, it had been eaten, while the other plate lay untouched. When I did not arrive in a timely manner, he must have commenced his meal."

"Which means he *did* make it back here before he vanished," my teacher said.

Then, most casually, he turned to Cardinal Cardoza: "Your Grace, were you aware of Cardinal Farnese's opium habit?"

The cardinal's face went instantly cold. "I beg your pardon?"

"I said, were you aware that Cardinal Farnese was a very frequent user of an opium pipe?" Mr. Ascham said innocently.

I got the distinct impression that my teacher did not like Cardinal Cardoza—his haughty manner, his ostentatious displays of wealth— and I wondered if he was trying to provoke the cardinal in some way by making such an allegation.

"No. I was not so aware." The cardinal's eyes narrowed. "I am also, I have to say, somewhat surprised that you might know this about my friend given you only became acquainted with him after his death."

"The dead sometimes tell tales," Mr. Ascham said.

"Communing with the dead is a sin against God, Mr. Ascham. You do not partake in witchcraft or sorcery, do you?"

"I do not. Nor did I commune with the dead cardinal," my teacher said. "I simply looked under his tongue. Do many cardinals of Rome indulge in such exotic pleasures?"

Cardinal Cardoza visibly hardened. "Even priests are men, Mr. Ascham, men who are sometimes prone to weakness and temptation. In my experience, an opium habit is not the worst of human vices."

"This is true." Mr. Ascham glanced at Latif and nodded to indicate that he was done. He turned back to the cardinal. "Thank you for your time, Your Grace."

"Not at all. I wish you God's speed and wisdom in your investigations."

We left.

———

Mr. Ascham strode quickly across the lawn outside the Catholic embassy, heading back toward the Third Courtyard. He moved so fast, Latif and I struggled to keep up with him.

"God save me from cardinals and religion," he muttered. " 'Even priests are men.' Balderdash. If priests truly had the Holy Spirit in them then they would not need opiates or other sins of the flesh. The cardinal knew something and he wasn't telling us."

"He did?"

"For one thing, he didn't want us examining Farnese's sleeping quarters," my teacher said.

"Perhaps he didn't want Protestants like us seeing the luxury in which he is accustomed to sleeping each night," I suggested.

"No, there is something he doesn't want us to *know*, and I would like to discover what that is."

I stopped walking. "You don't think that Cardinal Cardoza might have been involved in the death of the visiting cardinal?" I whispered.

My teacher also stopped and bit his lip in thought. "If he was involved, he is a most remarkably calculating fellow to stand there before us and lie to our faces. I wonder if he has his own suspicions about who might have killed Farnese. In any case, now we are back where we started. We still face the original question: why would someone want to kill the visiting cardinal *and* disguise the crime? We need to find someone with intimate knowledge of Cardinal Farnese and the schemers and plotters of Rome, and I think I know just who to ask. Come, the tournament is about to begin and we will find him there."

THE TOURNAMENT DRAW

IT WAS NEARING MIDMORNING WHEN we returned to our rooms to collect Mr. Giles and Elsie and depart for the tournament.

The matches were to be held in the largest hall in the world: the nave of the Hagia Sophia. The mighty mosque stood just outside the palace walls and was the only venue in the city capable of accommodating the enormous crowds the tournament was expected to draw.

As it turned out, even it wasn't big enough.

A vast crowd of at least ten thousand people massed around the entrances to the great building, pushing and shouting, all trying to force their way in to see the draw for the tournament and the first match.

Since we were escorting a player, we were permitted to enter the Hagia Sophia via the sultan's rear door. A short queue of similarly favored guests was lined up at that entrance when we arrived there. We spied Michelangelo chatting with some people in the line.

My teacher approached him. "Michel, a private word, if I may?"

Michelangelo excused himself from his conversation and joined my teacher and me off to the side. "What is it, Roger?"

"You know of last night's incident, do you not?"

"All I know is that the sultan himself came to my rooms to inquire about *your* skills as a solver of mysteries," Michelangelo said. "I said there was no one I knew more capable at such things."

"That is all you know?"

"There are whispers going around. Something about Cardinal Farnese falling victim to the fiend terrorizing the city. And no one has seen him this morning. Is it true? Is Farnese dead?"

"Yes, he is dead, but no, he was not a victim of the fiend. He was a victim of foul play. And now, based on your recommendation, the sultan has asked me to investigate the matter."

Michelangelo said, "Sorry, Roger. Although in my defense the sultan seemed well aware of your talents before he asked me about them."

"Tell me about Cardinal Farnese," Mr. Ascham said. "I know of his harsh views on the Moslem faith. Was he a marked man in Rome?"

"Not at all. He was actually *more* liked than his brother the pope. Farnese was known for avoiding plots and intrigues. I would be most surprised if someone came all the way from Rome to kill him here."

"He indulged in opium use."

"He was not alone in that, Roger," Michelangelo said. "They are priests, not angels. Opium use was the least of the good cardinal's diversions."

"The least of his diversions?" My teacher's brow furrowed. "Are you saying Farnese was a . . . sodomite?"

Michelangelo gave a single nod.

"Men or boys?"

"Both."

"Here in Constantinople?"

Michelangelo nodded again.

Mr. Ascham took this all in. "One more thing. What of Cardinal Cardoza? Might he have had a reason for doing away with Cardinal Farnese?"

"I would be shocked if that were so," Michelangelo said. "Cardoza and Farnese were boyhood friends and Cardoza owes his rise within the Church almost solely to Farnese's influence. They were brothers in all but name. Whoever did this, it certainly wasn't Cardoza."

"Thank you, Michel, these are things I need to know. It gives me a wider context for my inquiries."

"Good luck, Roger. And be careful. Do not let your inquisitiveness be the death of you."

———

We resumed our places in the queue and shortly after, entered the great cathedral-mosque.

If the Hagia Sophia was magnificent when viewed from the outside, then its interior offered a whole new level of splendor and wonder.

Its nave soared skyward, its immense lofty dome mounted atop a series of smaller semicircular domes. Once upon a time those domes had contained intricate mosaics of Christian saints but they had been crudely scraped off by the heathen Moslems. A few remained, including the centerpiece of the nave, a superb mosaic of the Virgin and child, since the Moslems venerate the Virgin Mary and Christ himself. They just do not accept Christ as the son of God.

We emerged from our private entry tunnel onto a stage facing the stupendous nave. Seats had been prepared for us on this stage not far from the sultan's huge throne.

Set up on a smaller platform out in the exact center of the hall was a square table at which sat two chairs facing each other. This was the playing stage—and right now, a great throng of spectators swarmed around it, a heaving ocean of humanity, the noise of their collective murmuring echoing in the vast space.

If the crowd outside was large, then this was its leading edge: five thousand fortunate citizens who had managed to shove their way inside. They pressed around the playing stage, gathered under the sultan's private prayer balcony (an elevated lattice-shrouded platform) and leaned out from the Hagia Sophia's lofty balconies one hundred and fifty feet in the air. Prime positions on those balconies, however, were occupied by the sultan's favored courtiers and the high-born families of Constantinople.

We were informed that at that moment, servants of the sultan were erecting large wooden displays that resembled chessboards (complete with movable pieces) outside the great building, so that the vast overflow of people out there could watch the progress of an ongoing match.

I imagined that not since the chariot races in Constantinople's long-lost Hippodrome had such a mass gathering been held in that ancient city. It was awe inspiring.

More players and their entourages filed into the hall from the rear entrance and took their places on the sultan's stage.

Suddenly trumpets flared and all fell silent as the sultan himself entered the hall. His retinue followed behind him while at his right hand walked Michelangelo, bearing a wide irregularly shaped object in his hands, covered with a sheet of shining gold satin.

"Ladies and gentlemen!" the sultan intoned. "Behold, the chess set on which the championship will be played!"

With a flourish, he whipped the satin sheet off the object in Michelangelo's hands to reveal one of the two chess sets the great artist had created for the event.

The assembled crowd gasped at the sight of it, myself among them.

It was astonishing in its beauty.

The board on its own was a work of the most supreme artistry, bearing squares of silver and gold that glinted with a radiance I had never seen before.

And then there were the pieces. One side was of gold, the other silver. Assembled in their ranks, glittering and sparkling in the sunlight that streamed through the dome's high windows, they looked like a treasure beyond compare, a prize beyond value.

I heard a voice behind me say in Spanish, "This sultan has some nerve. He makes his chess set from the gold and silver his pirates plunder from our galleons returning from the New World."

A surreptitious glance revealed the speaker to be the ambassador from the House of Castile.

Michelangelo strode out through the hushed crowd (flanked by four palace guards who I suspected were protecting the priceless chess set rather than the priceless artist) and ascended the playing platform. With great ceremony, he placed the chess set on the table. The four guards remained on the playing stage, where they would stay for each match of the tournament.

The *sadrazam* then brought forward a beautiful glass jar of substantial size in which one could see sixteen round stones, each the size of an apple and smoothed to a spherical shape.

He called in Turkish then Greek: "It is time for the tournament draw! Inscribed on the stones inside this jar are the names of the sixteen players in the tournament. Your Majesty, if you would do us the honor?"

The sultan stepped over to the jar, dipped his hand into it and stirred the rocks around playfully.

The crowd leaned forward.

The sultan shuffled the rocks some more, smiling for his subjects, enjoying the tension he was creating. They laughed.

Then he grabbed one stone and held it aloft, reading the name on it: "Zaman of Constantinople!"

The crowd cheered. It was one of the two local heroes, the royal cousin and *aliyat*.

The sultan dipped his hand into the big glass jar again and once again swirled his hand around theatrically before extracting another stone and reading the name on it:

"Maximilian of Vienna!" A chorus of boos and hisses came from the crowd as the Habsburg player's name was called. All were aware of the sharp-edged relationship between the Ottomans and the Habsburgs.

"This is a good match for Zaman," Mr. Giles whispered to my teacher. "Maximilian is one of the weaker players here. An *aliyat* like Zaman should make short work of him."

The rest of the draw took place in similar style, with great theatricality from the sultan and enthusiastic responses from the crowd. As each match was drawn, the players' names were put up on a large scoreboard not unlike those seen at jousts (I later learned that identical scoreboards had been erected for the crowds outside) and as he drew them, the sultan placed the drawn stones in a row on a bench near the scoreboard.

Mr. Giles drew a very tough opponent in his first-round match. He would play Talib, the aged librarian from Baghdad.

The pope's man, Brother Raul, drew Brother Eduardo of Syracuse, while the Muscovite, Vladimir, drew a wily little Egyptian from Cairo. The brutish Wallachian, Dragan of Brasov, drew the Venetian representative, who was not, those around me commented, regarded as a strong player.

But the greatest cheer of all arose when the name of the peasant champion, Ibrahim of Constantinople, was called. The crowd's cheers dissipated somewhat, however, when his opponent was called: the formidable young Prussian, Wilhelm of Königsberg. That would be a demanding match for both parties.

When the ceremony was over, the tournament draw filled the large scoreboard. It read:

1ST ROUND	2ND ROUND	SEMI- FINALS	FINAL

1. **ZAMAN**
   OF CONSTANTINOPLE

2. **MAXIMILIAN**
   OF VIENNA

3. **MUSTAFA**
   OF CAIRO

4. **VLADIMIR**
   OF MUSCOVY

5. **ALI HASSAN RAMA**
   OF MEDINA

6. **PABLO MONTOYA**
   OF CASTILE

7. **BR. EDUARDO**
   OF SYRACUSE

8. **BR. RAUL**
   OF THE PAPAL STATES

9. **GILBERT GILES**
   OF ENGLAND

10. **TALIB**
    OF BAGHDAD

11. **DRAGAN**
    OF WALLACHIA

12. **MARKO**
    OF VENICE

13. **NASIRUDDIN**
    OF THE MOGHUL EMPIRE

14. **LAO TSE**
    OF THE HAN PEOPLE

15. **WILHELM**
    OF KÖNIGSBERG

16. **IBRAHIM**
    OF CONSTANTINOPLE

The *sadrazam* announced, "The first match—between Zaman of Constantinople and Maximilian of Vienna—will commence exactly one hour from now! A single afternoon match will follow. Tomorrow, the remaining six matches of the first round will be played on two boards here in this hall. Now, honor your sultan!"

The massive crowd fell as one to their knees as the sultan swept out through the rear door. Once he was gone, they rose again and started murmuring about the draw and the matches.

Many of the players and their entourages also left the hall, their presence no longer required. The crowd, however, stayed exactly where they were: positions inside the Hagia Sophia were highly prized and would not be given up lightly.

"What say you, Giles?" Mr. Ascham said. "Would you like to watch the first match or would you prefer to retire to our rooms?"

"I think I should like to get used to the mood of this hall," Mr. Giles said. "It is a large space and the crowd is lively. I am also interested to see Zaman play."

"Splendid. I myself would be most pleased to sit still for a while and watch some good chess." He smiled at me and glanced at Elsie (who was studiously examining her fingernails).

Then he stood and strolled over to the bench by the scoreboard, the one on which the sultan had placed the drawn stones. I followed him.

Mr. Ascham picked up a few of the smoothed stones and rolled them around in his hand, marveling at their artistry.

I came up beside him. "The sultan certainly knows how to put on a spectacle."

"He does indeed," Mr. Ascham said as he inspected one stone closely before putting it down. "He also knows how to rig a draw."

"What?"

"Don't make any outward reaction, Bess, just feel this stone. It is the one marked with Zaman's name." Mr. Ascham handed me the rock.

It was warm.

"Don't react," he whispered sharply. "The stone for Maximilian of

Vienna is also warm, while the stones for Ibrahim of Constantinople and the Prussian are both cold, as if they have been kept in snow. The rest are all of normal temperature."

I was shocked. "Are you saying that a draw that just took place in front of five thousand people was fixed? That the sultan knew which stones to select?"

"It is not hard to heat up two stones in a fire or cool two others in snow. They still look like rocks to the crowd. I suspect His Majesty wanted his royal cousin, Zaman, to play in the first match of the tournament *and* to have an easy opponent. I also suspect that he did not want Zaman to be on the same side of the draw as the people's champion, Ibrahim. He does not want his two local heroes to clash, which is probably why Ibrahim also drew a very tough opponent in the Prussian, Wilhelm. The sultan looks after his royal relative."

My teacher moved away from the bench. I shook my head as I followed him. "You know, sir, sometimes I fear that you are too curious for your own good."

"Sometimes I do, too," he replied as we returned to our seats to await the first match of the tournament.

THE FIRST MATCH

AN EERIE HUSH GRIPPED THE HALL of the Hagia Sophia. It was unnerving to see so gargantuan a space filled with so many spectators yet be so perfectly still and silent.

In the center of the massive hall, surrounded by the enormous crowd, sat the sultan's champion, Zaman, and Maximilian of Vienna, a stiff-backed Austrian with a small pointed mustache trimmed in the style popular in Austria in those days. High above them sat the sultan, who had returned to his throne eager to observe the first match of his historic tournament.

The match began and the crowd watched it with rapt intensity. Every move was followed by a ripple of hushed whispers. The people of Constantinople certainly loved their chess.

As the *sadrazam* had explained the previous evening, each match was composed of seven games; the first player to win four games won the match.

I sat with Mr. Ascham, Mr. Giles and Elsie in the special seats reserved for players and their companions on the sultan's stage. About halfway through the first game, Mr. Giles leaned over to Mr. Ascham and whispered, "This will be a short match. Zaman has Maximilian's measure. The Austrian is out of his depth."

Sure enough, the first game finished within half an hour, with Zaman mating his opponent without losing a major piece. The second game was over even faster—as soon as Zaman took Maximilian's queen, the Austrian floundered and in his desperation lost first his bishops, then his knights, then his rooks. After less than an hour of play, Zaman was leading, two games to nil.

As the third game commenced and Zaman took an early lead, I noticed that my teacher was not watching the board at all. Rather, he was observing Cardinal Cardoza, who sat at the opposite end of the royal stage watching the match with profound disinterest. He was flanked by some junior visiting priests from Rome who looked equally bored.

My teacher's eyes narrowed. He was thinking about something.

"What is it?" I whispered.

"The two cardinals took their dinner in the embassy . . ." Mr. Ascham said softly.

"So?"

My teacher kept staring at the cardinal. "The rash . . . the swelling of the tongue . . . elephant's ear . . ."

He stood up abruptly. "I have to go."

When he rose, so did Latif, nearby.

"Where are you going?" I hissed, but my teacher was already leaving, so I hurried after him, out of the hall, back toward the palace.

———

Mr. Ascham strode purposefully back through the main gates of Top-kapi Palace and headed quickly up the tree-lined path that led to the inner Gate of Salutation.

"Can you *please* explain to me what you are doing?" I pleaded as I struggled to keep up with him.

"Do you remember when we saw the dead cardinal's body last night?"

"Yes."

"Do you recall the rash inside his mouth? And his swollen tongue?"

"Yes . . ."

"There is a poisonous plant called the elephant's ear which is known to cause rashes around the mouth, and if ingested in large quantities will cause the victim's tongue to swell to such an extent that it will block the air passage to his throat and suffocate him."

"Wait. Are you saying that Cardinal Farnese was killed by some poison?"

"I believe so, yes."

"Forgive me," I said, "but what about the *stab wounds* all over his body? Don't you think *they* might have played a substantial role in his death?"

"The cardinal was already dead when he was stabbed so energetically," Mr. Ascham said simply.

"How do you know this?"

"Because the cardinal's many stab wounds did not bleed. When its heart has already stopped, a body will not bleed when it is pierced. A *live* man stabbed so many times and in such a frenzy would have bled copiously—Lord, it would have been a bloodbath—but you told me yourself there was little blood around the pool in which Cardinal Farnese was found. For a man stabbed so vigorously, there should have been great swathes of blood around that pool—even if his killer had carried him to the pool on his shoulders, there should have been some kind of trail of dripping blood. But there was none. When we went to call upon Cardinal Cardoza earlier today, I examined the grounds around the Catholic embassy and found no trace of blood on the surrounding grass. Had the cardinal been stabbed to death inside that building, there would have been at least *some* blood left on the ground as he was conveyed away."

"Perhaps our killer is more careful than you think," I said. "Perhaps he cleaned up the blood trail, or perhaps he conveyed the body from the embassy in a wagon, or perhaps he did not kill the cardinal in the embassy at all."

Mr. Ascham nodded as we passed through the Gate of Salutation and headed across the Second Courtyard.

"All good points, Bess. All very good points. Nevertheless, I still believe Cardinal Farnese was dead when he was stabbed."

"Why?"

"Because he offered no defense against his frenzied attacker."

I stopped walking. "How can you possibly know this?" My teacher did not stop. He kept walking. I hurried after him. "How can you know this?" I repeated.

"When we saw the cardinal's corpse in the dungeon, did you happen to notice his hands?" Mr. Ascham asked.

"Yes. They were pudgy, gray and pale, and otherwise completely normal."

"Precisely. In the face of such a violent attack, wouldn't even the weakest man raise his hands in some form of defense and consequently receive cuts to his upraised palms? Yet the cardinal's hands were completely unmarked. A dead man offers no defense. Hence, my conclusion."

I fell silent. It was actually rather sound logic.

"All right, then. So why stab the cardinal so many times if he was already dead?" I asked.

My teacher turned to face me as we walked.

"To throw us off the scent," he said. "Like the flaying of the face, the stabbing was a ruse designed to lead the casual investigator to conclude that the cardinal was killed by the insane fiend. It was done to conceal the identity of the cardinal's true killer. Unfortunately for the killer, he could not know that the insane fiend was locked in the sultan's dungeon at the time."

I was beginning to see that the unraveling of this matter was giving my teacher a peculiar kind of thrill. I honestly think he enjoyed pitting his wits against those of the murderer. When he went on, he spoke quickly and with enthusiasm.

"If we accept that the cardinal was poisoned, we must now ask *how*: How was he poisoned? You will recall Cardinal Cardoza left the banquet to take his dinner in his embassy with Cardinal Farnese. I think the poison that killed Cardinal Farnese was slipped into his meal, a meal that was prepared in the kitchens and taken to the Catholic embassy. Which is why I must speak with the chef, Brunello of Borgia, right this instant."

It was only then that I realized that we had crossed the Second Courtyard and arrived at the kitchens.

———

My teacher hurried into the kitchen area, barging through wafts of steam and passing by several slaughter rooms as the apron-wearing slaughterers inside them flung water across their chopping blocks, washing away blood.

A small group of servants was gathered in the doorway of the farthest slaughter room, at the rearmost corner of the kitchen.

"Oh, no . . ." Mr. Ascham quickened his stride. "No . . ."

We came to the doorway in question, my teacher pushing through the group of aghast kitchen hands.

We stopped dead in our tracks.

The room was filled with six large sides of beef, hanging in a row from meat hooks, and hanging with them, their crooked necks bent at horrible angles in separate nooses, were the bodies of Brunello of Borgia and his wife, Marianna.

TWO MORE VICTIMS

THE SMALL CROWD THAT WAS GATHERED in the doorway of the slaughter room consisted of a cook, three slave boys and two servant girls.

With a loud boom, the door behind us suddenly slammed shut. I spun. Latif had closed it, sealing us all inside.

Latif glared at the slaves as he spoke in common Greek: "Not a word shall be spoken of this until the sultan has been informed." He thrust his head outside the door and called for some guards. Then he stood in front of the door, blocking the way—evidently, none of us would even be allowed to leave until the sultan had been advised about the situation, which could be some time, since he was at that moment still watching the opening match. Our escort clearly had orders of his own to follow.

My teacher sighed. He gazed up at the suspended bodies of Brunello and Marianna.

I said, "When we met Brunello last night, he did not strike me as melancholy or prone to taking his own life."

"I thought similarly," my teacher said. "Are we to assume that for some reason he poisoned a high-ranking visiting cardinal and then, in a fit of remorse, killed himself?"

"I fear I am still trying to catch up with your reasoning about Brunello poisoning Cardinal Farnese," I said.

Mr. Ascham leaned around and behind Brunello's body and peered up at the dead chef's hands. "That the cardinal was poisoned we can deduce from the rash in his mouth and the swelling of his tongue," he explained without looking at me. "That he was poisoned by Brunello, well, I am deducing that from the fact that the meal that poisoned Cardinal Farnese was brought to his rooms from the kitchens where it had been prepared by Brunello, the Christian chef in charge of meals for visiting dignitaries with weak stomachs."

"Ah . . ."

"And yet now the murderer would appear to have hanged himself," Mr. Ascham said. "The question is, why would he do such a thing?"

"All right. Why would he?"

Mr. Ascham nodded silently at the dead man's wrists. I followed his eye line. Red rope burns could be discerned there. I saw similar marks on Marianna's wrists.

Mr. Ascham whispered: "Their hands were bound when they were hanged, and then after it was done, the bonds were removed. The good chef and his wife did not kill themselves at all."

My eyes widened. "But then that would mean—"

"Let us keep our counsel to ourselves for a while, Bess. At least until the sultan gets here. This palace, it would seem, hides many secrets and I think we have only scratched the surface."

———

An hour passed. I assumed the sultan was busy enjoying Zaman's match and would not come to the kitchens until it was finished. The slaughter room had a rank odor—I was not sure if it stemmed from previous slaughters or the bodies or both.

My teacher and I sat on the floor, facing the six kitchen hands. Like us, their only crime, as far as I could see, had been to see the dead couple.

Only Latif stood. He still guarded the door.

At one stage, Mr. Ascham rose and walked in a full circle around the two hanging bodies. Oddly, though, he did not look up at them. Rather, he walked with his head bent, peering at the floor.

I went over to him. "Whatever are you doing?"

He crouched low. The floor in the center of the room was covered in a ghastly layer of sawdust intermixed with dried animal blood. The foul mush felt soft under my feet, like mud. Many overlapping footprints, including our own, could be discerned in the mixture.

"Sandals mainly," Mr. Ascham said. "Leather-soled sandals of the kind worn by the kitchen hands. But in several places I see *this* footprint, made by a flat *wooden* sole with a nick in it between the big toe and the second toe, a prominent *V*-shaped nick. It is the wearer's left shoe. Wooden sandals are a more expensive kind of shoe, worn by someone of moderate status."

"Why do you say *moderate* status?"

"Because, dear Bess, if the wearer was a person of high status, he could afford to buy new shoes or at least mend his nicked sandal." My teacher turned to the others in the room. "Latif. May I see everyone's shoes, please? Yours, too."

Upon examination, he found that all six of the kitchen workers in that room wore basic leather-soled sandals, so the print had not been made by any of them. Only Latif wore sandals with solid wooden soles, but his left one bore no incriminating nick.

"Am I above suspicion now?" Latif asked as he lowered his foot back to the ground.

"No," Mr. Ascham answered flatly. "Nobody is above suspicion, least of all anyone who keeps me confined in a room against my will."

"I serve the sultan's interests, not yours."

"Believe me, I am keenly aware of that."

Mr. Ascham then stepped over to the body of Brunello's wife, Marianna, and looked thoughtfully up at her. He reached up and touched the rosary beads looped around her neck, examining the black bow tied to them.

He turned to face the kitchen hands and spoke in Greek. "Do any of you speak Greek?"

One of the servant girls nodded. She said her name was Sasha and that she had lived in Macedonia before she'd been captured by an Ottoman force and brought to Constantinople.

Mr. Ascham said, "The chef's wife wore a black ribbon on her rosary beads, which means she was mourning someone. For whom did she mourn?"

"Her son," the girl said.

"Her son? But we met him only last night."

"No, you would have met Pietro, their older boy. The one who died was their younger son, Benicio. He was a quiet boy, a sweet little angel with the most beautiful snow-white hair, but he was slow, of diminished mind. He was only twelve years of age, but two weeks ago, he killed himself. He was found in one of these slaughter rooms with his wrists slashed."

"A boy of twelve committed suicide?" my teacher said. "Suicide is very rare in children so young."

"We were all surprised and most upset. Slow though he was, little Benicio was a lovely boy, gentle, well liked in the kitchens. He had a round smiling face and was a little fat because of all the trimmings the chefs would slip him. That the little angel even knew how to kill anything, let alone his own earthly body, came as a shock to us all."

"How did Brunello and his wife cope with his death?" Mr. Ascham asked.

"Marianna was devastated. She cried for days. Brunello was also upset but he was busy preparing the many banquets for the sultan's tournament. He became quick to anger, shouting at us for small transgressions. He even lost his temper with Cardinal Cardoza, shouting at the cardinal when he came into the kitchens one day, but I do not know what caused that outburst."

"Brunello raised his voice to Cardinal Cardoza?" my teacher said. "Tell me, have you or any of the others here seen Brunello meeting or conversing overmuch with any of the visiting players or dignitaries this past week?"

The slave girl relayed the question to the others in the room in Turkish. The cook answered her.

Sasha translated: "He says that Brunello had four separate visits from the Austrian player, Maximilian of Vienna, in the days before the opening banquet. He would arrive with a young girl, the one the Austrians later gave as a gift to His Majesty, the sultan."

"Helena," I said.

"Is it known what they discussed?" Mr. Ascham asked.

Sasha asked the cook. He shook his head. "No, he does not know what they talked about."

———

Some time later, I could not tell exactly how long, the door to the slaughter room opened and in walked the sultan, the grand vizier, and eight of the sultan's personal guards. The kitchen area behind them had been completely cleared. The six kitchen hands in the room all clambered quickly to their feet and stood to attention, gazing meekly at their toes.

The sultan peered up at the two hanging bodies—the look on his face more one of annoyance than sadness—before turning his stern gaze at my teacher, then me, then the kitchen hands.

"You six are the only witnesses?" he asked the workers in Greek.

Sasha spoke for the group. "We are, Your Majesty. I was about to run and tell the palace guards about it when these three"—a nod at Mr. Ascham, Latif and me—"arrived and the eunuch shut us in."

The sultan nodded sagely.

He turned to my teacher and switched to English. "Mr. Roger Ascham. Why do I find you here?"

"I made certain deductions, Your Majesty, but I must admit I didn't expect to find Brunello dead—"

"You may be cleverer than I thought," the sultan cut him off. "I might have to watch my own actions around you. You surmised that the chef was connected to the death of the visiting cardinal?"

"I did."

"And now the murderer is dead by his own hand?"

Mr. Ascham glanced at the kitchen hands nearby, clearly hesitant to speak about his investigations in front of them.

"You may speak freely," the sultan said calmly.

"That is what we are supposed to think, Your Majesty," my teacher said. "But I do not believe it to be the truth. Rather, I believe the chef and his wife were themselves murdered. The killer is still at large."

The sultan's eyebrows rose. My teacher said nothing more while the sultan appraised him. The great king eyed him very, very closely.

"A second and a third murder in my palace," he said. "This I do not like. Have you any suspicions about these new deaths, Mr. Roger Ascham?"

My teacher said, "There is a devious mind at work within these walls, Your Majesty. If each of these murders had been accepted at face value, we would have attributed the death of the cardinal to the insane fiend and these two to suicide. But no, *all three* killings have been deliberately designed to throw off further investigation. They are connected. Not only are my inquiries thus still unfinished, it is my advice to you to allow me to include the deaths of the chef and his wife in the existing investigation into the killing of Cardinal Farnese."

The sultan thought about this for a moment. "Fine. Do so and continue your investigation."

The sultan stepped aside, allowing us to leave. He indicated the six kitchen hands still in the slaughter room. "Have you spoken to these six?"

"I have," Mr. Ascham said.

"Have you any further need of them?"

"No. They are innocent. They just saw the bodies. They know nothing of value."

The sultan escorted us out of the slaughter room, turning to his chief guardsman as he did so and saying a few sharp words in Turkish.

I slowed my stride and turned to look back but Mr. Ascham gently pressed my shoulder, keeping me moving.

He was right to do so, for as we walked away from that slaughter room and its door swung shut behind us, the last thing I saw—to my utter horror and disbelief—was the chief guardsman and the other guards drawing their swords.

THE CARDINAL
AND THE WHOREMONGER

WE EMERGED FROM THE KITCHEN AREA to find that it was now midafternoon. The sultan and his entourage left us without another word. They headed off toward the harem.

I was in a state of some considerable dismay over the fates of Sasha and the other kitchen staff. "Mr. Ascham, why did the sultan order that those poor people be killed?"

"We are in a strange and unholy land, Bess," Mr. Ascham replied. "We should count ourselves lucky we didn't suffer a similar fate. I imagine it was only your royal blood and my deductive abilities that allowed us to escape that room alive."

We were standing in the Second Courtyard. Delegations and players were now milling around under its trees. Zaman's match was over—he had beaten Maximilian of Vienna four games to nil, a thrashing—and now the privileged crowd was taking in some air before the second match of the day began, that of Vladimir of Muscovy and Mustafa of Cairo.

"But why kill them?" I said, still appalled. "They did nothing but see the dead couple."

"The most dangerous thing in any palace is a rumor," my teacher said. "They would have told others, who would have told others still. Word is already spreading about the death of Cardinal Farnese. Whispers of more deaths cannot be tolerated. It would reflect poorly on the sultan: he would be seen to have lost control of his own palace. Your father has executed dukes for no less a reason, and should you ever become queen, you, too, will execute people for the dangerous things they say."

"I most certainly will not!"

My teacher sighed sadly. "Yes. You will." He stood straighter, as if reacquiring his bearings. "Now, though, we have inquiries to make. For one thing I would like to find Brunello's surviving son, Pietro—he delivered meals for his father and may be able to help us with our investigation. I am also intrigued by the visits to the kitchen of the Austrian player, Maximilian. Most of all, however, I would very much like to know why so pious a man as Brunello should forget his place and shout at a cardinal of the Church to which he was devoted. We must speak with Cardinal Cardoza again. Why, there he is—"

The cardinal was standing on the opposite side of the wide courtyard, talking with a small, bearded Persian. The Persian was a tiny runt of a man. He wore a shiny maroon outfit with gaudy gold shoulder braids. It was an outfit that was formal but at the same time a little too flamboyant and garish. The little Persian was gesticulating animatedly, jabbing a finger angrily at the cardinal's face. At one point, the Persian moved quite close to the cardinal and the cardinal's manservant interceded and physically pushed the smaller man back a step.

Mr. Ascham said, "It would appear that it was not only Brunello who was angry with the cardinal. Latif, who is that little fellow arguing with Cardinal Cardoza?"

"That is Afridi, a local whoremonger and owner of several brothels. His largest brothel is located just beyond the Ayasofya."

Mr. Ascham watched the exchange between the short Persian and the burly cardinal with great interest. It ended with the brightly dressed whoremonger turning on his heel, waving a hand dismissively, and storming away from Cardinal Cardoza.

Mr. Ascham said, "The whoremonger seems quite upset. Historically speaking, it is usually the holy man who is angry at the one who sells sins of the flesh." He watched Afridi leave the courtyard, heading out of the palace.

"Do you still wish to speak with the cardinal?" Latif asked.

Mr. Ascham was still watching the departing whoremonger.

"No," he said slowly. "I wish to speak with that whoremonger first. I would like to know what angers him so."

————

And so, led by Latif, we left the palace grounds and ventured into the bustling market district that surrounded the man-made mountain that was the Hagia Sophia.

People were everywhere: beggars, poultry sellers, spice merchants, men smoking pipes or sipping the rich dark tea that the Turks drink, women buying chickens. One bet taker had drawn in chalk on a wall a gigantic replica of the tournament draw and assigned every player odds on his chances of winning the tournament. Zaman's name had already been shifted into the second-round column. The crowd of gamblers seeking to wager on the matches was twenty deep. There were at least ten other bet takers doing similar business in the square outside the Hagia Sophia.

Entering a wide street beyond the square, we came to a most peculiar building: the lower half appeared to be made of ancient Roman marble while the upper half was constructed of more recent masonry.

"This is Afridi's establishment," Latif said.

"A profitable business?" my teacher asked.

"Very. Afridi owns several whorehouses in the city but this is the biggest of them. He is very successful."

Just then, two men emerged from the whorehouse, one of whom I recognized. He was the big swarthy Wallachian player, Dragan.

Dragan had a broad grin on his face and he staggered slightly, drunk. "That's better!" he roared in Greek. "I've been feeling poorly ever since I arrived in this dung heap of a city. A good fuck after lunch is most cleansing for the mind!"

The Wallachian spotted us, nodded sloppily at my teacher. "Ah, you are one of the Englishmen, are you not? I was led to believe that the English were too prudish for whoring, but you surprise me! Good for you! Or are you showing your girl there how a woman can earn a decent living simply by spreading her legs?"

My teacher said nothing.

Dragan staggered off, calling, "Send her to my rooms tonight and I'll break her in!"

My teacher just watched them go with a most sour look on his face. When they disappeared around a corner, he said quietly to me, "From this moment on, stay close to me both inside and outside the palace."

"Yes, sir."

"And, Bess, fortify your mind. What you are about to see may not be pleasant."

We went inside the brothel.

————

Upon entering it, the unusual construction of the whorehouse revealed its origins: the building had actually once been a Roman bath. Afridi had merely kept its ancient base and added the upper half.

The main room was a wide, high-ceilinged space, the centerpiece of which was a huge steaming bath. Islands of marble were scattered around it, while ten open-ended booths, all filled with cushions, lined the walls, encircling the central pool.

Nude women carried food and drinks on trays, delivering them to customers in the booths. Female masseuses wearing only neck chains massaged customers on marble slabs, occasionally interrupting their ministrations to mount their customers or pleasure them in other ways.

In nearly every booth, fornication was taking place. Most of the booths were open for all to see, while a small number of them had their curtains closed. Grunts and groans could be heard from every corner, but unlike Elsie's description of her sensuous night in the harem, there was nothing sensuous about the noises here. They were the sounds of men getting their money's worth.

I had heard about prostitutes and, indeed, brothels before (one only had to read the Bible), but I was not prepared for the cold, businesslike nature of it all: the reduction of an intimate act of love to a mere act of commerce.

And then I saw the children.

They were the same age as me, thirteen or thereabouts, young boys and girls, but they strolled about the bathhouse with their faces painted like adults, in various degrees of undress, bearing drinks, grapes or smoking pipes.

I felt sick.

Standing beside me, Mr. Ascham viewed the liaisons around us with unconcealed disgust. He absently put a protective hand on my shoulder.

At that moment we spotted the diminutive whoremonger, Afridi, still dressed in his gaudy maroon-and-gold attire. He was speaking to a pair of Romany gypsies, a man and an old crone, who led two dirty country children by their hands. As we watched, Afridi gave the gypsies some coins and the children were handed over to him. The gypsies left.

This, I realized with horror, was what happened to children who were taken by gypsies. They ended up in establishments like this.

Latif went over to Afridi and after a brief exchange brought the whoremonger to us. The eunuch made the introductions for everyone's convenience in common Greek. He also informed Afridi that my teacher asked his questions at the command of the sultan himself.

"I saw you arguing with Cardinal Cardoza a short time ago," Mr. Ascham said directly. "What was the cause of your disagreement?"

"That bastard is stealing my business, that's what it was about," the Persian spat. "Thieving sodomite! Until *he* came to Constantinople, visiting clergymen from Rome were my best customers!"

"How could he be stealing your business? He is a cardinal of Rome."

"Look around you, fool! Nearly all of the men here are visitors for the tournament. Not just players—bah, there are only sixteen of them—but their masters, their attendants, their servants. An event like this is tremendous for business! And yet the entire visiting delegation from Rome—twelve men of God, twelve gloriously lusty men of the cloth—remain each night in the cardinal's quarters, serviced by the cardinal's own collection of boys."

"The cardinal keeps . . . boys?"

"Lads he finds on the streets. Lads he finds himself. Pays them with silver or food. And he *knows* that I will deliver as many boys as he needs. All the other ambassadors use my women for their gatherings in the palace. But not the cardinal, oh no. And my boys are *skilled*, you know. They know how to—"

My teacher winced as he held up a hand, stopping Afridi from elaborating. "I think I understand," Mr. Ascham said, eyeing the whoremonger with considerable distaste. "So what does Cardinal Cardoza do in his quarters exactly?"

"He holds private *gatherings*. Oh, those priests and their appetites. That's why I'm so angry. If it weren't for Cardoza, those priests would be here, every day and night, fucking like queer rabbits and paying me for the privilege!"

"Good God . . ." my teacher breathed.

"I think God stopped watching long ago," Afridi said. "This may not happen in England, but it goes on in half the Church's embassies in Eastern Europe. The local cardinal provides—how to put this—*lodging and services* for any visiting priest. If you are a man who likes other men, then the Church is the organization for you."

"I see."

"It's just wrong, I tell you! You don't see me selling places in heaven to their customers! The church should not barge into other men's trades. Its business is selling salvation. It has no business elbowing in on mine."

As Afridi continued his ranting and they conversed some more, I ventured away from my teacher's side, drawn to a large gold-painted door. It literally sparkled with golden dust. It was ajar. Curious, I pushed it open.

I saw an elaborately decorated bedchamber with a huge four-poster bed draped in the finest red satin sheets. The bed was currently empty, but a pair of padded ropes dangled from the headboard. A sign above the bed read in Arabic:

شهزاده نڭ كنديسينڭ ده قوللاندغى كيبى

I peered at the symbols closely. I was getting better at understanding the local script and I managed to recognize one set of symbols: شهزاده نڭ They were Arabic-Turkish for "crown prince."

A rough hand came down on my shoulder. An unshaven man of Egyptian appearance stood over me. "I'll take this one!" he called out to Afridi in Greek.

"You most certainly will not." My teacher hurried to my side. "This girl does not work here. Get away from her."

The Egyptian skulked off. Mr. Ascham watched him go. Then he glanced into the room beyond the golden door to see what had drawn me to it, before saying, "Let's go, Bess. We're finished here."

As we strode out the main doors, Afridi called after us, "Hey, Englishman! While you are here, you want a woman? Since you're visiting on behalf of the sultan, I will give you a woman for no charge!"

Mr. Ascham said nothing as we hastened out of there.

———

We left Afridi's establishment and stepped back into the sunshine.

I was very pleased to be out of there. I was actually quite unnerved by the experience: the dark brothel was a place where a young girl like me could enter by accident and never leave. It was good to be back out in the light of day, in the freedom of the streets of Constantinople.

My teacher walked with a grim, determined look on his face, heading back toward the Hagia Sophia and the palace.

"Did you learn anything in there?" I asked. While I was a little disturbed by Afridi's descriptions of the indiscretions of the visiting priests, I had not derived much of relevance to our investigation from his remarks.

"Too many things," he replied. "Our world advances so quickly yet some men will always be slaves to their basest desires. Sometimes I think we are merely animals who wear clothes. I regret that you had to see that. Are you all right?"

I winced. "I didn't like seeing the children. I did not know such things happened."

Mr. Ascham nodded. "While I regret that you saw what you did, I must say I am not *sorry* you saw it. Bess, many would say that you should never see such awful things, that seeing them will offend your delicate sensibilities. But I do not think so."

"Even when it is painful to see them?" I asked.

"Precisely because it is painful. A potential future ruler like you *should* see the grim underbelly of the world, foul places like the one you just witnessed, for if you didn't, you would sincerely believe that all folk enjoy the same privileged life as you when in reality they do not. We live in a world where women sell their bodies to men and where children are kidnapped in the countryside and sold into slavery in brothels in the cities. You should know that these things occur."

"Couldn't you just *tell* me about them? Then I could know of them without having to see them."

"Not this time. There is no better lesson than seeing something with your own eyes."

We had arrived back at the Hagia Sophia. The enormous throng of people still crowded around the mighty cathedral.

I said, "So what is your plan now?"

"From what I have seen and heard so far," Mr. Ascham said, "I am increasingly intrigued by Cardinal Cardoza and his embassy. That is where Cardinal Farnese was poisoned by a meal that came from Brunello's kitchen. And the now-dead Brunello argued with

Cardoza, who feuds with the whoremonger Afridi. And now we hear from Afridi of most unholy gatherings that take place there at night. My plan, then, is to follow my own advice and see this embassy with my own eyes. I intend to observe the cardinal's embassy under the cover of darkness, perhaps as soon as tonight, and see what goes on there."

ANOTHER NIGHT
AT THE PALACE

WE RETURNED TO THE HAGIA SOPHIA in time to see the final stages of the second match of the tournament: Vladimir of Muscovy versus Mustafa of Cairo. Like the first match, it was a rather one-sided contest.

The burly Muscovite won the match by four games to nil, and when he mated the Egyptian in the fourth game, the young prince Ivan leaped up from his chair on the royal stage and punched the air with a cry of, "Good show, Vlad! Good show!"

A wooden placard bearing Vladimir's name was placed in the second column of the draw. The Muscovite would face Zaman in the next round and all knew that it would be a fine match.

———

The sun set on Constantinople and the delighted crowd dispersed from the Hagia Sophia. As the distinguished guests staying at the palace filed out of the great cathedral and back through the palace gates, Mr. Ascham held me aside so that they could pass us by.

"What are we—" I began, but then I realized.

He was looking at their shoes, searching for a wooden-soled left sandal with a nick in it. But he saw no such shoe among the many feet that went by.

The next day offered an abundance of chess: the remaining six matches of the first round would be played. To accommodate this, we'd been told, the single central playing stage would be converted into two playing stages.

Given the big day to follow, no formal dinner was held that evening and most delegations took supper in their rooms.

My teacher's plan to furtively observe the cardinal's quarters that night was also thwarted when he learned that, since Rome's own player was playing the next day, Cardinal Cardoza had ordered all his guests to retire early that night so as not to disturb Brother Raul.

"The cardinal is, however, scheduled to host a reception for the sultan in the Church's embassy tomorrow evening," Mr. Ascham said. "I might try to see what happens there after that."

I myself was glad for the early night. The events in the slaughter room and the visit to the brothel had shaken me. I wasn't sure what to make of them. On the one hand, I most certainly didn't like seeing such things. But then, on the other, I didn't want to be a naive king's daughter who knew nothing of the real world. That world might be unpleasant, it might even be dangerous, but it was *real*, and I found myself wanting to know about it, no matter how terrible its secrets might be. Having said that, after staying out so late the previous night, I was tired and another evening of grim investigation was not something I desired greatly, so I was happy for the reprieve.

It was still light when I dropped into my bed and quickly fell asleep.

I awoke later to find the world around me dark, the palace quiet and Elsie's bed once again empty. I rolled over and went back to sleep.

———

A shuffling noise woke me. I opened my eyes to see Elsie treading softly across the room toward her bed. The first purple rays of dawn were creeping through the window shades.

"Elsie!" I whispered. "Where have you been?"

"Oh, just to another delicious gathering with the crown prince and his friends," she said in a hushed but most excited voice. "This time it was in one of the ancient crypts underneath the Hagia Sophia, one that must have been built when the great mosque was a Christian church.

Zubaida had learned that a gathering was taking place there this evening and bid me join her."

She leaped to my side and, unbidden, launched into a description of her evening.

"When I arrived at the rear entrance to the Hagia with Zubaida, we were each handed a mask and instructed to disrobe. Can you believe it, Bessie, masks and nakedness! How exciting! We then descended some stairs and entered the crypt. Normally, it would have been the most frightening and ghoulish place but the prince's servants had decorated it with hundreds of candles that illuminated the old stone chamber in a rich, warm glow.

"Scattered around the crypt were perhaps two dozen young men and girls—including Crown Prince Selim himself—all of them naked but for their flimsy masks. Many sipped wine from gold goblets while others casually pleasured each other on the stone sarcophagi arrayed around the place, careless of any offense this may have caused the dead.

"I felt a thrill: congress is a delight in itself, but congress in illicit places has an extra excitement to it. I shouldn't tell you, Bessie, but I once allowed Mr. Trelawney, the gardener at Hatfield, to take me in his work shed while his wife tilled the vegetable garden not twenty paces away."

"Elsie!"

"Trust me, Bessie, a man will take it whenever he can get it, and, truly, the more risky the location, the greater the thrill—riding the gardener while looking out at his wife heightened my pleasure considerably."

I could not speak. I had thought Mr. Trelawney to be a decent and loyal husband. He went to church every Sunday.

Elsie went on. "Upon entering the crypt, I eyed the crown prince. He lounged on a marble coffin wearing a gold half mask, drinking wine and conversing with one of his male friends while a slave girl stood behind him massaging his shoulders.

"Zubaida said, 'See that man Selim is talking to? He is Rahman, the prince's closest friend since childhood. If you want to snare the prince, you must first impress Rahman.'

"'I see,' I replied, striding around the crypt, ostensibly gazing at the bodies around me but in reality assessing this Rahman. He was handsome in a rugged sort of way, with long black hair that flopped down over his bronze half-faced mask.

"I made three circuits of the crypt, sidling past Rahman and the prince each time, swiveling my naked hips as I went by. They noticed.

"A short time later, leaning against a stone coffin, I threw a nod at Rahman, which brought him over to me. He arrived before me and said in Greek, 'Good evening, I understand that you are a rose from England. I am Rahman—'

"I pressed my finger gently to his lips, silencing him. Then I took him by the hand and led him into a side crypt. Without uttering a single word, I sat him down on a stone seat and mounted him. Then I rode him, gently and sensually, until with the rhythm of my hips I brought him to a gasping climax."

"Goodness, Elsie . . ." I said. "How could you be so forward? Would a man really like that?"

Elsie smiled knowingly. "Believe me, they like it, Bessie. You'll learn. Once Rahman had caught his breath, I said most demurely, 'It is a pleasure to meet you, Rahman. My name is Elsie and I do indeed hail from England.'

"After that, we conversed most pleasantly for a short while before he returned to the prince's side and engaged Selim in a conversation which included many glances in my direction.

"I just nodded to them and the prince nodded back." Elsie shivered, giggling. "Oh, Bessie, I am getting closer to the prince."

"Elsie, what exactly do you hope to achieve by coupling with the crown prince?"

"Bessie, you silly, silly girl! What do you *think*? But of course, you do not think of these things because you were born a princess. I was not so born. The only way I can become a princess is by seducing a prince, and the only way I can become a *queen* is by seducing and marrying a *crown* prince. What better way to win one than by satisfying his manly needs?"

I suddenly felt very young. I did not like being called a silly, silly girl.

But then I thought of my father's long list of conquests. He must have bedded over two hundred women in his life and he certainly hadn't intended to marry all of them. There was only one exception to this rule: my mother, Anne Boleyn. A most confident and prepossessing lady—some said devious—she had not succumbed to his charms until she was absolutely sure he would marry her. But even that had not saved her. Once they had been wed and she had treacherously given him a daughter, me, his wandering eye had found other willing girls and his interest in her waned till the day he had her head cut off.

"Be careful, Elsie," I said, "the crown prince cannot marry every girl he plucks and it sounds to me like he and his friends have plucked many."

Elsie sighed. "That's easy for you to say, Bessie. But just think, if I were to marry Selim and become his queen and you were to become Queen of England, we would be queens together! What wonderful parties we could hold at our courts!"

"Elsie," I said, "I have one brother and an elder sister who both precede me in the line of succession. By the sound of it, you are currently closer to sitting on a throne than I am."

We talked a little more, but soon Elsie, exhausted from her nocturnal adventures, nodded off. By this time, dawn had come fully and sounds could be heard from the other rooms of our lodgings.

The second day of the tournament was about to start.

A DISCUSSION AMONG TITANS

WE ARRIVED AT THE HAGIA SOPHIA later that morning to find two chess stages erected before the royal stage and the eager masses crowding around them both. The sultan sat up on his throne, equidistant from the two boards, able to watch whichever match took his fancy.

The first two matches to be played were the remaining two from the top half of the draw: Ali Hassan Rama of Medina versus Pablo Montoya of Castile; and Eduardo of Syracuse versus Brother Raul of the Papal States.

At one point during those two matches, my teacher went over to sit with Ignatius of Loyola. He recounted to me later the conversation they had:

"Signor Ignatius, we have not met but my name is Ascham, from—"

"Please, I know who you are, Mr. Ascham. It is a privilege. I am told by our mutual friend Michelangelo that you are a man after my own heart: a lover of learning and teaching."

"I am indeed," my teacher replied. "Sir, if you don't mind, I'd like to ask you some brief questions."

"Certainly."

"On the night of the opening banquet, just before the main meal, did you engage Cardinal Cardoza in a conversation?"

"I did."

"He was leaving the courtyard, was he not?"

"He was. He was returning to his embassy."

"Was it a lengthy discussion?"

"Yes. And a passionate one, too. It was about the selling of indulgences by the pope and his cardinals to the wealthy. I find it outrageous. Cardinal Cardoza does not."

"I see. May I also ask if you are staying at Cardinal Cardoza's embassy while you are in attendance at this tournament?"

"No!" the Jesuit retorted sharply. "I most certainly am not. The selling of indulgences is not the only Church practice the cardinal and I disagree on. I am staying in more humble lodgings in the city, on my own."

"What of your player? Brother Raul?"

"He is staying with the cardinal, against my advice," the Jesuit said darkly.

They spoke briefly of other matters, but then Brother Raul's match reached a critical juncture and my teacher politely took his leave so that Ignatius could watch the match with his full attention.

In the end, the two matches were stirring contests that went to seven and six games respectively, with both the Spanish players winning. The second round would thus be most interesting: Spaniard would face Spaniard with one representing the Holy Roman Emperor, King Charles, and the other God himself.

———

I was very excited about the next session—the middle session of the day—for it would see the first appearance of our man, Mr. Gilbert Giles. Earlier that morning, he had sat with Mr. Ascham in our rooms discussing potential strategies. I watched, enthralled.

"So, Giles, what do you know of this Talib?"

"Only that he has been playing chess for nearly sixty years," Mr. Giles said, "and that his prodigious memory of past contests is famous. His mind is said to be a repository of chess matches that he can call upon at will."

"A powerful strength," Mr. Ascham said.

"But also, I think, a potential weakness," Mr. Giles said.

"How so?"

"Talib has written much on the subject of chess. He loudly praises the classical strategies—openings, pawn formations, attacks—while scorning newer methods of play. Talib is trapped in the old ways. If I use some of the more unusual recent techniques, I think I might be able to unsettle him, bamboozle him."

I said, "Play the man, not the board."

"Correct." Mr. Giles grinned as he then said, "You know, Bess, I think we should call this new strategy the 'Ascham Gambit' since it involves using unorthodox techniques to achieve one's goal."

Mr. Ascham cracked a rare smile, not taking the bait. "Why, thank you, Giles. I am honored."

They both laughed and for a brief moment, I was actually happy. In that strange city, under the constant shadow of our grim investigation, I enjoyed seeing two good friends smiling.

Mr. Ascham became his serious self once again. "Be watchful for any accelerating or delaying tactics he might employ. I hear he is wily."

"Yes, yes. Good point . . ."

"What do you mean, accelerating or delaying tactics?" I asked.

My teacher said, "Some chess players are known to subtly control the pace of a game through certain stratagems: sometimes they move quickly, immediately after you have moved, rushing you, making you feel as if they know every move you can make before you do. Others play excessively slowly, even when they have only one or two possible moves, to the point where you want to reach over and move the damned piece for them. Their goal is to frustrate you, put you off your game."

"Because if you are annoyed," Mr. Giles said, "then you are not thinking about the game at hand. An angry mind does not play good chess."

"An angry mind does not do anything well," Mr. Ascham said. "Many a king has lost his kingdom because of decisions made in anger. We're lucky this is only chess."

———

And so it was that just before noon that day Mr. Giles faced off against the hunched and gnarled figure of Talib of Baghdad, while on the other stage the great unshaven brute, Dragan of Wallachia, played Marko of Venezia.

The other match was over long before Mr. Giles's—the dirty Wallachian made short work of the Venetian. Whenever he took one of his opponent's pieces, Dragan would shout something in his Slavic tongue. Word spread quickly that he was saying: "Take that and fuck your mother!"

The spectators on the royal stage and in the upper galleries of the hall exchanged embarrassed glances at his exclamations, but the enormous crowd of regular citizens cheered with delight whenever he spat the crude phrase.

Dragan, it should also be said, happily drank mugs of mead while he played, belching loudly, wiping his mouth with his sleeve, and at one point, stomping out of the hall to urinate in an alley outside, in full view of the crowd.

Mr. Giles had a far tougher time of it against the little librarian from the House of Wisdom in Baghdad. Talib was indeed a seasoned and wily player who set many traps and oftentimes would groan sadly after a move—only to leap forward three moves later and pounce on one of Mr. Giles's pieces, revealing his groan to have been but a ruse.

He also, I noticed, engaged in the exact delaying tactics my teacher and Mr. Giles had discussed that morning. He took an excessively long time to make even the simplest move, but Mr. Giles just sat back in his chair, as if enjoying the extra time this gave him to admire the details of the Hagia Sophia's nave.

Their match was poised at two games apiece when Dragan finished off his Venetian opponent ("Take that and fuck your mother twice!"). The final score was four games to nil in Dragan's favor. The spectators around that table applauded appreciatively before turning their attention to the other playing stage.

As Mr. Giles's match became the center of attention in the vast hall, a familiar white-bearded figure appeared beside my teacher: Michelangelo.

"Roger," he said. "Your man plays well. He drew a difficult opponent in the first round."

"He most certainly did," my teacher replied. "Unlike others in the draw."

Michelangelo didn't seem to notice the barb. He said, "During the afternoon session, I will be venturing into the city for lunch with Ignatius. Would you like to join us?"

My teacher turned in his seat. "Why, that would be splendid! But—" He shot a concerned look at me.

Michelangelo saw it. "Bring the young princess, too. I like the sharpness of her eyes and, who knows"—he winked at me—"she might even learn something."

They arranged to meet in the square outside the Hagia Sophia at the conclusion of Mr. Giles's match.

As it turned out, that did not take very long: in the next two games, Mr. Giles employed some very unorthodox tactics (including a daring sacrifice of one of his knights after it went on a bloody rampage through Talib's carefully arranged pawns), which threw Talib completely. He blinked excessively and frowned at the pieces as if he were looking at a three-eyed man and not a chessboard. Mr. Giles's tactic had rattled him and it caused Talib to commit some small but fatal errors and Mr. Giles pounced, closing out the match, winning it four games to two.

It was now early in the afternoon and while the royal stage cleared for the luncheon intermission, none of the citizens dared move from their places: their hero, Ibrahim of Constantinople, would be playing in the final session of the day and they did not want to lose their spots.

Mr. Giles joined us on the royal stage. I noticed perspiration on his forehead and his gaze seemed to be fixed at a length of about two feet— the distance between his chair and the chessboard. The intensity of the match had taken a physical toll on him and I recalled my argument with my teacher about chess not being a sport unless one perspired while playing it. Clearly, I had been wrong.

"Nicely done, Giles," Mr. Ascham said. "A fine effort in forward planning."

Mr. Giles nodded in acknowledgment. "Goodness, I need a rest."

He retired to our quarters to take a nap, accompanied by Elsie who, in desperate need of sleep herself, said she would do the same.

As for Mr. Ascham and me, we ventured out into the mighty crowd massed on the wide plaza outside the main entrance to the Hagia Sophia, where we found Michelangelo and Ignatius waiting for us.

————

That afternoon, while the last two matches of the first round were played—the Moghul prince Nasiruddin versus Lao from the Orient, and Ibrahim of Constantinople versus Wilhelm of Königsberg—my teacher and I chatted and discoursed with two of the most celebrated minds of the age.

And what a discussion it was!

We dined at a small establishment on a hill about half a mile from the palace. With Constantinople spread out before us in the dusty afternoon light—its streets and minarets veiled in the perpetual haze, the great dome of the Hagia Sophia looming behind us—my dining companions talked about all manner of diverse and interesting things.

Their conversation ranged from a detailed examination of the sensational assertions made by the astronomer Nicolaus Copernicus in his recent publication, *De Revolutionibus orbium coelestium*, to fabulous stories of galleons overflowing with silver returning from the New World to Spain . . . and the privateers who had taken to plundering them; and of course, to matters of religion, including Luther's *Ninety-Five Theses* and the future of a bejeweled Catholic papacy in the face of this grassroots reform movement and, naturally, the exotic Moslem faith that surrounded us in Constantinople.

"Islam is a most beautiful religion but sometimes it saddens me,"

Michelangelo said as a veiled Moslem woman passed us by, walking obediently behind her husband, two young girls skipping happily beside her. "See that veiled woman. Islam does not in any way command that she be veiled. And see her little girls, so delightful and gay: in a few years, their smiling faces will be hidden behind gauze veils, too, and yet that need not be so. For in early Islam, it was only the Prophet's wives who had to be veiled, not all women."

"Then how did it come to be that all Moslem women now do so?" I asked.

"Interestingly, it is more about the nature of fashion than faith," the great artist said. "Let me ask you this: your father, Henry, the king of England. He is a handsome man?"

"He is." In his youth, my father had been positively dashing, a sportsman-king. As he aged now, he grew wider in the paunch, but I was not going to admit that.

"And a fashionable fellow?"

"Most assuredly."

"When he wears a new item of clothing, do others in the court and in the streets of London mimic him?"

"All the time," I said. "It is said that if he wears a new design of paned breeches—to further display his manly calves, of which he is ever so proud—within a week every man at Whitehall is wearing similar breeches."

"So it is with Moslem women and their veils," Michelangelo said. "When they saw Muhammad's wives wearing veils, they sought to imitate them, and so now nearly all Islamic women wear veils even though there is no stipulation in their Holy Koran that they do so."

"Now, now, Michel," my teacher interjected. "That's not the whole of it. As with many other faiths—including our own Christian one—a small group of zealots have distorted Islam to further their own agenda. When many women took to imitating the fashions of the Prophet's wives, some Moslem men saw an opportunity to put *all* women under their thumb. They espoused foul laws like those allowing a man to beat his wife or force her into his bed."

"But why?" I asked innocently. "Why do these men seek to dominate women? I mean, what have they to fear from women?"

"From the mouths of babes . . ." Michelangelo said wistfully.

"Indeed," my teacher agreed, smiling at me kindly.

I noticed, however, that Ignatius said nothing on this matter.

Mr. Ascham said, "Bess, not all men seek to dominate women. Only small-minded ones. Such men do so because it is a woman's choice whether or not she grants her body to a man. Small-minded men hate this, perhaps because at some time in their lives their advances were rejected by women. And so these men design laws that give them power over women. The shame of it all is that they do so in the name of God."

Ignatius raised his finger. "But what of someone like me, a member of an order composed exclusively of celibate men. I devote my entire being, including my sexual being, to my Church and my God. That is why I distance myself from women, not because I am one of your 'small-minded' men."

"You most certainly are not one of those." My teacher bowed his head. "And I respect you, your vows and the self-restraint you display in living in accordance with them. But your faith's attitudes to women are not so worthy. For instance, why can a woman not be one of your Jesuits or a priest in the Catholic Church? Can a woman not also devote her entire being to God?"

"Well, the early Church was composed almost entirely of men . . ."

"In a male-dominated ancient world. My good sir, times and customs have changed over a thousand years. In these times, queens rule, women own property, and young maidens walk the streets unaccompanied."

"Christ himself had only male disciples."

"And yet the majority of those who had the courage to stay by his side when he was nailed to the cross were women," Michelangelo pointed out.

My teacher said, "The Church's war against women occurred not under Christ—who by all accounts held women as equals to men—but through the writings of St. Irenaeus and Tertullian, and that most cruel woman hater of them all, St. Paul, whose hostile views on women were unfortunately included in the Bible. But let me be clear, it is not only a Catholic problem; it is a *Christian* one: Martin Luther, the scourge of the old Church, shares its views on women. He once wrote: 'Girls begin to talk and to stand on their feet sooner than boys because weeds always grow up more quickly than good crops.' Weeds! *Weeds!*"

I had not heard of this. I quite favored Luther's views on the Christian faith over those of the Church in Rome. But I did not like being thought of as a weed.

I was also, I must say, captivated by what they were saying. I had never heard *anyone* discuss so boldly and forthrightly the topic of women or religion, let alone a group of minds as distinguished as this one. I listened intently, determined to remember every word.

Mr. Ascham went on. "Consider Islam's promise of seventy-two round-bosomed maidens 'whom no man will have deflowered before them' to any man who martyrs himself in defense of the faith. To whom can that appeal *but* a small-minded man?"

"A most odd promise," Ignatius admitted, "and one that my translators of Islamic texts have struggled with."

Michelangelo said, "Indeed, for only a fellow who is a failure in the bedchamber would require virgins in heaven, as only virgins would be ignorant of how poor a lover he was. This also raises the question: do Moslem *women* who martyr themselves in the name of their faith encounter seventy-two strapping young virgin men in heaven? This I do not know but I doubt it."

Later, the topic turned to the sultan and the strength of his Moslem empire.

"*Is* Europe in danger of an Islamic invasion?" my teacher asked. "This sultan openly calls the Holy Roman Emperor the 'king of Spain,' he treats the Habsburgs with contempt, his forces hold Buda, he considers another attack on Vienna, and his navies recently defeated the Spanish at Preveza. Can the West stop this Islamic wave? Will we in England soon be reading the Koran at prayer times?"

The two great thinkers sitting with us contemplated this.

Ignatius said, "I foresee only one outcome: a great pan-European war to settle this. A new Crusade; not one fought in the Holy Land but rather at the gates of each and every capital in Europe, as we fend off this ever-expanding empire. While the West has bickered about popes, faiths and royal divorces, the Moslems have been rising and now they advance."

Michelangelo nodded. "I am inclined to agree."

"You really think so?" Mr. Ascham said.

"Oh, yes," Michelangelo said. "Let me ask you, did you bring a scarlet envelope with you to this event, sealed by your king Henry?"

"Yes, I did."

"Do you know what it contained?"

"No. I was forbidden to open it. I was merely instructed to deliver it to the sultan upon our arrival."

"You brought nothing else with that scarlet envelope? No trunk or chest or lockbox?" Michelangelo asked pointedly.

"No," Mr. Ascham said blankly. "Should I have?"

Michelangelo frowned at that and threw a glance at Ignatius. Then he looked away, his formidable mind turning. "How *very* interesting. Henry . . . Henry the Eighth. Ignatius, did you bring such an envelope with you from the pope?"

"I did, and like Mr. Ascham I did not know its contents. I also handed to the sultan, during our initial audience, a heavy locked trunk, filled—I guessed—with gold."

"As did every other delegation to this tournament," Michelangelo informed us, "except for one: the English one."

I felt a chill run through me. I was not certain it was a good thing to be so singular in this matter.

My teacher was also very confused by this. He looked from Michelangelo to Ignatius as if he were the only one present not included in a joke. "I do not understand. What was in the scarlet envelope?"

Michelangelo leaned forward and spoke in a whisper.

"Inside that scarlet envelope was your king's answer to a challenge from the sultan," he said. "Every king who sent a player to this tournament *also* sent to the sultan, in one of those red envelopes, his answer to Suleiman's challenge."

"And what was this challenge?" I asked, unable to restrain myself.

"I do not know the precise details," Michelangelo said, "but I am led to believe that the sultan, while inviting each king to send his chess champion to Constantinople, also dispatched a secret protocol to each king giving them a choice: pay Suleiman a hefty ransom in gold or face full-scale invasion after the tournament. And as we have now seen, only one king did *not* return his scarlet envelope accompanied by any kind of trunk or chest filled with gold: yours."

My teacher and I exchanged worried looks. My father was a great man, but as we both knew, he was also vain, impetuous and not given to taking threats well.

We could only wonder in horror at what King Henry VIII of England had written in the scarlet envelope my teacher had personally brought to the possible future ruler of Europe.

Thankfully, the conversation turned to another topic and over the course of that afternoon (we heard the wails of the muezzins twice), it was my privilege to hear those three great men discuss many things, until finally, as the dying sun touched the horizon and Constantinople shone in a magnificent orange glow, they concluded their philosophical musings and headed back to the palace.

We stopped at the Hagia Sophia on the way to find out what had happened in the afternoon matches.

It turned out that the Moghul prince Nasiruddin had defeated Lao over six games, while Ibrahim had overcome Wilhelm of Königsberg in a very tough encounter that had gone to the seventh and deciding game.

With the day's matches over, the *sadrazam* made an announcement: tomorrow would be a rest day, during which the successful players could put their minds at ease in preparation for the second round. In lieu of chess, festival activities would be held around the city, paid for by the sultan himself. The crowd cheered loudly at this.

And so as night fell, we arrived back at the palace. There Mr. Ascham and I took our leave of Michelangelo and Ignatius, thanking them for a most stimulating afternoon.

We returned to our quarters for supper, but I was keenly aware that we would not be staying there long, for having been thwarted the previous evening, tonight my teacher had plans: he wanted to observe Cardinal Cardoza's embassy under the cover of darkness.

THE EMBASSY

AFTER TAKING A LATE SUPPER, my teacher called for Latif and asked the eunuch to escort him, Elsie and me on a stroll around the palace grounds. After the mental exertions of his match during the day, Mr. Giles was fast asleep, snoring loudly.

I already knew that this was a ruse of Mr. Ascham's: to any observer, we would merely be visitors taking a late-evening tour of the palace, guided by an esteemed eunuch, whereas in reality my teacher had already asked Latif to take us to all possible vantage points from which he could observe Cardinal Cardoza's embassy later that night.

Guided by Latif, the three of us strolled around the nighttime palace.

We walked under a glorious full moon, and bathed in its silver light the palace was a magical place. With its high domes, vivid mosaics and intricate lattice walls that gave one tantalizing glimpses of the adjoining courtyards, Topkapi Palace was as fantastical and exotic as English castles were cold and utilitarian.

"Latif," my teacher said. "Have you discovered anything about the whereabouts of the dead chef's son, Pietro?"

"I fear not, sir," Latif replied as he walked. "The lad has vanished. My men have been making inquiries all day, but there has been no sign of the boy at all. He has not been seen since his parents' bodies were discovered yesterday."

I looked at my teacher. "A sign of guilt?"

"Or fear," Mr. Ascham said.

We continued our perambulations. For a time, I walked with Elsie a short distance behind my teacher and Latif.

I said, "Elsie, I have been thinking. About the awful things that people do to each other. Murder, torture, enslavement. Do you ever wonder *why* we do such terrible things to each other?"

Elsie thought for a long moment. Then she turned to face me, a look of sudden enlightenment in her eyes. "You know, Bessie, I think I should wear my hair up for tonight's gathering with the crown prince. It will show off my neck all the more."

I looked at Elsie as she continued walking and I said no more.

We arrived at the southeast corner of the palace, where we spied the white two-story structure that was Cardinal Cardoza's embassy.

"Did the cardinal host the sultan earlier?" Mr. Ascham asked Latif.

"He did," the eunuch said. "The sultan left an hour ago with his retinue. Now, only churchmen remain in the embassy."

As Latif walked in front of us, pointing to the string of small islands in the Sea of Marmara directly to the south, we essentially circumnavigated the wide lawn surrounding the cardinal's building.

Candlelight glowed within the embassy and we could hear voices and lute music playing inside. The curtains of all the ground-level windows were drawn.

"But those on the upper level are not," my teacher observed.

The upper level of the structure bore four tall windows on its southern and eastern faces, designed to take in the view. My teacher looked around us and beheld a balcony at the very end of the nearby south pavilion from which one might be able to see into the embassy's upper level.

"Latif," Mr. Ascham said. "That balcony, is it accessible? Or, rather, can we gain access to it unnoticed?"

"We can. It is the sultan's private viewing balcony. His Majesty only uses it in the daytime and then but rarely."

"I am sure he will not mind us borrowing it in the course of our investigation. It is the vantage point I seek. Take us there, please."

———

Getting to the sultan's balcony meant doubling back past our own rooms and Mr. Ascham gave both Elsie and me the option of retiring. Of course, Elsie took that option, although she and I knew exactly where she would be going. I, however, insisted on staying with my teacher.

"You may come," he said, "as long as you understand that you may again see unpleasant things."

"I understand." I felt I was becoming an old hand at seeing unpleasant things and could no longer be easily shocked. I must admit that maybe I was also becoming like my teacher: I didn't like unresolved events. I wanted to know what was behind the murders that had taken place in the palace.

"You promise not to make a sound?" he said.

"Not a sound."

"No matter what we see?"

"No matter what we see."

"All right, then," he said, but the final, doubtful look he gave me suggested that it might not be all right at all.

And so, guided by our eunuch, we made our way to the sultan's private balcony.

The wide balcony offered a glorious panoramic view of the Sea of Marmara and I could see why it was reserved for the sultan. It also, as my teacher had hoped, looked back down on to the Catholic embassy, offering a clear view into its upper-level windows.

My teacher and I settled into two wooden chairs at the rail and commenced our watch.

My confidence in my inability to be easily shocked was short lived.

What I saw appalled me. It was all I could do not to cry out.

I saw two rooms. In the left-hand one, I saw priests of the Church prancing around in various states of undress and drunkenness—some wore their holy chains around their naked waists instead of their shoulders, others wore nothing at all; a few gulped wine from holy chalices, spilling it down their chests, while others smoked opium. Among them was Brother Raul.

There were perhaps six priests in total in that room and with them were a gaggle of boys ranging in age from about thirteen to fifteen. The boys wore loincloths and laurel wreaths, making them look like a gang of Cupids, and they variously served and entertained the clergymen: one boy poured wine while another sang, and a third daintily stroked an old priest's hair.

Directing the whole affair was Cardinal Cardoza himself.

He sat on an elevated chair—a throne of sorts—holding a bejeweled chalice filled with wine, pointing and laughing and stroking the shoulders of a boy who sat at his side like a loyal dog. The big cardinal was also naked. Every now and then, he would pick up his little horsehair whip and swat away with it at some irritating insect.

"By the love of . . ." I whispered. "These are men of God . . ."

My teacher grimaced. "These men do not preach the Word of the Lord. They gorge at the trough of an organization that gives them wealth, influence and power. And it appears they have taken advantage of that organization to cater to their perversions.

"The Lord I believe in does not endorse men like these. Nor do the truly pious men of the Church, like Ignatius. The Church does many noble deeds and it has produced many genuinely great individuals, but it has been corrupted by men of low character who bring down its reputation: men like Boniface who sold indulgences and supposedly celibate popes who fathered many bastards."

"But this, sir," I said, "this is wickedness. This is the work of the devil."

"No, Bess, it is the work of men," Mr. Ascham said sadly. "The corruption of young boys by its priests has been a problem for the Church for over a thousand years. It was mentioned as far back as 309 A.D. when the lack of moral discipline among priests was so poor that the Council of Elvira was convened under the presidency of Felix of Accitum. St. Bede wrote about it in his *Penitential* in the eighth century and in 1051, the great reformist monk St. Peter Damian wrote in his *Liber Gomorrhianus* that interference with children by priests was rampant in the Church at that time. Worse still, Damian accused the Church's superiors of concealing the deplorable crimes of its clergy. And so it continues today, an absolute abomination. Is it any wonder that Luther has found a willing audience for his message?"

We continued to watch the gathering and as I gazed upon these men of God engaging in such impiety, I realized that they had no more connection with God than even the lowest criminal did. For my whole life I had thought priests and ministers had a special, higher relationship with our Lord. Now I could see otherwise. Priests were simply men with the same flaws and desires as other men.

I found myself thinking about Elsie's description of the crown prince's gatherings and her comments about the delightful thrill of copulation. I also pondered what I had witnessed in Afridi's establishment the previous day.

"Mr. Ascham," I said, "are all adult affairs really just driven by carnal desires?"

My teacher looked at me, thinking.

"I should very much like to know," I prodded, "especially now that I have reached womanhood and my father speaks of marrying me off to a foreign prince."

Mr. Ascham sighed. "In the end I'd have to say, yes, many if not most adult affairs are driven by such desires. And the powerful have long known that power itself can command certain carnal advantages: from the wicked doctrine of *jus primae noctis* that used to be practiced by landed lords to the lusty monarch who merely points to a girl and she is whisked to his bedchamber."

"Like my father?"

My teacher hesitated. It was one of the rare occasions when I saw him uncertain, unsure.

"You may speak freely, sir," I said. "I will not tell. I ask only to learn. I am keen to know your thoughts on these matters."

Mr. Ascham looked hard at me. "Yes, like your father."

"Please elaborate."

He turned back to face the cardinal's rooms as he went on. "Your father—with respect—has indulged his carnal whims almost every night of his adult life, whether with his wives, other men's wives, the queen's ladies of the bedchamber or the occasional kitchen girl. He does not respect other men's marriages or maidens' reputations. For him, free and ready fornication is one of the natural perquisites of being king. Perhaps the only time he ever restrained himself was when he was courting your mother."

"What of queens, then?" I asked. "Are female rulers any different?"

My teacher pondered this. "A good question. I'd have to say a life of such carnal abandon is more difficult for queens to maintain."

"Why!" I said, almost indignant. "Are you saying that a male ruler can happily indulge his sensual appetites while a female one cannot without being called a whore?"

"Sadly, that is exactly what I am saying," my teacher said. "I would hasten to add that a more reasoned foundation for my position is that the *consequences* of behaving in such a carefree manner are far more long-lasting for a woman than for a man. If a king plucks every girl he sees, the consequence is perhaps a dozen bastards whose paternity he can happily deny. But if a *queen* indulges in regular copulation, she might fall pregnant, and that is a condition she cannot hide. Nor can she deny ownership of the child."

"The Egyptian queen Cleopatra was a famous ruler," I said, "and she bore sons to both Julius Caesar and Mark Antony."

"And look at how she fared: she lost her empire to Augustus, both she and Mark Antony committed suicide, and she has gone down as one of history's greatest whores."

I said, "What of a happy marriage, then, to a loyal and faithful husband? Can a queen accomplish that in these times?"

Mr. Ascham pondered that for a moment. "It is possible, I'm sure, but I would also say it would be difficult to achieve."

"Why?"

"Because as you well know, a queen rarely gets to choose her husband. Royal matches are usually made when a princess is young, in a bargain between her father and the ruler of a foreign land for political reasons, not loyalty, love or fidelity. To marry for love is not common for a queen. It is the price of a royal life."

I frowned. "It would seem, then, that perhaps the best course of action for a queen might be to abstain from any sort of intimate relations entirely. Then one can be neither a vessel for producing the next king nor a harlot."

In the darkness, my teacher slowly nodded. "That might well be the answer—wait a moment, what is this?"

My teacher's eyes narrowed as he watched the cardinal's rooms.

A new participant had entered the upper-left-hand room.

My eyes widened as I recognized him.

It was impossible not to. It was Darius, the famous Persian wrestler who had performed at the opening banquet. He was handsome and enormous, his muscles bulging. He strode into the room and stood before Cardinal Cardoza, wearing only a small white cloth to cover his modesty.

The cardinal said something and the cloth was removed.

Darius stood naked before the cardinal. The cardinal bit his whip's handle, smiling lasciviously at what he saw.

Then he took Darius into the right-hand room. We watched as he circled the great wrestler, who just stood there staring stoically forward. It occurred to me that Darius had not gone there willingly. The cardinal stroked the wrestler's hairless chest. Still the wrestler just stared forward.

Then the cardinal instructed the wrestler to bend over a chair, which Darius dutifully did.

"Bess. Turn away," my teacher said sharply.

"But—?"

"Turn away. Now. This is not for innocent eyes."

I ducked below the rail, and so I did not see what happened next between the cardinal and the wrestler. I did, however, see the look on my teacher's face as he continued to watch for a few moments. It was a look of the most profound revulsion.

He stood abruptly, turning away from the sight. "Come," he said. "I have seen enough of this foulness."

We left the balcony with Latif in tow. As we did so, my teacher frowned in thought. "I do not understand. The cardinal treats the great Darius with contempt, using him as a plaything, and the wrestler just obliges. How can this be?"

I bit my lip uncertainly. "I might know why," I whispered.

My teacher turned to me as we walked, cocking a surprised eyebrow before he glanced sharply at Latif and said to me in German, "Later."

I nodded.

He shook his head. "God save me, I hope I have not completely corrupted your innocent mind by bringing you to this godforsaken city. One can observe cruelty for only so long before one loses one's own sense of decency. Bess, please learn from this night: these men are scoundrels, not because of their unnatural urges—men have loved men since the time of the Greeks—but because they use their status to take other people's bodies for their own gratification. Let us away now and sleep, for we must be alert tomorrow."

Following my teacher, I stole one final look back at the embassy—

I froze.

As my gaze passed over a series of lattice screens to the left of the embassy at the edge of its surrounding lawn, I thought I glimpsed a figure behind one of those screens, a tall man-shaped shadow standing deathly still *and looking directly at us*.

My eyes raced back to the lattice screen, but by the time I found it again in the moonlight, the figure—if there had been one at all—was gone.

I wasn't sure if it was my mind playing tricks on me or a quirk of the late-evening shadows, so I didn't mention it to my teacher, but as I followed Mr. Ascham back to our quarters, I had a most unsettling feeling that for the whole time we had been watching the embassy, we ourselves had been watched.

———

We returned to our rooms.

No sooner had Mr. Ascham closed the outer door, leaving Latif outside, than he turned to me and whispered, "Talk to me. What do you know about Darius?"

I shrugged. "I know how palaces work. Secrets are many and when they are discovered, keeping them is achieved through payment: sometimes with gold, sometimes with favors both political and carnal."

"And what do you know of this situation?"

"I am reliably informed that Darius and the queen are lovers," I said.

My teacher's eyebrows rose in surprise. "And how did you come to be aware of this?"

I nodded at the room I shared with Elsie. "One of our party has witnessed them together." I went on. "Perhaps Cardinal Cardoza discovered their affair and now he is holding this knowledge over Darius's head like the Sword of Damocles: the cardinal demands Darius's affections or else he will tell the sultan of the affair."

"By God, Bess, you know far more about such matters at the age of thirteen than I did at your age. What has become of the world!" He paused in thought. "But it is a fair surmise, and one that might, just might, provide us with another suspect in our investigation."

"It does?"

"You will understand better tomorrow."

"Wait, you have a theory about the cardinal's murder, then?" If he had one, I did not yet know of it.

"Oh, yes."

"And . . . ?"

Mr. Ascham bent forward and whispered in my ear, "I think Cardinal Farnese was murdered by mistake."

I leaned back, contemplating this. "By mistake, but then . . ."

Mr. Ascham stood. "Thank you for your help, Bess. You are proving to be a most capable assistant in this investigation." He made for his room.

"Sir, one more question. Why did you not want me to mention this while Latif was present?"

"Even though Latif stands at our side, do not be fooled. Our escort works for the sultan. Be assured that everything we see, hear and say in Latif's presence is being relayed to the sultan. There are schemes afoot in this palace and the sultan himself may not be entirely innocent of them. I imagine he is a dangerous chess player himself, and oftentimes, the best chess players feign ignorance when in fact they know everything.

"Now, off to bed with you, young lady. It is time to get some sleep. With the first round completed, tomorrow is a rest day as far as the chess is concerned. As such, it will give us time to further our investigation."

I liked how it had become *our* investigation.

"What do you plan to do?" I asked.

"I have two threads that I would like to pursue. First, I would like to speak with the defeated Austrian player, Maximilian of Vienna: I would like to know why he would wish to speak with the unfortunate chef Brunello on four separate occasions."

"And the second thread?"

"Having heard what you have just told me," he said, "I would like to contrive an audience with Her Highness, the queen."

———

I went into my room, my mind bouncing between visions of naked priests, shadowy figures, dead chefs and the prospect of my teacher questioning the formidable Queen Roxelana.

Of course, Elsie was not in our room when I arrived there, but I didn't care. It was very late and I quickly fell asleep.

When I awoke to the dawning sun, however, there she was, lying in her bed in the deepest slumber, with the most serene and contented smile on her face.

—IV—

QUEEN

Just as the bishop was once an elephant and the castle a chariot, the piece that we know as the queen was originally the "king's minister."

It is believed that the transition from minister to queen coincided with the rise of several strong queens in Europe. Some have suggested that the queen in chess owes her all-powerful status to Queen Adelaide of Burgundy, the most powerful woman of the tenth century.

Given that in many medieval kingdoms only sons could inherit the throne, it is somewhat astonishing that in such times it was happily accepted that the most powerful piece on a chessboard should be the only female one.

From: *Chess in the Middle Ages,*
TEL JACKSON (W. M. Lawry & Co., London, 1992)

*Just look at how well she governs! She is only a woman,
a mistress of half an island, and yet she makes herself feared by Spain,
by France, by the [Holy Roman] Empire, by all.*

—POPE SIXTUS V, ON QUEEN ELIZABETH I

A MOST UNUSUAL MORNING

SHORTLY AFTER I AWOKE, THERE CAME an insistent rapping at the door.

I waited in my room as Mr. Ascham answered it. I was unable to hear the quiet exchange that followed but I did make out my teacher saying, "Thank you," and a moment later, he appeared in the doorway to the room I shared with Elsie.

"Bess," he said. "It seems you have made quite an impression on someone."

He held up a golden envelope. "You have been invited on a morning tour of the sultan's menagerie—his famous collection of exotic animals—to see His Majesty's new Russian bear."

"*I* have been invited?" I asked.

"It appears that the invitation came not from the sultan but from the donor of the gift. The sultan's messenger said he specifically requested your presence on the tour."

"The donor of the gift?" I thought for a moment. "That boy? That insufferable boy Ivan?"

My teacher grinned. "I imagine he took a liking to you."

At this point, Elsie, who I did not realize was even awake, sat up in her bed. "Oh, Bessie, you have a little admirer! How positively adorable!"

"An admirer?" I blurted. "But I was mean and horrible to him. And he was most appalling to me, appalling and obnoxious and rude."

"Little boys who like little girls often behave in such a manner," Mr. Ascham said.

"Big boys do, too," Elsie said with a smirk.

"I could not possibly go," I declared.

"Oh, no, you most certainly will go," my teacher said.

"I beg your pardon?"

"You will go on this excursion to the menagerie," he said as if it were the most obvious and natural thing in the world.

"But I don't like this boy. He is a backward Eastern duke from a backward Eastern duchy—"

"Oh, come now, you only met him once and one cannot gauge *any* person's character from a single meeting. No. This is something you should definitely learn. Go, it will be good for you. Besides, what have you to lose? Today is a rest day for the tournament, so you will not miss any chess, and I have inquiries to make. It seems other royalty will be there, too, including the sultan and his son, the crown prince. It would be of benefit to you to observe them."

Elsie's head snapped up at the mention of the crown prince. "I can go with Bess, sir. As—well—as a chaperone, if you like."

"Why, that would be splendid, Elsie," Mr. Ascham said. "Excellent. An escort from the sultan will be here in an hour to collect you both. I shall see you after lunch."

———

Sure enough, an hour later a member of the sultan's personal guard came to collect us. He escorted us out of the inner palace and across the First Courtyard to a heavy, studded gate set into its northern wall.

I fumed as I walked. I couldn't believe my teacher was forcing me to go on this excursion. I dreaded the thought of seeing the short Russian boy again.

Elsie thought my discomfort was most amusing. "Oh, Bessie, what's worse: having the attentions of a rude boy or the attentions of no boys at all?"

The question actually extracted me from my seething.

"In all honesty, I am not sure," I answered. I was young, yes, but I had always watched people closely, and on this trip—out in the world, beyond my cloistered life at Hatfield—I had watched them more closely than ever. And the previous night's conversation with my teacher about kings and queens had also left a mark on me. "I am not entirely convinced that sensual or carnal attentions have *any* worth. And marriage might have the least worth of all."

"What!" Elsie said. "What on earth do you mean, Bessie?"

"On this trip alone, we have been witness to a married couple where the wife, Mrs. Ponsonby, reigns over her husband like a tyrant. He is not her equal. He is not even her friend. He is her servant. I do not think marriage is meant to be like that. It should be a bond between equals."

"Yes, but—"

"I have seen a brothel, where in return for payment to the owner, the customer uses the prostitute's body for his own gratification. I have seen men of God using others' bodies to satiate their desires."

Elsie made to speak again, but again I cut her off.

"And, lastly, you have spoken at length about your nocturnal adventures, where copulation is a pastime. An enjoyable one, clearly, but a pastime, an idle game, an act of mutual pleasure engaged in solely for pleasure's sake." I paused. "The conclusion I have drawn from all this is that our very animal nature drives us to engage in carnal activities. It is like eating or sleeping and entirely natural. The *problem*, as I see it, are the twin human creations of marriage and religion. It is marriage and religion that make copulation complex and hurtful. Marriage brings up notions of trust, cuckoldry and ownership, while religion makes certain kinds of intimacy sinful. It makes me wonder if my life would be better if I were never to marry at all."

I turned to Elsie, offering her the chance to respond.

But she just looked dreamily up at the trees and the sky and said, "Honestly, Bessie, you think overmuch and it will make you miserable.

Life is so much sweeter and easier when you let the wind sweep you along."

She whirled on the spot as she said this, a carefree twirl, and I looked at her askance and wondered if I did indeed think too much on things. I also wondered if perhaps Elsie did not think *enough*. She delighted in her late-night gatherings, for instance, and in her scheme for snaring Crown Prince Selim, but like a chess player who forgets that his opponent also has a plan, had she considered how *others* might be perceiving her behavior at those gatherings?

I further pondered whether or not Elsie was mentally capable of keeping up with me and my overthinking. Even though she was four years my senior, had I outgrown my friend? Had she even been my friend in the first place?

"Since we're on the subject," I said, "where did you get to last night?"

"Oh, Bessie," she said excitedly, her attention fully regained now that we were talking about her. "I'm getting closer."

"Closer to what?"

"Closer to bedding the crown prince!" she whispered eagerly. "Last night's frolic was in his private bathhouse and, goodness, it was even more delicious than the first two gatherings! Imagine, Bessie: marble baths polished to perfection and filled with steaming hot water heated by furnaces beneath the floor; rose petals scattered across the surface and the most soothing, relaxing oils scenting the air.

"It was a delight to the senses just to walk in there, but, of course, there were other delights on offer. It was a smaller crowd than the previous night and the rising steam from the baths made all of the lithe young bodies there glisten with perspiration. And goodness, Bessie, sweating bodies make for the most divinely slippery couplings."

"Is that so?" I said. "What happened with the prince?"

"Well, as I did the night before, I spotted the crown prince in the steamy mist and made sure I caught his eye. A short time later, I found his good friend Rahman in a corner and once again mounted him and brought him to a delighted climax. But the whole time I was riding

Rahman, I kept my eyes locked on the prince, across the room, as if to say, 'Look at the pleasure I could be giving you.'"

"And what happened then?"

"A short while later, after the prince had a whispered discussion with Rahman, Selim asked for me to come before him and spread my legs so he could examine me—which I am told is what he does.

"I lay before him and stretched my legs wide. I'm glad I have always danced, Bessie, for I can spread my legs wider than most other girls and I saw that this impressed him greatly. Then he waved me away with a grin and the words, 'Perhaps tomorrow night, English rose.'

"Honestly, Bessie, I spent the rest of the evening in a state of dreamy repose, lying on a hot marble island, beads of sweat glistening all over my naked body, with my head thrown back and my toes drawing circles on the surface of the water, but always keeping my eyes on the prince, even as he occupied other girls. I am making him desire me, Bessie."

"You do appear to be close to snaring him, Elsie."

"I most certainly am and I cannot wait for the next gathering tomorrow evening!" Elsie said excitedly. "For when it comes, I aim to get the crown prince between my thighs, and if I can do that, I like my chances of becoming his queen."

———

We arrived at the gates to the sultan's private animal enclosure, where we were met by a party headed by Ivan, the diminutive grand prince of the Duchy of Muscovy. With him were some local palace officials and a few foreign dignitaries.

The sultan's menagerie stood to the north of the palace complex, not far from some military docks on that shore of the headland, and it was enclosed by a high brick wall. The gates to the enclosure rose before us—black cast-iron bars set into a soaring arch. Behind the wall, animal sounds could be heard: the trumpeting of an elephant, the growl of a jungle cat, the agitated tweeting of birds surrounded by elephants and jungle cats.

Ivan saw me and smiled broadly. During the whole of our previous unpleasant encounter, I had not seen him smile once. It made me suspicious.

"Princess Elizabeth!" he said brightly, in heavily accented English. "I am so pleased you could come. When we met before in the line to meet the sultan I did not know who you were, but I asked after you and discovered you are a princess of England, daughter of King Henry himself. I am a keen student of England and a great admirer of your father's achievements. Please forgive me if I was rude when we last encountered each other. My party was late and I was angry with my men and then you and I met in unfortunate circumstances. I humbly apologize and beg your forgiveness."

I was momentarily speechless. The rude boy had vanished and a most pleasant young man had taken over his body. Mr. Ascham, curse him, might have been right.

"You are lucky that I do not make judgments of people based on first meetings," I said smoothly. "I have found it is sensible to view someone at least a second time before I make an adverse conclusion as to their character." I ignored Elsie's stifled cough behind me.

Ivan seemed relieved. "You are as wise as you are beautiful. Again, I am so pleased you have come."

No one had ever called me beautiful before. With my orange curls and pale freckled skin, not even I considered myself to be beautiful. But when this boy said it, it made me feel, despite my previous misgivings about him, far more partial toward him. I quite liked being called beautiful.

At that moment a horn blared, and we all turned to see the sultan and the crown prince coming down the winding path from the palace, leading an enormous retinue of guards, officials and other hangers-on.

Ivan said to me, "Please excuse me, Elizabeth. I have duties to perform. But I do hope we shall get the opportunity to converse later."

With a smile, he went off to greet the sultan.

Moments later, the great iron gates to the menagerie were opened and, led by the sultan, Crown Prince Selim and Prince Ivan, we were ushered through them. As he passed by, the sultan saw me and gave me a silent nod of recognition, while the crown prince spied Elsie and gave her a different kind of nod.

We went inside.

THE SULTAN'S INCREDIBLE MENAGERIE

THE SULTAN'S MENAGERIE WAS, ESSENTIALLY, a large four-sided courtyard that was open to the sky. It had barred cages on three sides and on the fourth was the arched entry gate. A paved path, framed by cleverly planted bushes that prevented one from seeing every cage at once, meandered past all the cages before arriving back at the main gate.

Upon seeing Suleiman's menagerie and his collection of exotic animals inside it, I vowed that should I ever become Queen of England, I would open up the animal menagerie in the Bulwark of the Tower to the public at large. Every man and woman, no matter what their station in life, should be able to see the wonders of the animal kingdom.

The sultan's collection of exotic beasts was simply extraordinary.

He had two elephants and one giraffe; five fearsomely large snakes; a dozen monkeys, cheeky and playful; a vast collection of birds from all over the world; a zebra; two ostriches; an aurochs; an oryx; and not one but two varieties of tiger—one from the jungles of India and a larger white one from the chill lands far to the east of Russia. In one of the bigger cages, I beheld three wolves: they had gray coats, powerful shoulders and cruel stares. They watched every individual who passed them by with calculating interest, their pale eyes unblinking. I found them quite unnerving.

In the very center of the beautiful compound, surrounded by the ring of bushes and with its own inner path so that the sultan could make an uninterrupted circuit around it, was a brand-new and very high iron cage.

In it was Ivan's gift to the Ottoman ruler: the mighty Russian bear.

It was, I must admit, a most magnificent beast. It paced on all fours inside its enormous cage, but then upon seeing the sultan and the crowd gathered behind him, it rose onto its hind legs, standing a full twelve feet tall, and bellowed angrily in the sultan's face.

The sultan stood his ground.

"He likes you," Ivan said in Greek, grinning. The sultan snorted a laugh. The crowd chuckled nervously. "But please don't get too close to the bars. He has a considerable reach," Ivan added.

As I looked at the great bear in its massive cage, occupying pride of place in that remarkable menagerie, I thought of the way my countrymen used bears: they tormented them, tied them down to stakes while fighting dogs were permitted to attack them for sport and wagers. I felt ashamed.

"The Russian bear," Ivan said in common Greek so all could understand, "is the largest predator to walk on land. It can kill a man with a single swipe. Fortunately for us, bears rarely kill men. They eat mainly berries and roots and sometimes young deer, but most of all, big bears like this one love salmon." On cue, the animal keeper beside Ivan threw a dead salmon at the bear. With surprising speed, the bear reached through the bars, caught the fish in its claws and ripped it clean in two with a great crunching bite. The crowd gasped in awe.

"The bear is slow to anger, but when angry, by virtue of its size and strength, it is a force to be reckoned with." Ivan grinned. "Much like the Duchy of Muscovy."

The sultan smiled indulgently, appreciating and allowing Ivan's show of pride.

I was aware that Suleiman's armies had had skirmishes with the Rus peoples to the north of his empire, but it was not an area that the Moslem sultan seemed interested in conquering. As Ivan had intimated, the population there was large. The Rus people were also notoriously tough folk, hardened by their bitter climate.

Crown Prince Selim, however, was not so indulgent. He said, "Your duchy still pays us tribute, little prince. Mark your words or my father may decide to send a governor there. When I am sultan, I might just do that."

Ivan's face went red, but he bit his tongue.

The sultan saved him. "Come now, Selim, the lad meant no offense. He was merely speaking out of pride, pride for his homeland and for this magnificent beast. Thank you for this gift, Prince Ivan. I shall treasure it."

A short while later, the sultan departed and with him the crown prince and most of his entourage. As he left, the crown prince smiled at Elsie and she returned his smile brightly; then he was gone. The remaining guests, perhaps twelve of us, were left to stroll through the wonderful menagerie at our leisure.

Elsie and I were peering into the monkey cage when Ivan came up beside me and said in English, "I have heard stories of your father, King Henry. He is a great man, a king who will be remembered as . . . I do not know the word . . . *grozny.*"

"*Grozny?*" I said.

"It means, how do I say this, to inspire fear or awe in one's enemies. Terrible—wait, no. No, that is wrong. 'Formidable.' *Grozny.*"

My father certainly met those requirements, at least in my eyes.

Ivan went on: "By breaking from the Roman Church and taking its lands, your father announced to the world that he was a true king, one who has no master under the sky but himself. He put cannons on warships and made England a powerful seafaring nation. But most of all, he crushes anyone who opposes him. I am informed that over the course of his reign, he has executed over twenty thousand men."

I had heard that the figure was almost three times that but I did not feel the need to correct Ivan.

Ivan said, "My nation is vast but it is largely populated by peasants. It is backward. If it were united under a strong king, then I believe it would be formidable, a bear among nations. I wish to modernize my lands, based on what your father has done in England. I must bend the Orthodox Church to my will, like your father did; I must build ports and a navy, like your father did; and I must act decisively and swiftly against any and all who oppose me, like your father has done."

This talk of emulating my father made me uneasy. I would have wagered that Ivan did not know that as he had aged, my father had become increasingly erratic in his behavior—erratic and paranoid—which in turn had made him even *more* brutal in his suppression of those who opposed him. This was, after all, a man whose capacity for brutality had included beheading two of his wives. And yet as a young man, my father had, by all accounts, been sweet and romantic, a poet, a composer, a dreamer. In those younger days, I was often told, he'd been dashingly handsome, clean-shaven and athletic. Now, as his mind grew paranoid and grotesque, his body followed: he was now hunched and paunchy, with a beard to hide the double chin that mocked his vanity.

"He is indeed his own man," was all I could say.

I looked at Grand Prince Ivan—in his midteens, but a few years older than I—and I thought of the two versions of him that I had witnessed: the charming young man on display today and the angry-faced boy of a few days previously. He seemed a lot like my father: two persons trapped in the same body.

And then it occurred to me. My father, for all his marriages and all his power, was miserable. Miserable in a way that only a person with two conflicting selves could be: he wanted to be loved by all his subjects, yet when he was loved by them, he doubted their motives.

I did not wish such a fate on young Ivan—or on myself, for that matter, should I ever become queen—and I was about to say something to that effect when he went on.

"Despite all his impressive achievements," Ivan said, "your father might do well to adopt a technique of the sultan's. The sultan employs a vast network of informants and spies in his city, a clandestine force that reports to him on the moods and actions of his people. I think when I am king I shall create such a force."

I felt that it was time to leave. I nudged Elsie. "Thank you for the invitation today, Prince Ivan. I enjoyed seeing your bear. It is a most remarkable creature and you are a most intriguing young man."

We started to leave.

"Princess Elizabeth!" Ivan hurried after us. "May I be so bold as to ask something of you?"

"What?"

"May I write to you? In England. After this tournament is over."

I looked at him for a long moment. It couldn't hurt and I imagined my teacher would certainly approve. "You may," I said, and then Elsie and I left the menagerie.

———

We returned to our rooms around lunchtime to find Mr. Giles practicing chess moves and Mr. Ascham standing at the window, staring out over the Sea of Marmara, so consumed by his thoughts that he did not even notice our arrival.

"Mr. Ascham," said I, "you really must see the sultan's menagerie before you leave Constantinople. It is a truly exceptional collection of animals laid out in a most ingenious fashion."

My teacher smiled tightly, but he did not answer me.

"Whatever is the matter?" I asked.

"I went to see Maximilian of Austria in his rooms this morning," Mr. Ascham said. "And I found him dead."

THE DEATH OF A PLAYER

MY TEACHER EXPLAINED.

After breakfast, he had informed Latif that he desired to visit Maximilian of Austria in his rooms, to interrogate him about his multiple conversations with Brunello the chef: Mr. Ascham was still very suspicious of the meal that had killed Cardinal Farnese and thus equally suspicious about anyone who had a connection with its preparation.

Like most of the other players, Maximilian had been quartered in a special pavilion of rooms that backed onto—but did not have access to—the harem. With Latif at his side, my teacher knocked on the Austrian player's door but received no reply.

He knocked louder. Still no reply.

Inquiries were made: Maximilian had not received breakfast in his rooms that morning. Nor had he been seen that morning by the guards stationed at the various palace gates. The night guard for the players' pavilion was found and he reported that he had seen Maximilian return to his rooms very late last night, with a veiled girl in his company, presumably a prostitute. Having been beaten in the first round of the tournament, Maximilian of Vienna did not need to worry about retiring early anymore.

But that was the last anyone had seen of Maximilian. He had returned to his rooms with the girl and neither of them had emerged.

A key to the pavilion was found and two guards were brought to act as witnesses. Then Latif unlocked the outer door to Maximilian's rooms.

My teacher entered behind the eunuch and immediately beheld a grisly scene.

Maximilian lay spread-eagled on his bed, stark naked, his blood-shot eyes wide with apparent shock, his mouth open, his wholly black tongue visible for all to see, an opium pipe lying askew on the mattress beneath his outstretched open hand. There by his side in the bed, equally naked and equally still, was the virgin girl Helena, who, two days earlier, Maximilian had presented to the sultan as a gift from his master, Ferdinand, the archduke of Austria. She, too, had a blackened tongue and was also dead.

"You, sir," I said, "are starting to look like a curse. Anyone to whom you desire to speak is suddenly found dead."

"It would seem so," Mr. Ascham said. "And this one was a player in the tournament. It would seem no one is safe in this palace."

"Were there any wounds on their bodies, as there were with the cardinal or the chef and his wife? Could you determine how they were killed?"

"There was no evidence that they *were* killed, Bess," my teacher said. "The scene bore all the signs of a simple clandestine love affair: the player from Austria had fallen in love with the virgin 'gift' he had brought to Constantinople for the sultan. They frolicked in his bedchamber, yet from the way we found them—naked, with blackened tongues—it was clear that their intimate activities were accompanied by opium use. And as far as I could tell, it was the opiates that killed them. Either they imbibed too much or perhaps the local variety of opiate was too powerful for their constitutions.

"One of the guards went and fetched the *sadrazam*. He arrived soon after and just shook his head sadly when he saw the bodies. It was something he had seen before: foreigners overindulging in the potent local opiate."

I said, "So you are saying that there have been two further deaths but they are unrelated to our investigation. An unhappy coincidence, but a coincidence nonetheless."

"So it would seem . . ." my teacher said slowly.

"You do not appear convinced."

"Because I am not. Because this is a coincidence that is explained *too* easily for my liking. I am starting to see a pattern. Cardinal Farnese's death was dressed up as the work of a lunatic, because you can't kill off a famous cardinal without an explanation. Brunello and his wife's deaths were made to look like suicides. And now Maximilian. He was a well-known chess player, a participant in the tournament. If someone wanted him killed, they would need to dress up his death, too, and I think they did. Which was why, when the guard went to fetch the *sadrazam,* I examined Maximilian's and the girl's bodies, and I found something odd."

"What?" My eyes widened.

"They both had some subtle but distinct bruising around their nostrils and their cheeks. Here"—he pressed the fleshy part of my cheeks on either side of my mouth—"and here"—he squeezed my nostrils shut.

"What do you make of such injuries?" I asked.

Mr. Ascham paused, looked about himself as if to see whether there was a listener in the room with us. "I do not think they accidentally overindulged in the use of an extra-potent local opiate. I think the opiate was forced on them. I think someone held them down, pinched their nostrils together and forced their mouths open by pressing their cheeks, and made them inhale the opiate in a quantity that killed them."

I gasped. "And yet it would appear to be an accident. Well, to anyone but you."

"Yes," my teacher said. "My suspicions aroused, while we waited for the *sadrazam,* I examined Maximilian's bedchamber. I noticed his trunk. It was filled with what one would expect: clothes, shoes, a chess set. But my attention was drawn to a pair of his shoes standing by the door. They were dress shoes, cut in the Austrian style, made of fine black leather with brass buckles."

I started. "Wait. Did they have wooden soles and a nick?"

"No. They had leather soles with only wooden heels. But the soles of these shoes did bear curious marks on them: dark spots of blood and other patches of wetness, and an odd gray powder. At some point, their wearer—Maximilian—had stepped on wet ground, for the fine gray powder had adhered to the moistened soles. I sniffed the powder: it smelled like charcoal, but infused with a curious salty, fishy odor."

"Salt and fish? Like in the kitchen perhaps?" I said. "It would explain the spots of blood. Maximilian may have stepped on animal blood when he was in the kitchen."

"Perhaps . . ." Mr. Ascham said, but clearly he thought otherwise. "In any case, as I turned the shoe in my hand, something very odd happened: its wooden heel turned outward on a hinge, to reveal a secret compartment inside it."

"No . . . !"

"And in that compartment, I found this."

My teacher pulled a small folded note from his pocket and showed it to me. It was written in German. "At the time I found it, Latif was at the door speaking with the remaining guard, and I had my back turned to them, so I'm certain they didn't see it. Here, your German is better than mine. Can you translate it for me?"

I did so. It read:

N–16 K 20 G, 6 R

HAVE NOT BEEN ABLE TO SEE SOUTH SIDE YET.

HELENA REPORTS SULTAN HAPPY IN PUBLIC BUT SULLEN AND MOROSE WHEN IN HAREM; SUSPICIOUS OF OUTSIDERS. EAGER FOR TOURNAMENT TO SUCCEED; DISTURBED BY UNEXPECTED DEATH OF FARNESE.

I asked, "What do those letters and numbers mean?"

"I do not know, but I think that Maximilian of Vienna was more than just a chess player," Mr. Ascham said. "Likewise, the girl was more than just a virgin gift to the sultan. I do not think they were having an affair; they were together for another reason. I suspect they were both spies for the archduke of Austria."

"*Spies?*" I gasped. "And their deaths?"

"The fate of spies who are discovered. I believe that Archduke Ferdinand saw this tournament as a chance to slip a new spy, the girl, into the sultan's innermost circle, his retinue of concubines. Look at the note: Helena was reporting on the sultan's moods behind the closed doors of the harem. I'm guessing that Maximilian was also a spy. Do you remember that Maximilian visited Brunello on four separate occasions? I think Maximilian saw Brunello as an excellent source of secondary information about the sultan. Brunello cooked for and talked with many of the sultan's powerful guests—we ourselves accompanied Michelangelo and saw exactly that. Brunello would have been an excellent repository of various people's opinions about the sultan and his intentions in Europe. But Helena and Maximilian were discovered, so their deaths were posed as an opiate accident so that whoever found them would not suspect anything nefarious."

"Anyone but you," I said again.

"Yes, anyone but me," Mr. Ascham said.

"So after all that, you are ultimately no closer to discovering Cardinal Farnese's killer?"

Mr. Ascham put the slip of paper into his satchel and then put the satchel inside his traveling trunk. "Oh, no, not at all. I am certainly closer."

"How do you reckon that?" I asked.

"Well, now I have two fewer suspects."

———

There was one other thing to do that day, something unrelated to chess or to our investigation. In the afternoon, Mr. Ascham, Elsie and I ventured across the city to check on the health of Mrs. Ponsonby.

We found her and her husband at the same inn where we had left them outside the Golden Gate. The six soldiers who had escorted us across the Continent were also lodged there and happily passed the time playing card and dice games.

Mrs. Ponsonby's condition had not improved. She lay in bed, pale and perspiring, repeating the same prayer over and over in a low, rapid voice: *"Hail Mary, full of grace, the Lord is with thee . . ."*

"She is still unwell?" Mr. Ascham said to Mr. Ponsonby. "She has not improved at all?"

"No, sir," Mr. Ponsonby said, "not a whit."

". . . blessed art thou among women . . ."

Mr. Ascham looked at her gravely. Then he stood. "Our prayers and thoughts are with you both. We shall return after the tournament is over."

". . . and blessed is the fruit of thy womb, Jesus . . ."

As we walked back in through the Golden Gate, my teacher said, "That is a strong woman."

"Mrs. Ponsonby?" I said a little incredulously. "Whatever do you mean?"

"Whatever poison she was given, it was potent, and yet her body is fighting it with all her might. A lesser person would be dead by now," Mr. Ascham said.

I had not considered it that way. I'd never thought I would find myself worrying for Primrose Ponsonby, or even respecting her strength, but right then I found myself doing both.

We returned to the palace, where the afternoon and evening passed quite peaceably.

At one point, Mr. Ascham tried to seek out Darius the wrestler—to question him about his actions in Cardinal Cardoza's embassy the previous night—but Darius could not be found anywhere inside the palace. My teacher was unperturbed. He resolved to find him the following day, hopefully around the time he managed to speak with the queen.

As for Elsie, to her great disappointment, the crown prince held no gathering that evening, so she stayed in our rooms with me. We spent the evening plaiting our hair while Mr. Ascham and Mr. Giles played chess. But they played by a strange rule whereby they each had to move their pieces immediately and without delay.

It was, above anything else, fun. And the two of them—perhaps releasing all the tensions of the tournament and of our grim investigation—seemed to delight in just having fun, laughing and teasing each other as they moved their pieces.

"Oh, come on, Roger, stop playing like an old maid!" Mr. Giles said at one point. Or: "My dear Ascham, that was predictable. And I know you can't stand being predictable!"

But my teacher gave as good as he got. "Really, Giles, I was told you once played for England, but I really can't see it in the way you're playing now."

Pieces were taken with flourishes. Reckless moves were followed by sudden sighs of realization. Mr. Giles won every game except for one—and when my teacher won that game, he leaped to his feet, arms raised in triumph, and Mr. Giles rolled his eyes. In the end, much enjoyment was had, and I was pleased to see it. When they finished, we all retired early.

Given what would happen the following day, I was glad we did.

THE SECOND ROUND BEGINS

THE FOLLOWING MORNING THE HAGIA SOPHIA was literally buzzing with excitement, for the four second-round matches were to be played that day. Two matches were scheduled for the morning, two for the afternoon, again to be played side by side.

An updated draw, written in the finest handwriting on the sultan's beautiful gilt-edged paper, had been slid under our door that morning. It read:

1ST ROUND	2ND ROUND	SEMI-FINALS	FINAL

1. ZAMAN
OF CONSTANTINOPLE

2. MAXIMILIAN
OF VIENNA

   ZAMAN
   OF CONSTANTINOPLE

3. MUSTAFA
OF CAIRO

4. VLADIMIR
OF MUSCOVY

   VLADIMIR
   OF MUSCOVY

5. ALI HASSAN RAMA
OF MEDINA

6. PABLO MONTOYA
OF CASTILE

   PABLO MONTOYA
   OF CASTILE

7. BR. EDUARDO
OF SYRACUSE

8. BR. RAUL
OF THE PAPAL STATES

   BR. RAUL
   OF THE PAPAL STATES

9. GILBERT GILES
OF ENGLAND

10. TALIB
OF BAGHDAD

   GILBERT GILES
   OF ENGLAND

11. DRAGAN
OF WALLACHIA

12. MARKO
OF VENICE

   DRAGAN
   OF WALLACHIA

13. NASIRUDDIN
OF THE MOGHUL EMPIRE

14. LAO TSE
OF THE HAN PEOPLE

   NASIRUDDIN
   OF THE MOGHUL EMPIRE

15. WILHELM
OF KÖNIGSBERG

16. IBRAHIM
OF CONSTANTINOPLE

   IBRAHIM
   OF CONSTANTINOPLE

In the morning session, the sultan's man Zaman would play the formidable Muscovite, Vladimir, while the two Spaniards, Pablo Montoya and Brother Raul, would face off alongside them.

Mr. Giles would have to wait till the afternoon to play the brutish but admittedly talented Dragan of Wallachia. Alongside that match would be played perhaps the most anticipated battle of the round: the people's champion, Ibrahim, versus the handsome Moghul prince, Nasiruddin, who had become something of a favorite among the women of Byzantium.

Every match brought with it some kind of rivalry or drama. It was little wonder the citizens of Constantinople were excited.

I was excited, too.

———

We took our seats on the royal stage, looking out over the two playing stages and the sea of humanity packed into the hall. Bright sunlight shone in through the great dome's high windows, bathing the space in an almost heavenly golden radiance.

The morning matches began.

The crowd sat in near perfect silence, hushed by the thrill of the occasion. The tournament had entered a new, more intense stage. You could hear the click of the pieces being moved from two hundred feet away.

At one point, my teacher went to sit with Ignatius. The learned Jesuit was watching the match between the two Catholic Spaniards anxiously (he was also, I concluded from the subtle but silent movements of his lips, offering the occasional prayer to the Lord to sway the outcome).

I remained with Elsie. In between watching the chess, I occasionally glanced over at the queen.

"Elsie," I said, "apart from the liaison you witnessed on the night of the banquet, what other things have you heard about the queen?"

"The queen?" Elsie glanced across at Queen Roxelana and lowered her voice to a respectful whisper. "This I can say with confidence: she is not to be trifled with. It was she who through intrigue, insinuation and outright murder engineered the rise of her son, Selim, to the rank of crown prince."

"Tell me more."

"Like every Ottoman ruler before him, this sultan has fathered many children with his concubines and prior to marrying Roxelana, he had already sired several sons. But only one of them can succeed him. Selim faced several challengers but his cunning mother managed to have them all dispatched to administrative positions in the outer provinces, strangled in their sleep or tossed into a dungeon, never to emerge.

"For, you see, in addition to holding the sultan's ear, it is said that the queen commands the loyalty of a small group of palace guards—notably those who control the dungeons. Apparently, she supplies these guards with gold, whores and liquor. Thus if the queen can convince her husband to send a rival of hers to the dungeon, that rival will most assuredly meet with a fatal accident in their cell soon after. She is most cunning and rightly feared."

I gazed over at the queen, sitting stoically at her husband's right hand. She was beautiful and poised, the picture of regal sophistication; but now that I looked at her more closely, I saw that her eyes were hard and cold.

Elsie concluded, "The young folk of the palace fear Roxelana greatly. They treat her with almost obsequious flattery, for to cross her is to take your life into your hands."

"I see," I said. Looking at the queen—at her cool stillness—I wondered what she thought about. Did she enjoy inspiring dread in others? Indeed, in a man's world, was it good for a queen to be feared? More than that, was it necessary?

I shook the thoughts away. Maybe Elsie was right: maybe I did think overmuch. I turned back to observe the chess matches once again.

At that moment, Mr. Ascham returned to my side and I was about to tell him what Elsie had said when suddenly the *sadrazam* appeared behind our seats.

"Mr. Ascham, Princess Elizabeth. His Majesty the sultan requests your presence at his side."

THE SULTAN

WITH SOME TREPIDATION, I FOLLOWED Mr. Ascham over to the two vacant seats to the left of the sultan's throne.

The queen sat stiffly on the other side of the sultan, staring resolutely forward. As far as I could tell, she was not looking at either chess match or at any actual object, for that matter. She did not acknowledge our arrival at the sultan's side.

"Mr. Roger Ascham, Princess Elizabeth," the sultan said. "Please sit down. My, the chess is tense this morning, isn't it?"

"It certainly is," my teacher said as we sat. From these more elevated and centrally located seats, we had an unsurpassed view of both boards. Being sultan had its advantages.

The sultan said, "I believe your man will be facing the Wallachian, Dragan, in the afternoon. First Talib, now Dragan. He has had a difficult draw."

"It is the nature of random draws, isn't it? No one could have known how those stones were going to come out of that jar," my teacher replied smoothly.

I am convinced that I saw a momentary grin flash across the sultan's face then. He said, "My people are thrilled by this tournament. Look at them: they come in droves, mass on the streets outside. Some, I am told, camp out overnight by the doors of the Ayasofya to get places nearest to the tables. I am pleased."

"Your Majesty should be," Mr. Ascham said. "It is a most remarkable event and it will be the talk of every kingdom in Europe for decades, even centuries, to come."

"You Europeans are impressed with my tournament?"

It was the classic king's question, because it could only be answered one way, in the affirmative. To answer any other way would be a profound insult.

My teacher, however, managed to find another way. "I myself am even more impressed that Your Majesty prefers to engage with other great kingdoms in a display of simulated warfare rather than actual warfare. I find this most enlightened and wish some European kings would act in similar fashion."

"You are most kind."

"Elizabeth," Mr. Ascham said, turning to me, "you may not be aware, but the West owes nearly all of its recent advancements to the Islamic world."

"Is that so?" I said.

"In the dark centuries after the fall of Rome, Europe became a wasteland. After the twin illuminations of the Greek and Roman civilizations met their ends, Europe regressed into crude tribalism and rule by force. And while Europe was wallowing in this filth of an existence, the Abassid caliphs were rescuing the great works of the Greeks—Aristotle, Xenocrates, Strato, Theophrastus—and translating them into Arabic so they could be widely studied."

The sultan nodded. "Your man's opponent yesterday, Talib of Baghdad, is the librarian at what was perhaps our greatest center of translation: the House of Wisdom in Baghdad. Is it not strange that your Bible, originally written in Greek, should return to Christianity after having first been translated into Arabic? Who knows, maybe a crafty Islamic translator inserted a few Koranic wisdoms into the Bible before sending it back to Europe."

But then the sultan's smile faded.

"Alas," he said, "those were the great days of Islam."

My teacher frowned. "But, Your Majesty, under your leadership, the Islamic world is as powerful and influential as it has ever been. Based on my observations here in Constantinople, your society—your *ummah* as it is called—could rise to heights reached by no empire before it, not even Rome. In five hundred years, I foresee a vast Moslem hegemony of the greatest technological and military preeminence, one that may subsume all of Europe."

Scandalous as such a view was, I couldn't disagree with my teacher.

The sultan smiled grimly. "You are most kind in your appraisal of my kingdom and I see that you are genuine. But the reality, I fear, is more complex."

The sultan caught himself for a moment, as if he was deciding whether or not to say more. He clearly decided that he would.

"Mr. Roger Ascham, you are a wise and clever man, so I will be candid with you. Imposing as my empire is, the *ummah* faces more internal challenges than external ones. I have worked very hard to make the Moslem world one of laws—so much so that my people call me 'the Lawgiver'—but it has been a struggle every step of the way.

"Ever since the death of the great Prophet, blessings and peace be upon him, Islam has been a faith divided. It is split into two competing factions: the Sunni and the Shia. The former are more progressive and believe in the legitimacy of the caliphs as leaders of the faith; the latter claim that only those who are descendants of the Prophet himself can lead.

"My people are most ingenious. When the Roman lands to the west fell to barbarism, we retained the Greek texts, learned from them, and built grand cities and machines of war. My greatest problem is that the Shia have decided that any advancements are distractions from paying due observance to Allah. Worse, they preach that to advance is to be *against* Allah.

"I have grave issues with this because it preaches honor in backwardness. And now I see the West rising again, rising every year, and it observes no similar restriction on advancement. I worry that the more the Shias preach backwardness as a virtue, the more the *ummah* will be overtaken by the West. How sad would it be if in five hundred years from now the kingdom of Islam is no further advanced than it is to-day?"

"Can that be possible?" Mr. Ascham asked.

"You would be amazed at what people can do and say in the name of piety. Right now, the most zealous of the Shia are agitating for even stricter laws against women: they want to ban women from showing their faces in public, their *faces*."

I glanced at my teacher. I wanted to mention what had been discussed the day before with Michelangelo and Ignatius, but Mr. Ascham shook his head imperceptibly.

The sultan went on sadly, "The Prophet loved women, loved what they bring to this world. The world is beautiful precisely because of the balance between masculine and feminine energies. A society that is too masculine is destined to forever be at the mercy of men's anger. My great fear is that my culture has reached its peak and is poised to decline from here, riven from within."

The sultan stared at the floor.

My teacher said softly, "I was aware of the schism in your faith but I was unaware of how bad things had become."

I was also surprised. I was amazed at the notion that the culture that had built the magnificent metropolis of Constantinople might be at the zenith of its achievement. I looked at the sultan's grave expression and I saw a man staring into the abyss of a dark and frightening future.

In the West, royal courts worried about an all-conquering Islamic army rampaging across Christendom, and here the sultan was seriously contemplating the possibility of his empire collapsing in on itself.

At that moment, the *sadrazam* appeared at the sultan's side and handed him something, a note of some sort, accompanied by a whispered message.

"Thank you." The sultan waved him away, then turned back to Mr. Ascham. "So, how go your investigations?"

"I am discovering many things," my teacher said, not untruthfully.

"But have you discovered who murdered Cardinal Farnese yet?"

"No. It seems everyone I seek to question on the matter meets an untimely end. First, the chef and his wife, then most recently the Austrian chess player, Maximilian."

"Do not concern yourself with the death of the Austrian player," the sultan said simply, looking away.

"But he was seen speaking with Brunello on several occas—"

"You are to concentrate on the murder of the cardinal. The chess player's death does not concern you." The sultan then held up the note that the *sadrazam* had just given to him.

I caught my breath at the sight of it.

It was the same note Mr. Ascham had shown me the night before, the one he had taken from the secret compartment in Maximilian's shoe heel. While we had been here in the Hagia Sophia, the sultan's men had been in our rooms.

The sultan indicated the code at the top of the note. "See these numbers and letters: 'N–16 K 20 G, 6 R.' It is a reference to my northern military dock. Right now, in that dock sit sixteen warships— or as they are known in German, *Kriegsschiffe*—twenty galleys— *Galeeren*—and six ramming ships, or *Rammschiffe*. Maximilian was a spy for Archduke Ferdinand of Austria, reporting back to him on my naval strength."

At that moment, something became clear in my mind: the fishy-salty smell on Maximilian's soles. It was not the smell of a kitchen but of a dock. The gray powder was gunpowder and the spots of blood found on them were the specks of spilled blood commonly found on a military dock.

The sultan continued: "The virgin was also a spy. Her task was to report on my unvarnished moods, opinions, reactions and demeanor, as witnessed by her in the privacy of my harem. As I said, I would prefer that you target your efforts on deaths that I do *not* know the cause of."

My teacher swallowed hard. "As you wish."

Just then, perhaps fortuitously, the *sadrazam* reappeared at the sultan's side. "Sire, that other matter has been taken care of. And your lunch with the imam is prepared."

The sultan nodded. "Thank you. I shall come when this game is over—"

A collective gasp from the crowd made us all look around.

Vladimir had just taken Zaman's queen.

The crowd murmured uncomfortably.

A familiar voice from my right piped up and said something in a Slavic tongue. It was Prince Ivan encouraging his player.

He saw me and said in English, "Princess Elizabeth. My man has the measure of this Persian. Zaman is good but he is no match for a player of Vlad's skill."

"Do not speak too soon, Ivan. Pride goeth before a fall," I said.

Ivan said, "We take chess very seriously in Muscovy and we breed our players tough. Vlad has him figured out. I hope that your man does not find himself sitting across the board from Vlad, for I fear that Vlad will make short work of him, too."

As Ivan turned back to watch the match, I observed him for a moment. There was a definite intensity to him, but it was an earnest type of intensity. More than anything, he just wanted respect; for himself, his people, his duchy. I saw him as a future ruler: intelligent and proud but forever vexed by the way other nations looked down their noses at his principality.

A short time later, Vladimir won the first game—and rather easily, too, it must be said. Ivan looked over at me and gave me a knowing nod.

At that point, the sultan abruptly stood and thus so did everyone else in the hall. "Please excuse me," he said to my teacher, "I must depart for a short time. The duties of a ruler never cease. It has been most interesting talking with you. Please, continue your investigations."

Then he bowed politely and left the hall.

I was about to head back to our regular seats when my teacher did a most presumptuous thing. He leaned over to the queen and said in Greek, "Your Highness? Might I indulge in a word?"

The queen eyed my teacher coolly, but after a moment nodded. "A very brief one."

THE QUEEN

AS THE SECOND GAME OF ZAMAN'S and Vladimir's match began, our chairs were brought beside the queen's throne.

"Are you enjoying the tournament, Your Highness?" Mr. Ascham whispered politely.

"Very much so."

"You play chess yourself?"

"A little."

"Forgive me, but I have never had the opportunity to ask this of an actual queen and I must take this chance: Do you, as a queen, delight in the fact that the most powerful piece on a chessboard is the queen?"

"I confess to taking some pleasure in the notion, yes."

She was speaking blandly, idly, indulging my teacher, her eyes fixed on the match.

Then Mr. Ascham whispered, "Are you aware that Cardinal Cardoza knows of your affair with the wrestler Darius and extracts unnatural favors from Darius in exchange for keeping your liaison secret?"

The queen blinked.

Once.

Her head did not move as she continued to gaze out at Zaman's ongoing match. It was barely perceptible, but I saw her swallow before she turned to face my teacher.

"I am aware, Mr. Roger Ascham of Cambridge, England, that my husband has enlisted your aid in unraveling the murder of the visiting cardinal. I was not aware that I had become the subject of your investigation."

"Your Highness, I seek only the truth."

"The truth is not always worth finding."

"Are you aware that Cardoza knows of your affair and extracts favors from Darius in exchange for keeping it secret?"

A long pause. Then the queen said, "I am and I am not."

"You will have to explain that to me further."

"I do not *have* to do anything, for I am a queen and you are not. Remember this, Englishman. I am aware that Cardinal Cardoza knows of my dalliance. He has known for two weeks now and in that time he has pressed *me* for certain favors. Not of the carnal variety—the cardinal does not like women—but of a royal nature. Intervening when his priests are caught molesting boys in their confessionals, freeing them from the sultan's jail with a word to the guards."

"And how, then, are you not aware?"

The queen bowed her head.

"I was not aware that my Darius had given his body to the cardinal as payment for his silence," she said softly. "I fail to see, however, what connection this has with your inquiries into the death of Cardinal Farnese."

"If my theory on the matter is correct, it holds a most important connection."

"And what is that theory?" the queen asked.

I leaned forward, listening intently, for until then, beyond a single cryptic comment about Cardinal Farnese being murdered by mistake, I myself did not know the theory that had been formulating in my teacher's mind.

Mr. Ascham said, "I believe that Cardinal Farnese was killed by accident and that the mutilation of his face in the manner of the lunatic was a sham perpetrated by the killer to disguise his, or her, error."

"An accident?" the queen said, giving voice to my own silent confusion.

"Yes," my teacher said. "For, you see, Cardinal Farnese died from poisoning, not from his ghastly wounds. But this is something of a paradox because, as I see it, no one in this palace had a truly compelling reason to murder the visiting cardinal. But several people, including you and your lover, the chef and a whoremonger, had great reasons to murder Cardinal *Cardoza*."

My breath caught. This was the first I had heard of this and it made an odd kind of sense.

"It is my theory," Mr. Ascham went on, "that Cardinal Farnese, dining in Cardinal Cardoza's private rooms, ate from Cardinal *Cardoza's* plate and inadvertently ate poisoned food intended for Cardinal Cardoza. I am of the belief that every murder is committed for a reason, a logical reason that benefits the murderer. I am thus on the hunt for the person or persons who would benefit from Cardinal Cardoza's death, and you, Your Highness, are one such person."

I couldn't believe what I was hearing. My teacher, speaking ever so boldly, was all but accusing the sultan's wife of murder.

The queen did not move, kept staring forward.

Then, oddly, her lips curved into a smile.

"Mr. Ascham, one does not rise from slave to concubine to queen without knowing how to navigate an imperial court and arrange for the removal of certain rivals. If I desire someone to be killed, then killed they will be. If I were to tell my dear husband that you, for example, were vexing me, by tomorrow morning you would find yourself at the bottom of the Sea of Marmara with your ankles tied to an old cannon. On the other hand, I could simply order that you be strangled in your sleep tonight.

"I do not need to kill in secret or via the subterfuge of poison, sir. Like the queen in chess, I wait for my moment, and when I move, I move brutally and decisively. But the queen in chess is not invincible— she can be taken by any other piece; likewise, she can also be trapped on a square and be forced to bide her time before she can emerge to wreak her vengeance."

The queen's tone was icy and perfectly calm despite the subject matter.

I found myself shaking, my heart beating ever faster.

Clearly, Cardinal Cardoza had boxed her in, but from what I was hearing—if I was interpreting her correctly—the queen was planning retaliatory action against him.

"Your Highness is very direct in both her words and, apparently, her actions," my teacher said. "I hope I do not find myself on the receiving end of them merely for carrying out the sultan's investigation."

"If you maintain my secret from my husband, then you have nothing to fear, Englishman."

"Consider your secret safe," Mr. Ascham said. "I am, however, intrigued by one thing: Darius was *also* being extorted by Cardinal Cardoza. You act directly, swiftly, without the need for subterfuge, but Darius may not have been so free to act. It might have been he who attempted to poison Cardoza and mistakenly killed Farnese."

The queen glanced at my teacher and nodded. "That could indeed be so," she said. Then, abruptly, she waved us away. "I am wearying of this conversation and the match is reaching a critical stage. Please, leave me."

We returned to our original places where we resumed our observations of the match and found that it had indeed reached a pivotal and most unexpected juncture.

THE SULTAN'S MAN STRUGGLES

AS ZAMAN'S MATCH AGAINST VLADIMIR UNFOLDED, it quickly became apparent that it was not unfolding according to plan.

Vladimir was not only beating the sultan's champion, he was thrashing him. The Muscovite had just won the second game and had now—as the sultan returned from his meeting and resumed his place on his throne—taken an early lead in the third.

The sultan's brow furrowed with concern. The match could be over by midmorning and his champion humiliated.

The crowd seemed to sense this, too. Every time Vladimir took one of Zaman's pieces, they cast nervous glances at the royal stage and whispered animatedly.

Having survived his bristly conversation with the queen, my teacher now watched the game with renewed interest. I noticed that his eyes narrowed curiously as he followed each move.

And so as that third game progressed, I followed it in an unusual way: by glancing alternately from the playing stage to my teacher's face and back again—like someone watching one of my father's tennis matches. For, yes, Mr. Ascham was watching the game but I sensed he was seeing something else in it that the other five thousand people in that hall were not.

Then, most abruptly, my teacher excused himself. "Stay here. I shall return shortly," he said before leaving the royal stage.

I shrugged and kept watching the match, my eyes fixed on the forlorn, helpless-looking figure of Zaman.

Head bent over the board, he was clearly flustered and confused, bamboozled by his opponent's strategies. Beads of sweat glistened on his forehead. Every now and then, he sat back in his chair and looked skyward, searching the domed ceiling of the hall as if he were looking to Allah himself for aid. But today it seemed that Allah was elsewhere.

After a time, Mr. Ascham returned to the stage and resumed his seat beside me.

"How goes the match?" he asked.

"Zaman is down both knights and a bishop," I reported. "But he is countering the Muscovite's attacks a little better in this game."

"Hmmm," my teacher said.

As it happened, that third game lasted much longer than the first two—Zaman, behind from the outset, battled valiantly and in a few daring moves almost recouped his early losses—but the result was the same: Vladimir won.

The Muscovite was now up three games to none. If he won the next game, he would take the match, provide the first big upset of the tournament, and do some considerable damage to the sultan's pride.

"I have a strange suspicion that Zaman is about to stage a remarkable comeback," Mr. Ascham whispered to me as the pieces were reset for the fourth game and Zaman and Vladimir conversed with their respective supporters (players were forbidden to speak with their entourages during games but in between games it was allowed).

I snorted. "I should think not. The Muscovite is far too good for him."

"Watch and see."

————

The fourth game began and Vladimir opened boldly, moving his pieces firmly and with confidence. On one occasion, he glanced over at his patron, the young Ivan, and threw the youth a cocksure wink.

Then Zaman took Vladimir's leading knight.

In none of the previous three games had the local champion taken one of the Muscovite's major pieces first.

Vladimir frowned, refocused, moved a few other pieces, only for Zaman to suddenly check him, forking his king and queen with one of his own prancing knights: the very move Mr. Giles had warned me about during our journey to Constantinople.

Vladimir moved his king out of check and Zaman thumped his knight on top of the Muscovite's queen and five thousand spectators erupted with cheers and applause and the entire hall sizzled with excitement.

The local champion was coming back.

Just as my teacher had predicted.

When Zaman won that fourth game half an hour later—to the evident delight of the sultan, the consternation of Vladimir and the utter rapture of the crowd—I threw a questioning glance at Mr. Ascham.

He just nodded and said, "Keep watching."

———

I did, and to my astonishment, Zaman won the next game and the next and suddenly the match was all square: three games apiece with the seventh and deciding game to be played.

It was almost lunchtime and the other match had long ago finished (the Church's man, Brother Raul, had defeated his fellow Spaniard, Montoya, four games to one, proving, some said, that God is still more powerful than the Holy Roman Emperor) but few in the hall had much interest in that match. The crowd only had eyes for this enthralling struggle between the skilled Muscovite and the surging local champion.

As it unfolded, I heard several people on the royal stage comment that the seventh and final game of their match might go down in history as one of the greatest games of chess ever played.

Zaman took Vladimir's queen early, but the Muscovite leveled the score a few moves later, and so they battled queenless, slowly removing pieces from the board until all that remained was a perilous endgame of pawns and kings.

The audience, both on the royal stage and among the masses, was on the edge of their seats. Every move caused loud intakes of breath, open applause or terrified gasps.

But then Zaman—after an utterly daring play that involved sacrificing one promising pawn—promoted a seemingly isolated pawn to queen and with a few swift, brutal, sweeping moves, promptly cleared the board, and Vladimir—stunned at being so suddenly and ingeniously outwitted—toppled his king and the Hagia Sophia shook with deafening applause, the entire crowd rising to their feet in appreciation of the epic contest they had just witnessed.

I stood and clapped, too, but as I did so, I saw that my teacher— alone in that crowded hall—remained rooted in his chair. He did not stand, nor did he clap.

Indeed, as the raucous cheering subsided and the sultan went over and shook the exhausted Zaman's hand, my teacher said flatly, "Come, Bess. Let us go and have some lunch with Giles before his important match this afternoon. I have seen enough of this."

Confused, I followed him out of the Hagia Sophia.

———

I had thought we would take lunch in our rooms, but Mr. Ascham decided that we would eat picnic style on a blanket out in the sunshine on the main lawn of the First Courtyard.

Mr. Giles ate in silence, contemplating, thinking, calming his mind for his upcoming match. Elsie kept looking about herself to see who passed by, hoping no doubt for a glimpse of the crown prince.

I asked my teacher why we were eating in such a manner: out of doors and in our own company.

"The walls of our living quarters have ears," he said. "And some of them have eyes, too. The sultan knew of the secret note I found in Maximilian's shoe heel and yet I am certain Latif never saw it. The only time I mentioned its existence to anyone was to you in our rooms and I am certain you did not tell anyone about it."

"Absolutely not!" I said, suddenly trying to think of what else might have been spoken in what we had thought was the privacy of our own rooms. Elsie's tales of her nocturnal adventures came to mind.

"We sit out here," Mr. Ascham said, "because I do not want the sultan to hear the answer to the question I know you want to ask me about the chess match we just witnessed."

I asked the question to which he was alluding. "How did you know that Zaman would win? He was so far behind and had lost the first three games roundly."

Mr. Ascham nodded. "Zaman had help. From above."

I cocked my head in disbelief. "Divine aid? From the Moslem god?"

"No, nothing so miraculous. He had human aid. You may have noticed how, in between moves, he often sat back and scanned the heavens. Zaman was not seeking divine assistance but rather signals from a team of local chess experts sitting up in the sultan's private worshipping balcony. Five men were up there, hidden behind its lattice screens—out of sight from the crowds on the floor and up in the galleries—watching and analyzing the match."

"Zaman was cheating . . . ?"

"Yes. When I left the royal stage halfway through the match, I strolled to a vantage point over by the sultan's entrance from which I could just see up into the sultan's balcony—and there they were, five of them, huddled over a chessboard of their own, the pieces of which were laid out in replication of those in Zaman's and Vladimir's game, their heads bent together in furious discussion and debate.

"And Zaman needed all the help he could get. Vladimir is a very strong player and I don't think either Zaman or his helpers anticipated just how quickly the Muscovite would win the first game. You'll remember that Zaman lasted a little longer in the second game and longer still in the third—his helpers needed that time to figure out defenses and counterstrategies to foil Vladimir's attacks."

"But this is outrageous," I said. "We must tell someone—"

"You will do no such thing. Besides, who would we tell? The sultan? Zaman's helpers sit in his own private balcony. They clearly act with his express knowledge and consent. We are aware that the sultan rigged the draw in Zaman's favor. We suspect he tried to have Mr. Giles poisoned on the way here—and, who knows, maybe other players, too: that Wallachian, Dragan, said that he had been feeling poorly since arriving in Byzantium. And now we know that the sultan will go to great lengths to ensure that his man wins the tournament in front of his subjects."

"What of our rooms?"

My teacher sighed. "I imagine there is someone listening to our conversations behind the thin walls or perhaps through the ceiling. We must be circumspect about what we say when in our lodgings from now on."

I shook my head. My teacher was brilliantly clever sometimes.

"In the end," Mr. Ascham said, "Zaman's cheating is of no matter to us unless Giles here reaches the final, since according to the draw he will not meet Zaman unless they both make it to the deciding match. And that is a long way off, for this afternoon Giles must overcome a most daunting opponent, Dragan of Wallachia."

———

As they had done before the match with Talib, Mr. Giles and Mr. Ascham began strategizing about the match ahead.

They discussed Dragan's previous effort against the Venetian, Marko, which the Wallachian had won without dropping a game and while drinking, belching and cursing liberally.

"That Dragan is the crudest brute I have ever seen," I offered. "It surprises me that one so boorish and uncouth could have *any* talent whatsoever at a game as intricate as chess."

"Now, now," my teacher said. "Dragan may indeed be harsh and coarse, but that does not mean he is unintelligent. Cleverness is not the exclusive domain of the wealthy and the cultured, Bess. Don't confuse someone's outward appearance with their inner acumen; just because a man is well spoken and well tailored does not mean he has a brain. Incidentally, and with respect, this is an error I believe your father makes at court regularly and one you would do well to avoid should you ever sit on the throne. Employ competent people: the state of their mind matters far more than the state of their clothes."

"If Dragan is so smart, why must he be so belligerent?" I asked. "If one is clever, one need not be hostile."

"I would not be surprised to learn that Dragan has had a hard life in Wallachia and perhaps a brutal upbringing. Whatever the cause, he is aggressive. Further, he knows this and at the chessboard, he uses his natural hostility and his imposing physical presence to his advantage. His crude insults are not idle slurs: they are deliberate attempts to intimidate and rattle his opponent, to make his opponent worry more about Dragan and think less about the game at hand."

"Likewise his drinking at the table," Mr. Giles said. "I have seen this sort of thing before. It is a distracting technique, designed to make his opponent underestimate Dragan and believe that he may be prone to foolish drunken moves. Throughout his match against the Venetian, during which Dragan drank happily and loudly, Dragan did not make a single errant move and his eyes were always sharp. He can indulge in his liquor and yet still be very precise in his chess play."

I leaned back in surprise. Where I had seen a common dirty thug, my teacher and Mr. Giles had seen much, much more.

"So how do you beat him?" I asked.

At first, silence answered me.

Then Mr. Ascham turned to Mr. Giles. "There's an Oriental saying I like: 'If aggression meets empty space it tends to defeat itself.' Let Dragan's aggression meet empty space. Whether it is a king in a court or a thug in a tavern, a bully gains strength from seeing a reaction. They enjoy seeing their victim squirm and this only makes the bully more confident. If you just smile back at him when he insults you, Giles, there's a good chance that this will infuriate him and he will then turn his aggression back on himself."

"Oh, I like that, Roger." Mr. Giles grinned. "I like that a lot."

"Either way, my friend, this is going to be a most challenging match."

MR. GILES VERSUS DRAGAN

ONCE AGAIN, MY TEACHER TURNED OUT to be correct in his prognostication: Mr. Giles's match against Dragan of Wallachia was a most torrid battle.

And the Wallachian was at his most aggressive. He threatened Mr. Giles in both his native tongue *and* in Greek. He glared at Mr. Giles in between moves and spat filthy challenges at him when he would take one of Mr. Giles's pieces, including the constant exhortation, "Fuck your mother, Englishman!" and the sophisticated extension of it, "Fuck her again!" He also scorned Mr. Giles's moves: "Now why the fuck would you do that!" or "I didn't know Englishmen were fucking fools as well as fucking dandies!" When he won the first game, Dragan yelled, "Ah-ha! Dragan is doing what all of France's armies wanted to do but couldn't: bend an Englishman over a barrel and fuck him up the arse! Ah-ha!"

Yet all the while, Mr. Giles remained unflappable.

Whenever Dragan insulted him, Mr. Giles just smiled happily back at the brute—and he quietly won the next two games.

It should also be noted that the Wallachian did not fight fair. After the fourth game (which Dragan won, leveling the contest at two games apiece), Mr. Giles complained to Mr. Ascham of a severe headache. We arranged for a calming brew of tea to be brought to him, which seemed to help—but then, during the next game, both my teacher and I observed a strange glinting of light that appeared to strike Mr. Giles in the eyes at crucial moments in the game.

Mr. Ascham searched the hall and found the source of the glinting: a small female gypsy holding a shard of mirror and angling it in such a fashion that the sunlight was reflected into Mr. Giles's eyes. She did not do it overtly or for long periods, but just enough to subtly irritate Mr. Giles.

My teacher quietly called over a palace guardsman and indicated the mirror-wielding woman and the offender was discreetly removed from the hall—but not before Dragan had won that game and taken the score to three games to two, putting that beastly man only one game away from victory.

With the removal of the distraction, however, Mr. Giles regained his focus and his play stepped up a notch. In the face of Dragan's increasingly coarse insults, Mr. Giles displayed almost unnatural calm, which—as my teacher had hoped—finally caused Dragan to start cursing *himself* ("What were you thinking, Dragan!" "You should have beaten this English fool two games ago!").

He also started looking up at Giles after hurling his insults, searching for some kind of reaction, any kind of reaction, but when he got none, Dragan would just move his piece sullenly, slamming it down on the board. Mr. Giles did not even blink. The Wallachian continued to curse himself even more.

Thus Mr. Giles won the sixth game, taking the match to a seventh and deciding game.

To my surprise, Mr. Giles took control of this final game early on and with uncharacteristic ruthlessness. (He created a powerful wedge of pawns that Dragan simply could not penetrate, and using them as a foundation, started launching devastating attacks with his knights and a bishop.)

By this time—he told me later—Mr. Giles had figured out the Wallachian's main tactics and in that final game, Mr. Giles saw them coming and thus anticipated every attack and returned it twofold, removing the Wallachian's major pieces from the board one at a time until the brute had only his king and some pawns up against Mr. Giles's full rank of knights, bishops, queen and rooks.

Then Mr. Giles swept a rook all the way down the board and said something to the Wallachian that no one but the two of them could hear.

The move mated Dragan, although Mr. Giles clearly said more than "Checkmate." The match was over and the giant Wallachian stomped off the stage, muttering and gesticulating with a profound lack of grace.

When Mr. Giles joined us later, smiling wearily, I asked him what exactly he had said to Dragan when he'd mated him.

Mr. Giles shrugged bashfully. "I said, 'Checkmate, you bastard, and go fuck *your* mother.'"

———

Whilst Mr. Giles's match had gone to seven games, it was over long before the other quarterfinal match being played on the second stage, that of Nasiruddin and Ibrahim.

Despite the unsporting tactics and crude insults, strategically speaking, Mr. Giles's match with Dragan had been a very direct affair with many bold moves and forced exchanges of pieces. Nasiruddin and Ibrahim's match was a more intricate and tortuous duel. In the same time it took Mr. Giles and Dragan to play seven games, Nasiruddin and Ibrahim had completed only four, with each player sitting on two wins apiece.

Leaving Mr. Giles to accept the hearty congratulations of the other delegations (Mr. Giles also wanted to watch the remainder of the other match), Mr. Ascham, Elsie and I left the Hagia Sophia. My teacher had decided to use the afternoon to carry out further investigations.

Specifically, he wanted to speak with Darius the wrestler.

We spent the entire afternoon searching the palace for him, moving from courtyard to courtyard, asking guards, servants and guests if they had seen the famous wrestler.

But not a soul had seen him or knew of his whereabouts.

Darius had disappeared.

THE WORLD BENEATH

THAT EVENING, AFTER THE EXCITEMENT of Mr. Giles's victory during the day and our afternoon search for Darius, my teacher retired immediately after supper, quickly falling into a deep slumber. Mr. Giles did likewise, his mind exhausted from his battle against the Wallachian.

Which left me in Elsie's charge, and Elsie had only one goal that night.

"Come, Bessie! Come and see with your own eyes one of the crown prince's gatherings. Tonight, I have word that he is holding a party in his *father's* private bath. I am meeting Zubaida over by the entrance to the harem shortly. Come! Tonight is the night I give the future sultan a taste of my English rose!"

And so off I went with Elsie, wrapped in a hooded cape, my mind hopelessly caught somewhere between innocent trepidation, hidden excitement and sheer curiosity. It was one thing to listen to Elsie speak of her frolics but another thing entirely to see them for myself. I hurried to keep up with her, my small legs pumping to match her long purposeful stride.

We met Zubaida at the main entrance to the harem. Zubaida wore a light cloak buttoned at the top—every now and then it blew open with the breeze and I saw that beneath it, she wore a very short dress made of a flimsy, almost translucent, cloth with long slits up both thighs. The three of us approached the guards.

Elsie gave that night's entry phrase but the guards did a strange thing: they said that they would admit only her.

"Prince Selim was most specific," one of the guards said to Elsie.

"This evening only a special few are to be granted admittance. You are one of the few, but they"—he jerked his head at Zubaida and me—"are not."

Elsie turned to face us, a stricken look on her face. Loyal as she was to her friends, she had intentions that night, and she needed us to let her go so that she could carry them out.

"Go on, Elsie," I said. "I shall have to see the crown prince's activities some other time."

Zubaida seemed less keen to let Elsie go in without her, especially given that it was she who had granted Elsie access to these exclusive gatherings in the first place.

"Zu-zu?" Elsie pleaded. "Do you mind—?"

"Oh, go," Zubaida said stiffly. "Just go."

Elsie squeaked with delight. "I shall tell you both everything tomorrow!" Then she hugged us and dashed past the guards into the secret world of the harem.

I was left standing at the guardhouse with Zubaida, disappointed and deflated.

But then Zubaida pulled me away from the guards, out of earshot. "You know, there are other ways to gain access to the sealed areas of the palace. Come with me."

We hurried off into the night.

———

Zubaida led me to a small garden at the northern end of the Fourth Courtyard.

This somewhat remote region of the palace was known for its many groves and gardens, all arranged in an extending sequence of lattice-walled miniature courtyards. Most of the flower arrangements were of tulips but this little garden was devoted to roses. A small fountain in the garden's center gurgled happily away.

Zubaida looked around furtively before guiding me into the rose garden. Once inside she snatched a flaming torch from a bracket on the wall and quickly knelt on the ground by the fountain, where she extracted a small square grate set into the paved stones.

"I grew up inside this palace and as a little girl, the older children introduced me to its underworld," she said. "Like all children, we loved playing in the palace's old Roman sewers and cisterns. The tunnels and chambers down here pass directly underneath the harem."

Darkness yawned beneath the opening. I could hear the sigh of moving air down there: a large space.

Zubaida stepped down into the hole, descending a ladder of some sort just below the rim.

"Not afraid of the dark are you, little princess?" she taunted before she disappeared into the hole, holding the torch with one hand, her echoing voice adding, "Make sure you replace the grate behind you."

I hesitated a moment, unsure and a little frightened, but ultimately pride and curiosity got the better of me and I hastened into the hole after Zubaida.

———

At the bottom of the ladder was a downward-curving spiral staircase of stone. Staying close to Zubaida, I descended those stairs until, unexpectedly, they plunged into water. I stopped short and found myself looking out over an enormous man-made cavern.

A forest of columns stretched away from me, two dozen of them, all in perfect alignment, holding up the high ceiling. They were of the Roman style: made of chiseled marble and featuring at their tops and bottoms heads carved in the shape of Artemis, Aphrodite and (on a few of them) Medusa. They all rose up out of a wide subterranean lake.

"A cistern," Zubaida whispered. "For storing freshwater. The Romans built scores of them around the city, to hold the water that they funneled here from the mountains. In the centuries since, Constantinople has been built and rebuilt over the top of them. But the Roman cisterns are so sturdy that they still stand today and, indeed, still collect groundwater. To this day, many city dwellers hammer out holes in the floors of their cellars and lower buckets into the ancient cisterns to gather water. Don't worry, it's not deep."

Zubaida stepped out into the lake and sure enough, the water came only to her knees. She sloshed away from me, heading into the darkness, the glow of her torch creating a small corona around her head. I hurried to keep up with her.

That first cistern was also filled with many small mountains of rubbish and debris—discarded iron gates and pipes, wooden planks, doors with hinges still on them and old sandstone blocks—all heaped against the columns in a very ugly manner. Narrow alleys had been carved through the heaps and many of the piles leaned precariously over me as I passed by them.

"The entrance used to be wider," Zubaida informed me, "so palace dwellers would bring their refuse down here. To stop the practice, the entry was reduced in size to that small grate in the rose garden."

There were other dangers. In the second cistern we came to, hidden underneath the knee-deep water, were a series of irregularly spaced deeper holes into which the unfamiliar explorer could suddenly drop bodily. I almost fell into two of them.

"These are all actually *smaller* cisterns," Zubaida said. "There's an immense one over by the Ayasofya that dwarfs these."

I tried to stay close to my guide and I was glad I did: after those first two chambers, Zubaida led me through a veritable labyrinth of tight passages and magnificent cisterns, a subterranean maze worthy of Minos himself.

We passed through soaring chambers that had not seen the light of day for over a thousand years—some had arched doorways and high windows (now bricked in) and even steps and staircases leading to other levels.

Zubaida seemed to use these chambers as reference points in the underground maze.

"Hmmm," she said, pausing in one such chamber. Three archways branched off it in three different directions. "Now. This one is underneath the queen's quarters, which means we must take that passageway to get to the sultan's private bath . . ."

We continued in this fashion for some time until Zubaida stopped suddenly in a new cistern. Evidently, she had taken a wrong turn somewhere because when she stopped, she spun around with a confused and angry look on her face.

"Damnation. I must have . . . oh . . . *oh*—"

Her face went pale as she saw something over my shoulder.

"I'm terribly sorry . . . I didn't mean to—"

I turned . . .

. . . to find myself confronted by several pairs of eyes emerging from the darkness, malevolent eyes that belonged to some residents of these caves, all of them dressed in rags and advancing menacingly toward us.

THE INHABITANTS
OF THE UNDERWORLD

THE GROUP OF DANGEROUS-LOOKING SOULS stepped into the light of Zubaida's torch and I was shocked to discover that they were children.

There were perhaps twelve of them and they ranged in age from about eight to sixteen. They all had grubby, dirty faces and the hollow eyes of the starving.

I took in the grim cavern around me: islands made of garbage rose above the waterline and on these islands were a collection of crude shanties and burrows. We had stumbled upon their home. For these children, a squalid life in the dark was better than one on the streets of Constantinople.

A tall, rangy boy who was the biggest of the group stepped forward and said in common Greek to Zubaida, "You know not to come here, rich girl."

"Omar, please, I'm so sorry," Zubaida stammered. "We . . . we got lost."

The boy—Omar—stood over her, stared lasciviously at her chest. "You know that no intruder leaves our cavern without paying a tax. I hope for your sakes that you both have something to trade other than your bodies."

Zubaida looked like a trapped dog. She wore only her light cloak over her very short dress—one that she had clearly put on in anticipation of a different kind of carnal adventure that night. She had nothing else on her person and certainly nothing to trade.

As this exchange took place, I gazed at the cluster of children gathered behind the taller Omar. Small girls with frightened eyes, little boys with defiant frowns, all dressed in soil-covered rags. And then among them I saw, not with a little shock, someone I recognized—

But at that moment the leader, Omar, rounded on me. "And what of you, little girl? I have not seen you before. You are a visitor to the palace? From whence do you hail?"

"I am from England," I said firmly in Greek. "Where I am the daughter of the king," I added, thinking a royal addendum might play to my advantage. It was not a good move.

The boy grinned through broken teeth. "The daughter of a king, eh? Let me add to your education then: royal blood means nothing in the deep places of the world. You are a long way from home, princess." His eyes ran over my wrists and neck, as if searching for jewelry. "My question still stands: what can you give me in exchange for safe passage out of here?"

Like Zubaida, I had nothing of value on my person, no rings, necklaces or coins.

My eyes, however, found those of the individual I knew among the gang of lost children—another tall boy, thin and gangly, perhaps fifteen years of age.

I said boldly, "I can give *him* information about the deaths of his parents."

"Information!" the leader spat. "That's not going to be—"

The boy I recognized stepped forward.

"Wait," he said softly.

Omar turned, surprised that his leadership might be challenged in front of outsiders. But the second boy—as I had noted—was of roughly his age and height and thus a legitimate challenger to his authority.

"I would like to hear what she has to say." The boy came up to me, stepping fully into the light of the torch, and I beheld the face of Pietro, the missing son of the murdered chef, Brunello of Borgia, and his wife.

———

I had wondered where Pietro had gone after his parents' suspicious deaths. I had also wondered why. One who flees a death scene, I assumed, did so because he was guilty of the crime. My teacher, I recalled, had offered a different reason for Pietro's flight: fear.

Now I had one answer: he had come here, to the place where orphans, runaways and other urchins of the street eked out an existence.

I hoped I was about to find out the answer to the second question.

Pietro stood before me.

I recalled meeting him in his father's kitchens on the night of the opening banquet. I had thought him shy then, quiet. Here, however, in the firelight of Zubaida's torch in the underground cistern, his features seemed sharper, more alert.

"I will give you one chance before I leave you to Omar," he said with a deferential nod to Omar. "What can you tell me of my parents' deaths?"

All eyes fell on me. I stood my ground and held my head high as I had seen my father do when he wanted to appear particularly regal.

I swallowed. Then I said, "My teacher, whom the sultan himself has consulted about both the cardinal's and your parents' deaths, believes that your mother and father did not take their own lives, but were murdered."

———

At first Pietro did not move. He just stared at me with unblinking eyes.

Then he said, "Thank the Lord. I didn't think anyone would ever believe me. My father would never commit suicide. Never. I was convinced there had been foul play, but I did not know how to prove it. I fled here because I thought I might also be in danger. Your teacher must be a most clever man."

"He is." He had also been right about the reason for Pietro's flight.

Pietro turned to Omar. "She has earned their passage."

Omar didn't seem exactly pleased about this, but he did nothing to contradict Pietro.

My mind, however, was racing. Mentioning the murder of Brunello and his wife had caused a storm of thoughts to rush through it.

First, my teacher's theory that someone—the queen or the wrestler Darius or even Brunello himself—had attempted to poison Cardinal Cardoza but had instead accidentally poisoned the visiting Cardinal Farnese.

Mr. Ascham had not believed that it had been Brunello. But I recalled my teacher's discussion with the slave girl Sasha in the slaughter room: she had said that Brunello had argued angrily with Cardinal Cardoza in the kitchens recently.

"One moment," I said as Zubaida backtracked toward the archway through which we had entered the children's cistern. "Before he died, your father argued with Cardinal Cardoza. What did they argue about?"

Pietro said, "My father was furious with the cardinal because he would not give my dead brother a Christian burial."

I had forgotten about Pietro's younger brother. What was his name? Benicio. About three years younger than Pietro and of diminished mind, the younger boy had killed himself a few weeks before our arrival in Constantinople by slashing his own wrists.

Pietro said, "Because my brother had taken his own life, Cardinal Cardoza denied him a Christian burial, thus condemning Benicio to an eternity in hell. My father was appalled. All his life he had been a good Christian and he had always been obedient to the cardinal, obedient to the point of fawning. He could not believe that the cardinal could be so heartless. But the cardinal would not budge from his stance. Suicide, he said, was a crime against God. Those who took away the greatest gift God had given them, life, were forever to be denied access to the gates of heaven. That was why they argued."

I had to tell Mr. Ascham. Perhaps, driven by rage at the cardinal's intransigence, Brunello had indeed tried to poison Cardinal Cardoza. But upon the death of the visiting Cardinal Farnese, the cunning Cardoza had deduced the true target of the poisoning attempt, himself, and had had the chef and his wife killed in a manner that made it appear they had committed suicide.

"Thank you, Pietro," I said. "If this matter is resolved and it is safe for you to come out of hiding, I will know where to find you—"

"Hey!" A sudden shout from the far end of the darkened cistern made us all turn.

I saw torches: three of them, small in the distance but growing larger as they approached.

The children of the cave scattered behind columns and into their mounds of debris and garbage. Zubaida and I also ducked behind the archway toward which we had been heading and peered back around it to observe what happened next.

Omar alone waited to meet the three men who appeared out of the darkness, holding torches aloft.

They were priests.

Young priests whom I had seen in Cardinal Cardoza's rooms the night before last.

"Greetings, young man," the first priest said in Greek. "Peace be with you. How are you this fine evening?" The priest said this in a bright voice that belied the somewhat foreboding surroundings.

"Speak plainly, priest," Omar said.

"Right, well," the priest said. "We bring you food"—at this, one of the other young priests held open a cloth on which sat a freshly cooked shank of beef and a collection of baked potatoes—"in exchange for your presence at a gathering we are holding tonight."

Omar's eyes were glued to the shank.

I saw the other children's heads appear from their hiding holes, drawn by the delicious smell of the hot food.

"How many?" Omar said.

"Three boys, one girl," the priest said as if he were at a market stall.

Omar turned and spoke gruffly to the darkness in Turkish.

"What is he saying?" I whispered to Zubaida.

"Omar just said, 'Whose turn is it this time?'" Zubaida said.

At length, four children stepped out from the shadows—three boys and a girl—and the lead priest reached out a hand to guide them but

Omar barked, "No! We eat the food first. Then you get what you desire. That's how it works."

The food was handed over and to my surprise, Omar gave the first bites to the four children who had stepped forward. Once they had eaten from the proffered delicacies, they went off with the three priests, and only then did Omar and the others—Pietro among them—partake of the remaining food, eating hungrily.

I felt a profound sadness as I watched this. So this was where the trade in human bodies began, with food for the starving given in exchange for favors for the depraved.

Zubaida and I scurried away and after some hurried searching, found our way back to the entrance in the rose garden. Once back on the surface, we went our separate ways toward our respective rooms, glad to return to the world we knew, the world of sun and air and light, a world that for all its wickedness was still safer and more palatable than the one we had just witnessed.

MOVEMENT IN THE NIGHT

AFTER BIDDING ZUBAIDA FAREWELL, I HURRIED back to my lodgings. I wanted to tell Mr. Ascham about my new theory.

Arriving at the hallway leading to our quarters, however, I slowed my pace and trod with more caution—while Elsie was clearly very accustomed to sneaking back into her bed without waking anyone, I was not, and I did not want to disturb anybody in the neighboring rooms and betray my nighttime adventuring.

But then as the door to our quarters came into view, it opened suddenly and I threw myself back behind some curtains.

Fast footsteps came down the hallway and, risking a peek, I spied my teacher—clad in his oilskin overcoat and hat—striding purposefully down the corridor. He walked quickly past my hiding place, too preoccupied with wherever he was going to notice me.

Where was he going—alone—in the middle of the night?

The answer, of course, was obvious. Only something to do with the investigation could draw him out of doors so late.

Although all I really wanted to do at that time was crawl into my bed and go to sleep, I worried for him. Already five people connected with our investigation had met unnatural and suspicious ends—Cardinal Farnese, the chef and his wife, Maximilian of Vienna and the virgin "gift," Helena—and I did not want my teacher, venturing out alone, to be the sixth.

And so, despite my weariness, I followed him.

My teacher's destination was, of all places, the sultan's animal menagerie.

Getting there meant passing through three guarded gates, and at each gate I lied to the gate guards, saying that I was traveling with my master (I never called him that at any other time, as he was not my master at all, merely my teacher) and had fallen behind. Bored, or not caring, they let me pass.

I descended the broad, grassy hill leading to the menagerie. A light rain fell. Leafless branches spread out above me like claws in the darkness. Then, out of the rain, the high brick wall of the menagerie appeared and there I saw the shadowy figure of my teacher pass through the menagerie's main gate.

I could only assume he was meeting someone—discreetly, in the dead of night—to further his investigation. I darted toward the main gate and slipped through it after him.

———

The sultan's animal enclosure was a different place after dark. I heard the shuffle of small creatures moving over branches in the monkey cage, the deep inhalations of the sleeping bear, the grunts of a pacing tiger. The elephants, however, stomped and trumpeted anxiously, as if something was bothering them.

The light rain made the slate stones slippery, and I trod with soft, halting steps, searching for Mr. Ascham.

But the decorative trees and the ring of bushes surrounding the central bear cage now became a most inconvenient barrier to viewing the whole menagerie. All was bathed in shadows and the veil of slow-falling rain—

The scream of rusty hinges cut through the air, then—*clang!*—there came the sound of a heavy gate slamming shut, followed by the click of a lock turning, then hurried footfalls outside the wall.

My heart stopped. I spun.

Someone had closed the main gate behind me, and then locked it, locking me—and Mr. Ascham—inside the menagerie.

I turned quickly, my eyes searching for my teacher, for another exit, for something, anything, and then in that desperate state I beheld something even more terrifying than the closing of the main gate.

I saw that the door to the cage housing the three gray wolves lay open.

THE WOLVES
OF TOPKAPI PALACE

I WOULD HAVE SCREAMED THEN and there from the sheer fright of it but at that moment a leather-gloved hand clamped over my mouth and yanked me back into a thick bush.

"Bess, shhh," my teacher hissed, his eyes peering out into the darkness. "Be very quiet. We're in danger. We've walked into a trap."

"What are you doing out here?" I asked in a whisper.

His eyes surveyed the menagerie as he spoke. "I should ask you the same question. I received a note tonight. It said that if I desired to know who killed the visiting cardinal, I was to come here after midnight, alone, without Latif, and all would be revealed."

"The wolf cage is open . . ."

"I know."

"Which means the wolves are out . . ."

"I know."

One of the elephants trumpeted again, this time more loudly. I looked over in that direction and—abruptly—through the veil of drizzling rain I saw the shadow of a large wolf slink by in front of the elephant, its head low, its legs tensed, searching for prey.

I tapped Mr. Ascham on the shoulder to point it out when without warning my teacher was thrown violently forward by a second wolf that had hurled itself into his back. That wolf now stood astride Mr. Ascham, snarling and snapping, and it lunged at his neck, but my teacher rolled and lashed out with his forearm, striking the animal in the snout, and it yelped as it was hurled sideways and Mr. Ascham leaped back up into a crouch.

We hadn't even heard it. It had stolen around behind us without so much as making a sound—

And then I heard a snort and felt a warm wash of air touch my right ear.

I turned my head very slowly. The third wolf stood *right next to me*, not a foot away, looking directly at me with its pale, pitiless eyes.

It leaped at me. I dove sideways. It missed. I rolled. It stood, its paws slipping on the wet slate stones, readying itself to leap again. It wouldn't miss me a second time. It leaped again. I shut my eyes and threw up my arms in pathetic self-defense as I heard Mr. Ascham, too far away, yell, "No!"

Nothing struck me.

Instead, I heard a pathetic yowl and the crack of breaking bone and I looked up to see the Russian bear, impossibly huge in the darkness, one of its hairy arms stretched through the bars of its cage, gripping the wolf in one of its mighty claws. It had caught the wolf by the throat in midlunge and snapped its neck like a twig. My sideways dive had brought me alongside its cage. The bear began to eat the wolf. I like to think the great beast rescued me, but I think it just saw the opportunity to snatch a tasty meal.

Mr. Ascham grabbed me at a run. "This way! Move!"

I didn't know where he was taking me and I didn't care so long as it was somewhere safe.

I saw the two remaining wolves pair up and watch us, as if regrouping to decide how to catch this unexpectedly troublesome prey.

Mr. Ascham never stopped moving. He thrust me in through a cage door, hurried through it after me and slammed the barred door shut behind us before reaching through the bars and ramming the bolt home.

Then he sat, breathless and panting. It took me a moment to realize where we were and when I did, I snorted appreciatively at my teacher's solution to our predicament.

We were in the wolves' cage.

A moment later, the two gray wolves stood before us, confused and confounded, pacing in obvious frustration at the easy meal that was now out of their reach.

Mr. Ascham turned to me. "Now. What on earth are *you* doing here?"

"I saw you leave our quarters and I was worried for you, so I followed you."

"*You* were worried about *me?*" He laughed softly. "I suppose subsequent events have proved your fears to have been well founded." He tousled my hair. "Thank you for worrying about me, little princess. I'm honored to be so highly regarded in your thoughts."

"What do we do now?" I asked. My teeth began to chatter. I suddenly felt very cold.

My teacher saw this and he put his arms around me. "There's nothing much we can do until the animal keepers arrive in the morning. While these lodgings are not quite up to the usual standards expected for a princess, they are adequate for our current predicament. Here, stay close to me and keep warm. This excitement has put you in a state and your body is reacting adversely. Stop talking now and just breathe deeply. Hopefully, you will sleep."

I did as he told me, enclosed in his strong arms and his wonderfully large cloak, warmed by his body. I burrowed my head into his chest. Despite our grim surroundings, I had never in my life felt so protected, so totally *enclosed* by another human being. I could have stayed in his arms forever. Handsomeness be damned. With his soft round features and his big nose, Mr. Roger Ascham may not have been considered fetching by the ladies of London, but with his razor-sharp mind, his kind heart and his extraordinary ability to see things through other people's eyes, as far as I was concerned, he was the most beautiful man in the whole world. All those silly girls who had rejected Roger Ascham's invitations to dance would never know what they had missed out on.

And, of course, he was right again. My body *was* in a state, reacting to my twin excitements of that night—in the cisterns with Zubaida and here in the menagerie with the wolves and the bear—and as my heart gradually slowed and my body warmed, I could feel a heavy sleep coming on.

The two wolves took up sentry positions right outside our cage, lying there in wait, while in the center of the menagerie the great bear feasted happily on his catch, the sound of crunching wolf bones echoing throughout the walled enclosure.

I couldn't resist the heaviness of my eyelids any longer and they closed and, forgetting all the things I had to tell my teacher, I fell into a deep sleep.

Mr. Ascham held me close that whole night. He did not sleep. He guarded me. My teacher. My knight. My protector.

———

Just before dawn, the sultan's chief animal keeper and his assistant arrived at their menagerie to find the natural order of things overturned: two wolves in the central area, two humans in the wolf cage, and one very satisfied bear in its cage with fresh blood all over its mouth.

At first, the animal keepers refused to release us, despite our claims to be agents of the sultan. I think they suspected us to be poachers whose plans had gone awry. The *sadrazam* was called and when he arrived some time later with a cohort of guards, he just looked at my teacher and me with a shake of the head.

"Why am I not surprised?" he said. Then, to the animal keepers, he said: "Get them out."

At length, the keepers lured and captured the two loose wolves and reversed our situations. Mr. Ascham and I thanked them profusely and hurried back to the palace. By this time, dawn had come, although it was still raining.

Before we hastened back up the hill from the menagerie, however, Mr. Ascham did one last thing. He crouched to examine the muddy ground outside the main gates of the menagerie.

"What are you looking for?" I asked.

"I assume that you, I, the animal keepers, the *sadrazam* and his men all kept to the paved path to get here. But I'm guessing that whoever trapped us inside the menagerie hid somewhere out here and then stole across the muddy ground to close the main gate behind us. I'm looking for . . . *this.*"

I crouched beside him and saw what he saw, and I marveled at his acumen.

There in the mud was a fresh set of footprints, footprints made by a pair of wooden-soled sandals, the left one of which had a V-shaped nick in it.

ELSIE AND THE CROWN PRINCE

FOR ONCE, ELSIE HAD GOTTEN TO bed before me. When I returned to the room I shared with her, I found her curled up in her bed, blissfully asleep.

Exhausted from my stressful nighttime adventures with first Zubaida and then Mr. Ascham, I dropped into my bed, an act which unfortunately woke her.

She leaped to my side, excitement personified. "Bessie! Bessie! I did it! I did it! I snared the crown prince!"

I could barely keep my eyes open. "Really?"

"I had him inside me, stiff as a flagpole. Oh, Bessie, it was simply *divine*. And after the raptures I gave him, I think I might have a very good chance of becoming his queen after all!"

———

Tired as I was, I was keen to hear her tale. And she was ever so keen to tell it.

Elsie said, "After I was granted access to the harem—leaving you and Zubaida outside, I'm so sorry!—I was escorted to the sultan's private bath chamber, which was simply a paradise on earth, far grander than the prince's bathhouse. It had several hot-water pools made of marble, all built at different levels and all connected by tumbling waterfalls. Steam rose everywhere, making every nubile young body in there shine like polished bronze.

"But while the bathhouse might have been larger, the gathering was smaller: only the crown prince, a handful of his friends and six girls, including me.

"When I entered the bathhouse, I saw that Crown Prince Selim had ensconced himself on a marble platform that jutted out into one of the larger pools and on which sat a wide marble throne. Two naked Persian girls fed him grapes while a third with gigantic breasts bent over in front of him, offering him her body.

"He saw me enter the bathhouse. We locked eyes.

"While I held his gaze, I loosened my dress, letting it fall to the floor, exposing my body to him. But my nakedness was different that night. Remember how I told you about that fashion among the Persian girls: to increase their allure, they shave the hair around their pudenda, with some even shaving it all off to create a sleek, smooth look. Well, so had I. My nether region was completely hairless. The crown prince saw this and he smiled.

"Then, while still maintaining eye contact with me, he stood from his marble throne and entered the bent-over girl in front of him, all the while watching me. The girl squealed with delight as he pumped her, but his every thrust was clearly directed at me, across the chamber.

"And so, still watching him, I just sidled over to the nearest bath and slid into its gloriously heated waters. Then I lay on a marble island a short distance from his throne, my body glistening all over with wetness.

"Then, while he was still pumping the Persian girl, the prince called over one of his friends and whispered to him, nodding at me.

"The friend, a muscular fellow named Fariq who would have been the catch of any ball back home, strode over to my island and offered me his manhood.

"What to do, Bess? Do I wait for the prince's attentions? Or do I let this lesser man occupy me? In the end, I decided that since the prince had sent him to me, what followed would be done for the prince's gratification.

"So I nodded to Fariq, rolled over, knelt on all fours and let him, still standing in the pool, enter me from behind.

"Fariq was actually quite skilled and, I must say, gave me genuine pleasure with his slow, measured movements, but I had positioned myself so that as Fariq thrust himself into me, I faced the crown prince—thus while the prince and I engaged with different lovers, in truth our eyes never parted and in reality we were making love to each other.

"Clearly, the crown prince also knew this was the case, for after a short while, he extracted himself from the Persian girl and called in Greek, 'Fariq! Enough! English rose, over here, now!'

"I removed myself from Fariq and sauntered over to the crown prince's platform while he handed the three Persian girls off to his friends. I stood before him. He gazed approvingly at my entirely hairless body.

"'English rose, I hear that you are magnificent,' he said. 'Prove it.'

"'If it pleases Your Highness,' I said. I knew that he favored girls bending over before him so that he could enter them at his leisure, so instead I mounted him face-to-face, kneeling on the armrests of the marble throne on which he sat and lowering myself onto his member. This allowed me to control the rhythm of our lovemaking.

"And so I called upon all the sensual skills I have gained and I pleasured him as he had never been pleasured before.

"I rode him like a stallion, Bessie. Rolling my hips, arching my back, extending my breasts skyward—to the point where I could feel his manhood harden even more inside me and I had him groaning with my every rise and fall. When this happened, I knew I had him under my spell.

"I should say that by this time most other men would have succumbed to an involuntary climax, but the prince was clearly an experienced fellow and possessed considerable stamina. But eventually I outlasted him and his breathing quickened and I increased the speed of my hip motions, enhancing his pleasure as he rushed toward climax, and finally he yelped with delight and fell back onto his throne, spent and exhilarated, a broad grin spread across his face.

"I had him three more times during the night, Bessie. I should mention that he genuinely pleasured me and on each occasion I shouted in ecstasy, his skills setting off fireworks throughout my body. The prince is a seasoned and skilled lover.

"Anyway, as dawn approached and all the others were fading off to sleep—they had been indulging in their own pleasurable acts in the various corners of the bathhouse while I had been frolicking with the prince—Selim said to me, 'English rose, you are a lover fit for a king. I thank you.'

"With those words, I took my leave and just before dawn, I returned to our rooms. Oh, Bessie. 'A lover fit for a king.' What do you think that means? In any case, I have had my chance to cast a spell over a prince and I have given it my best possible effort. It is now up to him to decide if he wants me in his bed forever."

I was happy for Elsie, and I wanted her to be happy, but I had my doubts. From observing my own father, I knew that kings and princes accepted the favors of many women while offering absolutely nothing in return, except in some cases the enduring shame of a bastard.

But Elsie was excited, deliriously excited, and so all I said was, "I am happy for you, Elsie. After this night, you may well be closer to queenhood than I am."

She hugged me tightly. "Oh, Bessie. Oh, Bessie." She wanted to continue talking about her night with the crown prince and becoming a queen, but I begged off, buried my head in my pillow and turned away.

I'd had enough of chess and wolves and princes for one day. All I wanted to do was sleep.

— V —

KNIGHT

Only one piece in chess is allowed to leap over other pieces: the knight. This curious L-shaped move makes him both unpredictable and particularly dangerous.

If chess is a metaphor for medieval society, then the placement of the knight on the board is worth noting. He does not stand at the side of his king; rather, he is separated from his master by both the queen and a bishop.

Even in the Middle Ages, a knight was simply a king's enforcer both on the battlefield and on his estates. Real power resided at court with queens, ministers and religious advisors.

This is also reflected in the "relative values" placed on chess pieces: bishops, rooks and the queen all outrank the knight. It is better to sacrifice a knight than any of them.

The loyal knight, astride his prancing horse, is designed only to be sent into battle by his king to die. In chess as in life, the knight is ultimately expendable.

From: *Chess in the Middle Ages,*
TEL JACKSON (W. M. Lawry & Co., London, 1992)

I have had good experience and trial of this world . . . I know what it is to be a subject, what to be a sovereign, what to have good neighbors, and sometimes meet evil willers.

—QUEEN ELIZABETH I

THE SEMIFINALS

AFTER TWO ROUNDS OF THE HIGHEST quality chess—and some of the highest quality cheating at chess—only four players remained in the tournament: the sultan's cousin, Zaman; Brother Raul from the Papal States; our own Mr. Giles; and the people's champion, Ibrahim from Constantinople.

Once again, an updated draw was slid under our door that morning. It read:

1ST ROUND	2ND ROUND	SEMI-FINALS	FINAL

1. **ZAMAN**
   OF CONSTANTINOPLE

2. **MAXIMILIAN**
   OF VIENNA

ZAMAN
OF CONSTANTINOPLE

3. **MUSTAFA**
   OF CAIRO

4. **VLADIMIR**
   OF MUSCOVY

VLADIMIR
OF MUSCOVY

ZAMAN
OF CONSTANTINOPLE

5. **ALI HASSAN RAMA**
   OF MEDINA

6. **PABLO MONTOYA**
   OF CASTILE

PABLO MONTOYA
OF CASTILE

7. **BR. EDUARDO**
   OF SYRACUSE

8. **BR. RAUL**
   OF THE PAPAL STATES

BR. RAUL
OF THE PAPAL STATES

BR. RAUL
OF THE PAPAL STATES

9. **GILBERT GILES**
   OF ENGLAND

10. **TALIB**
    OF BAGHDAD

GILBERT GILES
OF ENGLAND

11. **DRAGAN**
    OF WALLACHIA

12. **MARKO**
    OF VENICE

DRAGAN
OF WALLACHIA

GILBERT GILES
OF ENGLAND

13. **NASIRUDDIN**
    OF THE MOGHUL EMPIRE

14. **LAO TSE**
    OF THE HAN PEOPLE

NASIRUDDIN
OF THE MOGHUL EMPIRE

15. **WILHELM**
    OF KÖNIGSBERG

16. **IBRAHIM**
    OF CONSTANTINOPLE

IBRAHIM
OF CONSTANTINOPLE

IBRAHIM
OF CONSTANTINOPLE

Since there were now only three matches to be played (two semi-finals and the final), the second playing stage had been removed so that once again only a single stage occupied the center of the Hagia Sophia.

For reasons that only the functionaries of the sultan knew, today the *lower* half of the draw would play first, in the morning. I suspected this was because the sultan's cousin needed more coaching before his match.

Thus the first semifinal to be played would be that between Mr. Giles and Ibrahim. In the afternoon, Zaman would do battle against Brother Raul. That match would be a battle of faiths if ever there was one. Bet takers in the streets were apparently calling it "The New Crusade."

The citizens of Constantinople gathered both inside and outside the Hagia Sophia, their enthusiasm almost tangible. The day promised to be a most gripping one.

It would be more than that.

———

As Mr. Giles strode out through the crowd to the playing stage, Mr. Ascham, Elsie and I ascended the royal stage. Latif, as usual, followed behind us.

I yawned deeply as I looked out at the chessboard and the sea of people around it. Not an inch of floor space was bare and the crowd laughed and chatted amiably, enjoying the occasion. Beside me, Mr. Ascham stifled a yawn, too. We had both managed to get a few hours' sleep during the morning, and though outrageously tired, I was awake enough to take in the remarkable occasion before me.

Having said that, I could not help but compare this luminous, gay world to the subterranean one I had seen the previous night. The people of this world happily went about their lives—lives of work and play, food and joy, watching and gambling on spectacles like this chess tournament, blissfully unaware of the cruel existence going on in the cisterns beneath their feet.

Or maybe they were aware of it. The priests who had come down to the cistern to rent those children's bodies were certainly aware of their plight. People, I surmised, were actually keenly aware of any superiority they had over other people.

I shook my head, clearing it of such thoughts.

Mr. Ascham's and Mr. Giles's pre-match strategy discussion had been short on this occasion. Ibrahim was roughly the same age as Mr. Giles and played in a similar way. He did not appear to employ any unfair tactics or stratagems. This contest would, they decided, simply be a battle between two evenly matched and talented players, and whoever played best on the day would win.

As we made our way to our seats on the royal stage, the *sadrazam* appeared before us and discreetly took Mr. Ascham and Latif aside for a quiet word.

Elsie and I took our seats, and within moments, Elsie was winking and waving coquettishly at the crown prince a dozen seats away. He smiled back, grinning knowingly.

Mr. Ascham and Latif rejoined us. My teacher sat down beside me. Curiously, as he did so, a pair of the sultan's personal guards took up positions behind our chairs.

"Why are these guards here?" I asked.

"A precaution," my teacher said. "The *sadrazam* says there have been death threats made to Mr. Giles and to us should he beat the local man in this morning's match. Giles does not know."

"Oh, my." I glanced at the two stony-faced guards.

"And given our little incident in the menagerie last night," Mr. Ascham whispered, "a little protection seems like a nice idea to me."

I agreed. I also wanted to speak with Mr. Ascham about my encounter in the cisterns the previous evening, before the excitement in the menagerie. It had not occurred to me to raise the matter while I had been shivering in his embrace in the wolf cage; my mind, I hope it will be understood, was on other things at that time.

And so, as Mr. Giles and Ibrahim took their seats on the playing stage and began their match, I leaned close and told Mr. Ascham in a hushed voice about my adventures in the palace's underworld, how I had found Pietro and what I had learned from him.

My teacher listened in studious silence, offering me the occasional astonished look.

By the time I finished, the first game of the match was well under way but neither I nor Mr. Ascham had noticed. (At this stage, Elsie got up to take her toilet. I imagined she did so because it afforded her an opportunity to sidle past the crown prince.)

My teacher looked seriously at me. "You are not to venture alone into the palace grounds at night again, young lady."

"But you did the very same thing—"

"I am a full-grown man! You are a thirteen-year-old girl! Imagine if you had come to harm in those cisterns. You might never have been found." He said this last statement with genuine concern.

He softened. "Bess, I know Elsie takes off on nocturnal adventures, but Elsie is older than you are. She is also a sprite and a fool who does not fully understand the implications of giving her body to every man under the sun. Yes, I am aware of her predilections—both at home and here—and I suppose I could stop her, but she is a young woman who can make her own decisions. I also see her as an example to *you*, an example that you may choose to follow or to ignore. In my opinion, Elsie is almost certainly going to get herself into trouble one day. You, however, are not, at least not while you are in my charge."

I bowed my head. "I am very sorry, sir. I won't do it again." I was also somewhat startled by his knowledge of Elsie's promiscuity. Until that moment, I had thought that Elsie barely registered on Mr. Ascham's consciousness at all, but he was obviously aware of far more than I gave him credit for.

"Thank you, Bess," he said, visibly deflating. "I must add that I am also just rather fond of you. I would be devastated if something were to happen to you."

I smiled at that.

He straightened in his chair. "That said, with your discovery of Pietro, you have provided us with a very helpful new piece in this jigsaw puzzle of intrigue. So, Cardinal Cardoza refused to give Brunello's younger boy a holy burial, thus angering the chef. But was such a slight enough to drive Brunello to poison the cardinal? Of that I am not sure."

A cheer from the crowd made us turn. Ibrahim had just taken one of Mr. Giles's knights.

I took a greater interest in the match.

As it progressed, I noticed Mr. Giles wiping his brow with his kerchief a lot. He seemed to be perspiring more than he usually did but I attributed this to the tension of being in a semifinal against a talented player on such a historic stage.

Occasionally, however, he looked over at Mr. Ascham and me and smiled weakly—something he had not done in any of his previous matches. It was most unusual.

Then I saw him make a mistake. A mistake he would never make.

He moved his queen to a square that would allow Ibrahim—on his next move—to fork Mr. Giles's queen and king with a knight.

Of course, Ibrahim took this gift and checked Mr. Giles's king with his knight. Mr. Giles moved his king and—thump—a moment later, his queen was removed from the board and the crowd roared with delight.

From that moment on, the result of the first game was set. Deprived of his queen, Mr. Giles could only battle on valiantly but in vain. Ibrahim gradually wore him down, slowly taking all of his major pieces, until Mr. Giles—with only three pawns to protect his king, against Ibrahim's queen and a rook—toppled his king and extended his hand in congratulations.

The crowd went into delirium. They cheered and clapped. Their man was up one game to nothing.

And Mr. Giles just glanced again at Mr. Ascham and me on the royal stage.

———

During the break between games, Mr. Ascham and I went over to Mr. Giles.

"Giles, are you all right?" my teacher asked. "You look pale. Are you unwell?"

Mr. Giles blinked away his perspiration. "I'm . . . fine, thank you, Roger. Fine. Perfectly all right."

But he did not play like a man who was fine.

He lost the next game in a short time and only managed to win the third game when Ibrahim castled at a poor moment and Mr. Giles sallied forth with his signature queen-and-bishop checkmate. Yet still he appeared greatly unnerved, perspiring and generally looking very uncomfortable.

He lost the fourth game in a tense endgame tussle.

He was now down three games to one.

Once again, in between games, my teacher and I met with him by the playing stage. My teacher handed him a cup of tea.

"Giles, whatever is the matter?" Mr. Ascham whispered. "I doubt anyone in the crowd here can see it but I can. You are not yourself. You are not *playing* like yourself—"

"I have been told they will kill you and Elizabeth if I win, Roger," Mr. Giles said softly.

Mr. Ascham stiffened. "What? Who said this?"

"The *sadrazam*, this morning, as I took my seat on the playing stage. Your new guards"—Mr. Giles threw a look at our guards up on the royal stage—"they are not here to protect you. They are assassins. They are here to kill you—and later, me—should I beat Ibrahim today."

My teacher bit his lip in outright fury, looked back at the sultan on his throne. "First the poison on our journey here, and now this. The scoundrel. The dirty, scheming scoundrel."

He turned back. "Does Ibrahim know of this?"

"I do not think so. But he must suspect something. He knows he is winning too easily."

Mr. Ascham's eyes narrowed in thought. "This has probably gone on in all of Ibrahim's matches: his opponents have all had their companions' lives threatened, so they have deliberately lost."

"Are you saying the sultan *wants* Ibrahim to win?" I interjected. "That doesn't make sense. The sultan wants his man Zaman to win."

"That is not entirely true," Mr. Ascham said. "It would suit the sultan if *either* Zaman or Ibrahim won this tournament: in both eventualities, a Moslem wins and the Ottoman Empire emerges as the home of the greatest player in the world. Remember this, Bess: all rulers act to please their subjects at home, not to impress other nations. If Zaman *or* Ibrahim wins, the sultan's subjects are thrilled, for the world will have been beaten. Thus if the sultan can contrive an all-Moslem final, he cannot lose.

"Having said that, I wouldn't be surprised if he were to aid Zaman in that final, just to make sure that a Moslem of royal lineage wins. *This* was why he rigged the draw—to ensure that his two local players did not meet until the final. Then he helped Zaman win by cheating and he assisted the unknowing Ibrahim by threatening his opponents."

"What do I do, Roger?" Mr. Giles said desperately.

Mr. Ascham bowed his head in thought for a very long time. Then he looked up at Mr. Giles and me.

"Whether it be in war or in a game," he said seriously, "the outcome actually does not matter. Winning or losing is incidental. The brilliant Greek general Pyrrhus *won* the Battle of Asculum, but at such a cost, he has gone down in history as a fool—while the three hundred Spartans who fought to their deaths against an impossibly large force of Persians at Thermopylae are still honored two thousand years after the event. What matters both in war and in sport is that you *exhaust* yourself in the effort. That is all. You have done this, Gilbert, so you can hold your head high. But when you come up against an opponent who does not respect the game—an opponent who *only* desires to win and who will do any foul act to achieve victory—then the game loses any value it had and your efforts are wasted.

"Gilbert, my good friend, you've played a marvelous tournament. You've beaten two genuinely talented opponents in two genuinely difficult matches. You have nothing more to prove—to me, to Elizabeth, to King Henry or to yourself. Let us not waste your efforts any further. Give the sultan what he wants and let us be done with his doctored tournament."

Mr. Giles nodded silently.

I glanced at my teacher and I knew that he was right.

———

And so Mr. Giles lost that last game and thus the match. The crowd was ecstatic. They rushed the stage and hoisted Ibrahim onto their shoulders. Their champion was in the final but they were acting as if he had won the whole tournament. And, lo and behold, our new bodyguards vanished as quickly as they had appeared.

A break was held during which the sultan left the hall to take his lunch. Again, no one in the crowd moved.

As our party was leaving the Hagia Sophia, a messenger from the crown prince—I believe it was his friend Rahman—came over and asked Elsie if she would like to join the crown prince for lunch in the city.

Elsie, of course, was completely ignorant of the machinations behind Mr. Giles's loss and the danger that had been hanging over our heads. She threw Mr. Ascham a beseeching look. He just nodded wearily: "Do as you wish, Elsie."

With an excited squeal, Elsie dashed off and once again I was left to dine with my adult companions and not my friend.

After the lunch break, the playing stage was reset and the combatants in the second semifinal, Zaman and Brother Raul, ascended the stage and took their places at the board. I returned with my teacher and Mr. Giles. Mr. Ascham was particularly keen to see if Zaman received help from on high again.

By the time play commenced, Elsie had not returned from her lunch with the crown prince.

As the first game between Zaman and Raul entered a tense middle period, I again found myself watching my teacher rather than the chess.

Whenever it was Zaman's move, Mr. Ascham would gaze closely at Zaman and then look up at the sultan's private balcony. I myself saw shadows moving up there.

On other occasions, my teacher would look down the length of our stage at Cardinal Cardoza. The burly cardinal seemed bored. His loyal manservant, Sinon, stood alertly behind him, also careless of the chess but watchful of everything else. Even though the Church's representative was playing, it was as if the cardinal was watching the match out of duty, not interest, as if it was keeping him from other matters. From time to time, he would lash his face lightly with his little horsehair whip.

"That whip . . ." my teacher whispered.

I alone heard him and looked over at it, too. I saw its multicolored strands: brown, black, blond . . .

Mr. Ascham was staring at it intently when it dawned on him. "The chef's younger son, Benicio, had blond hair. Snow white blond hair. Oh, God. That's not horsehair. That's *human* hair. Cardoza keeps a lock of hair from every boy he violates."

I now saw the little whip in a horrifying new light. My eyes nar-

rowed on the section of snow white hair among the many other different colors.

"Cardoza, you monstrous bastard . . ." my teacher said, his mind
clearly moving very fast now.

Just then, however, a palace guard appeared at the cardinal's side
and whispered something in his ear and the cardinal quickly left the
Hagia Sophia, followed by Sinon, all the while observed by my teacher
and me.

This sent Mr. Ascham into a trance of even more intense thought.
He stared blankly into the near distance, ignoring the match, his face
set in a frown of concentration.

Then abruptly he stood. "Come, Bess. This match has some time
to run. There is still a mystery to solve, and the broad interest in this
match will give us an opportunity to visit your underworld unnoticed
and seek out the elusive Pietro."

"Pietro?"

"Yes. I want to ask him one question, a single question that will end
this matter once and for all."

PIETRO

THUS WHILE NEARLY THE ENTIRE CITIZENRY of Constantinople was massed in and around the Hagia Sophia to watch Zaman do battle with Brother Raul, my teacher and I returned to the deserted palace, shadowed as ever by our eunuch, Latif. Not far ahead of us, we saw Cardinal Cardoza and Sinon, guided by the guard who had fetched them, pass through the Gate of Felicity and head in the direction of their embassy.

"Latif," my teacher said. "I need you to keep watch over the cardinal for me whilst I visit a secret place."

"My orders are to accompany you at all times," Latif said, "*especially* to secret places."

"If you want to help me solve this riddle, you will watch over the cardinal now. If I'm right, everything that has happened here has happened because of Cardinal Cardoza, and he himself has blood on his hands. I believe this matter is about to come to a head and we will need to know his whereabouts when it does."

Latif hesitated. "But—"

"Good God, man, let me solve this thing! *Help me* solve this thing! Surely you realize by now that I seek only the truth! I do not wish to embarrass your master or his tournament. I seek only the truth! Please, just help me!"

Latif seemed to soften at that. He nodded slowly.

Mr. Ascham said, "Keep track of the cardinal. If he goes to his embassy, go to our observation balcony from the other night and make sure he stays there. If he ventures elsewhere, follow him. Bess, where is the entrance to your underworld?"

"It's in the rose garden in the Fourth Courtyard."

"Latif, meet us there in half an hour," my teacher said. Latif nodded and then, still somewhat hesitantly, left us.

Mr. Ascham and I found Zubaida lounging beside a fountain with some of the younger harem girls and, after a little exhortation on the part of Mr. Ascham (and his threat to inform the sultan if she refused to assist us), she agreed to guide us through the labyrinth and take us to Pietro.

After a brief stop in the kitchens—at my suggestion—we made our way to the rose garden where we would begin our descent, my second, into the underworld of Topkapi Palace.

———

As it turned out, the cistern world was a far different place in daylight than it was at night.

While it was still a dank and dark maze, it was less sinister. This was largely thanks to small cracks in the ceilings of its many chambers—from these cracks tiny shafts of sunlight lanced into the gloom like diagonal lengths of thread pulled taut. While Mr. Ascham and Zubaida still carried flaming torches aloft, these thin shafts of light gave off enough extra illumination to actually make certain chambers seem familiar. Finding one's way back out through the maze would certainly be easier so long as it was done while the sun was still shining outside.

Led by Zubaida, we navigated the early chambers—including the first two with their piles of rubbish and dangerous submerged holes—until after a time the three of us came to the cistern where Zubaida and I had encountered the feral children.

Of course, they were nowhere to be seen.

I called out, "Pietro! Pietro! Do not be afraid, this man means you no harm! He is my teacher, the one I told you about, and he has a question for you! I have also brought"—I held up the sack of roasted chickens we had taken from the kitchens—"some food."

Heads appeared from the various shanties and rubbish burrows in the cistern. The children edged forward, tentative at first—they eyed Mr. Ascham with much fear—but the smell of freshly cooked chicken was too much for their starving bellies.

Pietro appeared from behind a column.

"Why have you returned here? What do you want?"

Mr. Ascham stepped forward. "Blame me for this intrusion, young man. It was I who compelled these girls to bring me here. I have one simple question for you: on those occasions in the past when Cardinal Cardoza took his meals in his embassy, was it your little brother Benicio who delivered them to him?"

Pietro's eyes snapped up.

He looked as if my teacher had slapped him in the face.

But then—taking me completely by surprise—his entire face crumpled.

"Yes, yes he did," Pietro said, before he fell to his knees in front of my teacher and broke down entirely, sobbing. "Oh, sir! Good sir! That cardinal, that cruel bastard Cardoza, he did things to my brother! And Benicio was a dullard, slow but sweet and as innocent as the day is long. And that wretched cardinal had his way with him, night after night, and Benicio, sweet little Benicio, slow little Benicio, not even comprehending that these perversions were not of his doing, did not tell me what had happened until the night I found him dying in a puddle of his own blood, distraught and ashamed, his wrists slashed by his own hand."

I shot a look at Mr. Ascham but he shook his head.

"Did you tell your father?" Mr. Ascham asked.

"What could I have told him! Should I have told my father that, night after night since we had arrived in Byzantium three months ago, he himself had dispatched his weak-minded son into the hands of a rapist? No, I didn't tell him. I took matters into my own hands and on the night of the grand banquet I delivered a fateful meal to the cardinal, but then . . ."

Mr. Ascham said, "But while you left the poisoned meal in Cardinal Cardoza's private rooms, it wasn't Cardinal Cardoza who ate it, it was Cardinal Farnese. You killed the wrong man."

"Yes."

"You didn't know Cardinal Cardoza had been delayed?"

"No."

"And you didn't know the visiting Cardinal Farnese was staying in Cardoza's private rooms?"

"No."

"And when you went to check a short time later to see if your plan had worked, you found the wrong man dead, and so in an attempt to throw off any investigators, you mutilated Farnese's face in the manner of the insane fiend known to be on the loose in this city and hurled the body into the reflecting pool."

The boy nodded sadly. "Yes."

Mr. Ascham said, "You told Elizabeth here that your father argued with Cardinal Cardoza about the cardinal's refusal to bury Benicio with holy honors."

"It was the height of hypocrisy. The monster drove my brother to suicide and then he himself denied Benicio a Christian burial on the grounds that by killing himself *Benicio* had offended God. It was the final insult."

"It surely was," Mr. Ascham said quietly. "It was also, I believe, the reason why the cardinal had your parents killed."

"The cardinal did *what*—?"

"It is my theory that Cardinal Cardoza—having realized that the poison that killed Cardinal Farnese was actually intended for him— erroneously believed that your *father*, having somehow learned of Cardoza's sodomizing of your brother, had poisoned his meal, and so Cardinal Cardoza had both your father and mother murdered."

The boy looked horror-struck as he realized the depth of his error: his failed attempt on the cardinal's life had led to his parents' deaths.

"Oh, Lord in heaven . . ." he breathed, his eyes staring downward but seeing nothing.

My teacher gazed at him with a look of great kindness. "You couldn't have known this chain of events would happen, Pietro. You couldn't."

The boy said nothing.

"You understand, I must tell the sultan about all of this," Mr. Ascham said. "Which means staying within the palace walls could be dangerous for you. It might be wise for you to leave this place and disappear into the larger city for a time."

Still Pietro said nothing. He just stood there, head bent.

"I am truly sorry, Pietro," my teacher said. "Be at peace." And with those words Mr. Ascham led Zubaida and me out of the cistern.

———

As we made our way back through the maze of high-ceilinged chambers, Mr. Ascham said to me, "I made the same mistake Cardinal Cardoza did: I thought that Brunello had attempted to poison him. But it wasn't the furious father who had laced his meal with poison, it was the furious brother."

Sloshing through the water, we came to the second-to-last cistern.

"I need to speak with the sultan," Mr. Ascham said. "Cardinal Cardoza must be arrested for the murder—or at least for ordering the murder—of Brunello and his wife. I will tell the sultan that it was the boy Pietro who was responsible for the visiting cardinal's death."

"Will the sultan want to arrest Pietro as well?" I said.

"I would imagine so," Mr. Ascham said.

As we were passing through that second-to-last cistern with its dangerous submerged holes, so engaged was I in the conversation with my teacher that I made a misstep and my right foot went plunging into one of those concealed holes.

My foot struck something. Something soft.

Something that felt like . . .

I squealed. "There's something down there!"

Zubaida and Mr. Ascham grabbed my arms and righted me. Then we all looked down into the hole that had swallowed my errant foot. It was illuminated by a thin shaft of outside light, just enough to enable us to see what it was I had touched.

The drowned face of Darius the wrestler stared up at us with wide, unblinking eyes.

He stood upright in a seven-foot-deep hole, his hands bound behind his back, his hair floating in the watery haze, his feet presumably weighted down with chains or something similarly heavy.

"Darius . . ." Zubaida gasped.

"So this is where he went," Mr. Ascham said.

"Is the wrestler's death connected with our puzzle?" I asked.

"No," he replied firmly. "His death is another matter. But that can wait. Now it is time to confront the cardinal."

Mr. Ascham strode into the last cistern, toward the steep stone stairs at the far end that led up and out into daylight. I hurried after him and we arrived at the base of the stairs together, only to stop short as we were suddenly confronted by a figure blocking our way.

I saw the fellow's feet first and I noticed immediately that his left sandal had a prominent V-shaped nick in its wooden sole, beside his big toe.

My gaze rose upward and as it did I beheld the owner of those mysterious sandals—sandals that had left their mark in the slaughter room where the chef and his wife had been found hanged and in the fresh mud outside the menagerie after my teacher had been lured there to die—and as my eyes came up I found myself meeting the cold, impassive stare of Sinon, the towering manservant of Cardinal Cardoza.

THE CARDINAL'S MAN

"SINON," MY TEACHER SAID. "I had wondered if the cardinal would send you to kill me."

The manservant said, "The cardinal says you know too much, Englishman. He has ordered you and your girl to die, and I am here to carry out the sentence."

He loomed above us, his face completely devoid of emotion. He stood with an unnerving stillness, a stillness, I realized with a start, that I had seen before: on the night my teacher and I had observed the cardinal's debauched gathering in his embassy, I had glimpsed a tall, shadowy figure observing us from behind a lattice screen by the lawn, standing with a similar eerie stillness. It had been Sinon watching us that night.

He stepped down into the shallow water of the cistern, advancing on my teacher and me. Mr. Ascham pushed me back protectively. Zubaida just scurried away.

"You hanged the chef and his wife for your master," Mr. Ascham said.

"I do as my master commands."

"And you laid that trap for me in the menagerie."

Sinon kept advancing. "I do as my master commands."

My teacher kept backing away. "Including murder?"

Sinon kept advancing. "For your murder, he has given me absolution in advance." He nodded at me. "And for hers. My master says I will go to heaven for this."

"Your master is a pederast. There is no place in heaven for him or any who serve him."

"We shall let God decide," Sinon said, drawing a short glistening sword. "The Lord will guide my hands."

We were now standing among the scattered rubbish that had been carelessly tossed into the cistern: the heaped piles of discarded wooden objects overlaid with rusted iron poles and heavy barred gates.

"Bess, get back," Mr. Ascham whispered. "If this fellow gets the better of me, flee into the cisterns and get out some other way. Then tell the sultan everything." He glanced at me. "And know that I cared for you deeply."

I backed farther away as instructed, as suddenly, with a great cry, Sinon lunged at Mr. Ascham.

But my teacher had been moving with a purpose I had not noticed: as Sinon lunged at him, Mr. Ascham found himself standing beside a heap on top of which sat a length of iron piping, and he quickly grabbed it and used it to parry Sinon's blow and a mighty clang rang out.

The manservant raged and advanced on my teacher with greater speed, swinging his sword with shocking violence. My teacher fended off his blows with the pipe, backing down an alleyway. Every clang rang out in the vast cistern.

At one point, they came together and Sinon—a full head and shoulders taller than my teacher—used his free hand to punch Mr. Ascham in the face most powerfully and Mr. Ascham fell into the knee-deep water with an ungainly splash and the manservant leaped forward and swung down with his sword, only for my teacher to roll sideways in the water, spraying it everywhere, and the blade struck empty waves.

Mr. Ascham moved desperately, his body now soaked through. Sinon chased him into another alley, yelling with rage, his lusty swipes missing my teacher by inches.

But then Mr. Ascham saw that he had made an error. In his desperation, he'd fled into an alleyway that finished at a dead end.

He was trapped.

Sinon now advanced slowly. He regripped his sword menacingly.

Mr. Ascham backed up against the rubbish heap behind him, but there was nowhere for him to go.

I watched from the entrance to the next cistern, helpless and horrified.

"God will decide . . ." Sinon said in a monotone as he closed in on my trapped teacher. "The Lord will guide my hands . . ."

He stood over Mr. Ascham and raised his sword for the deathblow when suddenly my teacher did something most unexpected: he kicked with all his strength, not at Sinon but at the leg of one of the broken wooden tables in the rubbish pile immediately to his left.

The table leg snapped, causing the table to dislodge from its place in the heap and jerk suddenly downward, which in turn caused a heavy iron gate lying on top of the table to slide with considerable force off the pile . . . right into Sinon's face.

The big iron gate struck him with all its weight and a sickening crack echoed throughout the cistern—the sound of the gate's leading edge breaking Sinon's nose and some of his teeth—and the tall manservant fell, his head jerking unnaturally backward.

The gate's leading edge drove his head under the surface of the water with a great splash, before the rest of the huge iron thing landed flat on top of his body.

Sinon now lay before my teacher, trapped under the bars of the heavy gate, his face a gruesome mess, his nose smashed inward, bloody and deformed. He was lying in barely two feet of water, but he was gasping for air as the water sloshed over the wreckage of his nose, the weight of the gate pinning him down. Both of his hands were trapped underwater, including his sword hand, held down by the gate.

Mr. Ascham stood over Sinon, the cruel assassin now a helpless soul trying desperately to breathe. As the water sluiced over his face, it mixed with his blood and invaded his mouth and Sinon started gagging, coughing.

My teacher did nothing.

Sinon strained to lift the gate, but it was no use. It was far too heavy. The water flowed more freely over his face.

Still my teacher did nothing.

"Help . . . me . . ." Sinon said between the waves lapping over his face.

Mr. Ascham looked down at the struggling killer. My teacher's usually kind and open face had gone hard, not with coldness or anger, but with what can only be described as a look of calm justice. He said, "To those who show no mercy, no mercy shall be shown. Brunello and his wife died in helpless fear at your hands, Sinon. It is only fair that you die in the same state of terror."

And to the end Mr. Ascham did nothing as the great weight of the iron gate pushed Sinon's face fully under the water's surface. Sinon began to kick desperately, and the water around him began to churn. A few moments later, however, he went completely still and the water did, too. In two feet of water, the assassin had drowned.

When I rejoined Mr. Ascham, I saw Sinon's face under the water's surface, broken and bloody, the eyes staring at nothing. The angel of death was himself dead and he had died in abject fear. His death had not been a pleasant thing to watch, but somehow, even at that tender age, I knew it was a just and fitting end for a cruel man.

"Come, Bess." Mr. Ascham led me to the stairs. "It is time to end this. It is time to confront Cardinal Cardoza."

INTO THE CARDINAL'S DEN

IT WAS NEARING SUNSET WHEN we emerged from the underground world. My teacher—saturated from head to toe and bearing many scrapes and scratches from his fight with Sinon—led the way, striding quickly and strongly. Zubaida had rejoined us and simply followed behind, silent and no doubt unsure what to make of it all.

We had gone but a few steps when Latif arrived in the rose garden. He paused momentarily when he saw my teacher, sopping wet, bloody and filthy, but he just said, "Mr. Roger Ascham, the cardinal is in his embassy. By all appearances, he has been waiting there for someone, someone who had not yet arrived by the time I came here to find you. However, he sent his manservant, Sinon, on an errand soon after I began my observation of the embassy."

"He sent his manservant to kill us," my teacher said as he strode right past Latif, heading for the lawn that ringed the Catholic embassy. "But it was the manservant who will meet his maker today. Bess, go and fetch the nearest guards, any you can find, and send them immediately to Cardinal Cardoza's embassy. Latif and I will go there now."

And so we separated: my teacher and his escort hastened southward while Zubaida and I hurried back into the Third Courtyard to find some guards.

We had gone perhaps thirty yards when I noticed two palace guards standing in the arcade to our left, in an alcove there, peering through a lattice window that overlooked the Church's embassy.

"Guards!" I cried in Greek. I ran over to them. "Guards! Please! A moment—"

"Let us be, child," one of them said tersely, waving me away.

"But—!"

"Begone, little girl!" he barked and I stepped away, shocked.

I looked at the guard and suddenly I stopped. I had seen this man before but I could not picture where. He had a neatly trimmed beard and a Y-shaped scar on his right cheek—

The dungeon.

He had been one of the guards in the sultan's main dungeon.

I spun where I stood, taking in the two guards in their alcove. They were observing the Catholic embassy through the lattice screen, and nervously, too. The one who had just dismissed us so rudely carried a set of empty manacles in his right hand.

Empty manacles . . .

My eyes darted farther down the arcade . . .

. . . where I beheld *another* pair of dungeon guards also keeping watch over the embassy.

Then I looked through the lattice itself and saw my teacher and Latif entering the embassy's front door.

Zubaida said, "Come, Bess, there will be more guards over by the entrance to the harem—"

But I wasn't listening.

My veins had turned to ice as I realized what I was seeing.

Empty manacles . . .

"The queen commands the loyalty of a small group of palace guards," I said aloud, recalling Elsie's words. "Including those who control the sultan's dungeon."

I spun again, to face the first two guards. "And just now the cardinal was called from the chess to his embassy, where he has been waiting, presumably for someone important enough to warrant his immediate presence . . . someone like the queen . . ."

My eyes locked again on the manacles dangling from the first guard's hands.

These two dungeon guards had conveyed someone in manacles to the cardinal's embassy . . .

A prisoner of some sort . . .

A dangerous prisoner . . .

A wave of horror flooded through me.

The queen had finally made her play against the cardinal: *she had sent her assassin.*

But my teacher, my beloved teacher, was right at that moment entering the cardinal's embassy, unaware that he was walking into her deadly trap.

"What are you doing!" Zubaida shouted, but I had already broken into a run, racing out into the Fourth Courtyard in the direction of the cardinal's embassy.

———

I can't imagine how I must have looked: a gangly girl of thirteen running at breakneck speed out across the wide green lawn that surrounded the Holy See's embassy to the sultan.

I think one or two of the watching dungeon guards gave chase, but I didn't care. I just ran for all I was worth.

The great white two-story embassy rose before me, somber and silent in the light of the setting sun; the only sign that something was amiss: its massive front door was slightly ajar.

I hurried toward it, desperate to save my teacher, heedless of the very danger I sought to rescue him from.

I dashed inside the wide ornate door and found the atrium of the embassy enveloped in shadow, all of the wooden shutters drawn. Shafts of dusty sunlight shot sideways through the gloom.

Three bodies lay on the floor before me—Mr. Ascham and Latif were nearest to me, several paces inside the atrium. They both lay facedown, slumped and unmoving. I saw a welt on the back of Mr. Ascham's neck and a slick of blood trickling from a wound to the back of Latif's bald head.

Farther from me, by one of the shuttered windows to my right, I saw the body of Cardinal Cardoza, lying faceup, also still, but I didn't care about the cardinal. I was concerned only for my beloved teacher.

I slid to the floor beside Mr. Ascham and cradled his head in my lap.

He groaned. My heart leaped. He wasn't dead—

Thud.

The big front door slammed shut behind me and the room was plunged into deeper darkness.

There came a grunt from over by the door.

I turned—

—and the concern that had drawn me to the embassy turned to outright terror as I beheld a figure standing by the now-closed door, his dirty body hunched like that of an ape, his harelip twitching, his insane eyes opened unnaturally wide.

It was the demented fiend who had terrified the peasants of Constantinople before our arrival, the same unholy soul my teacher had seen in the sultan's dungeon on the night of the banquet—only now he had been released by the queen's men, released here to carry out the queen's plot and kill Cardinal Cardoza in the foulest possible way as revenge for his blackmail and degradation of her lover, Darius.

The fiend grunted again, snorting like a pig, blocking the way out. His head was bald, his skin leathery and brown, like the skin of one who has labored too long in a tannery. And he held in his hands two blood-smeared blades: the first, a rusty scimitar like those carried by the dungeon guards, and the second, one of Latif's glistening short-bladed cutlasses.

I stood up very slowly, like someone confronting a wild animal, my eyes searching the room for some kind of escape, when suddenly a pained moan called my attention to Cardinal Cardoza's upturned body.

I hadn't been able to see his face before, but now I saw it: the skin of the cardinal's jaw had been crudely and violently torn from his face, exposing flesh, teeth and bone. A shocking amount of blood stained the shoulders of his robe. The fiend had begun his mutilation of the cardinal while he was still alive. My teacher and Latif must have interrupted him while he had been skinning the cardinal.

I held back the vomit in my throat.

Suddenly the fiend scurried forward, his knuckles propelling him across the floor.

He was circling me.

The only avenue of escape open to me was the nearby door to the embassy's little chapel.

I dashed through it and he gave chase, his footfalls thumping loudly behind me.

I rushed inside the little chapel and saw a half dozen pews on either side of a central aisle that led to a small elevated altar.

I dived over the nearest pew, flinging my body over it in one desperate leap, then rolled under the pew in front of it in a scrambling attempt to hide myself from my attacker.

Thud. The wooden pew above me rocked as he landed on it. In the distance, I heard some guards banging helplessly on the embassy's closed front door.

Moving madly, I was crawling under the next pew on my hands and knees, sliding over a kneeler, when suddenly my pursuer dropped in front of me and brought down his scimitar in a great lusty swipe, but I rolled away and it lodged in the kneeler and as he tried to extract it, I slithered under the next three pews before leaping up and over the first pew, landing in a clumsy heap before the altar—

—just as I was yanked up by the scruff of the neck and hurled onto the altar.

I landed on my back with a smack and looked up into the yellow-rimmed eyes of the insane fiend. He panted like an animal and I saw his hideous harelip surmounting a collection of deformed teeth and malnourished gums.

He had abandoned his scimitar but still had Latif's cutlass, and now, as he raised it above my throat, he began to laugh a crude idiot's guffaw.

I was done for. What could a child do to hold off one so much larger and stronger?

And then it came to me.

With all my fingers extended, I thrust my hand forward with all my might and hit his left eye square and his right in a glancing way, but it was enough to make the fiend cry out in pain and lean back, clutching at his eyes, giving me the moment I needed to roll off the altar—

—only to have him reach out and snatch my arm at the last instant. *No!*

He hauled me back onto the altar, pushing me down with one firm hand, raising his cutlass with the other. Saliva from his mouth dripped onto my face as he stared into my eyes with his hideous demented grin. Then he brought the cutlass down with shocking violence.

THE BATTLE WITH THE FIEND

I HEARD IT BEFORE I SAW IT. The sound of a speeding arrow penetrating the insane fiend's flesh was horrible: a thick, wet slap.

The arrow struck him in the right shoulder—hard—causing him to snap backward and drop his cutlass.

I looked up . . . and saw a sight that I shall remember to my dying day.

I saw my teacher—my kind teacher, my glorious teacher, my magnificent teacher—in the doorway of the chapel, at the far end of the central aisle, crouched on one knee in a perfect firing stance, Latif's bow held in his outstretched left hand, having just loosed the arrow.

"Run, Bess! *Run!*"

I needed no second urging.

With my assailant recoiling, I rolled off the altar and dashed down the carpeted aisle, running toward the crouched figure of my teacher.

A terrifying howl rang out behind me.

I glanced back to see that the fiend had yanked the arrow from his shoulder—spraying flesh and blood—and was now giving chase, bounding after me, slashing the air with his retrieved cutlass.

I ran. Ran as fast as my knock-kneed legs would carry me.

And then, in a strange way, all time slowed.

I could hear nothing but the sound of my own breathing and the pounding of my heart inside my head.

I saw everything clearly. I saw my teacher ahead of me, crouched on one knee in the doorway at the end of the aisle, trying to nock a second arrow in his bow—I even saw the leather archer's ring on his right thumb. I could also see the shadow of the fiend looming up behind me, flashing over the pews as I passed them—and in the deepest corner of my mind I knew that this could end in only one of two ways: either my teacher nocked that arrow and loosed it or the madman caught up with me and slashed his cutlass across the back of my neck and ended my short life.

"Bess! Dive!"

In my panic, my mind barely registered the order, but somehow I obeyed.

I threw myself forward, onto the carpet of the aisle, just in time to glimpse my teacher whip up his bow—arrow perfectly nocked—and, with the most intense expression on his face, release the arrow.

This arrow flew down the length of the aisle and struck the fiend directly between the eyes, right through the bridge of his nose, the iron-tipped arrow driving deep into the man's head, stopping him in mid-stride, causing him to snap upright, his yellow eyes wide with shock, his right fist still dumbly gripping the cutlass, before he collapsed to the floor.

I lay on the aisle a bare yard from him, not daring to move lest he wasn't dead.

But then my teacher appeared above me and loosed a final arrow into the fiend's head from a range of one foot, and I knew the animal was dead.

Then I was in my teacher's arms, crying deep, heaving sobs into his shoulder, saying, "Thank you, Mr. Ascham! Thank you! Thank you!"

He held me out from him and looked into my eyes. "What are you thanking me for? If you hadn't come here, I would have become another victim of this madman, dead, flayed and mutilated. But because of you, he didn't get the chance and I awoke to see him chasing you into this chapel. Bess, don't thank me. You came here, heedless of any danger to yourself, to save me. Honestly, God help the world if you ever become queen of England!"

I didn't care.

I just hugged him tightly and cried my eyes out, honestly believing that I would never let him go.

———

Of course, shortly after, we let the dungeon guards in and they secured the embassy. Latif awoke with a painful headache, and after a long while, the sultan himself appeared, accompanied by the *sadrazam* and his personal guards.

The sultan gazed without emotion at the grisly scene: Cardinal Cardoza's barely alive body lying in a pool of blood; the dead fiend sprawled in the central aisle of the adjoining chapel, two arrows protruding from his skull at awkward angles; and the wounded Latif, sitting on the floor rubbing his head.

"Mr. Roger Ascham," the sultan said at last. "Am I to assume that your investigation is concluded?"

My teacher stood before the sultan, bloodied and cut, his clothes sodden, his hair wet. Yet he returned the sultan's gaze with perfect English dignity. "It is, Your Majesty."

"Enlighten me. Please."

"You may wish to have your men leave the room," my teacher said.

With a nod from their ruler, the guards left us. The *sadrazam* stayed.

"Him, too," Mr. Ascham said.

The sultan paused, no doubt unused to being ordered to do anything, but he nodded again and the *sadrazam* also departed, so that only Mr. Ascham, the sultan and I remained in the atrium.

"There have been six murders and one attempted murder—that of Cardinal Cardoza here—within your palace walls, but there have been four different killers," Mr. Ascham said. "The visiting Cardinal Farnese was killed by mistake. He was poisoned by the chef's elder son, Pietro. But the poison had been intended for Cardinal Cardoza, a sodomite who had taken to molesting Pietro's feeble-minded little brother, Benicio, when he delivered the cardinal his supper."

"Benicio? That was the boy who took his own life a few weeks ago?" the sultan asked.

"Yes. Pietro blamed his brother's suicide on Cardinal Cardoza and sought to poison him. Upon discovering that his poison had killed the wrong man, however, Pietro skinned Cardinal Farnese's body in the manner of the insane murderer in an attempt to lead any investigators astray. But he did not know that you, Your Majesty, had already captured the fiend. If you hadn't, we all may have been none the wiser and his plan would probably have succeeded.

"The second and third murders, those of the chef Brunello and his wife, were carried out by Cardinal Cardoza's manservant, Sinon, on the cardinal's orders. The cardinal, having surmised correctly that the poison that had killed Cardinal Farnese had actually been intended for him, assumed *incorrectly* that it had been the chef Brunello who had tried to poison him. I suspect the cardinal believed that Brunello had discovered his violation of the younger boy, the same boy the cardinal himself had denied holy burial. Angered that Brunello had tried to poison him, Cardinal Cardoza sent Sinon to kill Brunello and his wife out of retribution. His manservant, however, left his footprint—a most distinctive footprint—at the scene of Brunello and his wife's murders."

"And he made it look as if they had hanged themselves?" the sultan said.

"Yes. But Sinon bound their hands too tightly when he hanged them, leaving marks on their wrists that I was able to see. Fearing that I was on a path that would lead to his exposure, the cardinal then sought to eliminate me—so he sent me an anonymous note, inviting me to your menagerie late last night. It was a trap which Bess and I only just managed to survive, but it was there, again, that we saw the footprint of his manservant, Sinon. Then we come to the deaths of Maximilian of Vienna and the young Austrian virgin, and also the death of Darius."

The sultan said nothing. He did not blink as he waited for Mr. Ascham to continue.

"As you intimated to me, *you* had Maximilian and the girl killed, because Maximilian was a spy for your great European rival, Archduke Ferdinand of Austria. Maximilian's conversations with Brunello had nothing to do with any of the other murders; he was merely doing the work of a spy: assessing your moods and opinions as expressed to visiting dignitaries so as to report them back to his master in Vienna. I imagine it was Maximilian's *other* communications, about the size and strength of your fleet, that required he be killed."

The sultan's face gave away nothing. "And Darius?"

"At one stage, I thought that Cardinal Cardoza had had Darius killed," my teacher said. "For the same reason that he killed the chef Brunello: the cardinal knew of Darius's affair with the queen and had been using that knowledge to extract favors from the wrestler. Thinking, however, that perhaps he had been mistaken in killing the chef and that it had actually been *Darius* who had poisoned his meal, Cardinal Cardoza had the wrestler drowned."

"How appalling . . ." the sultan said.

"As I say, that *was* what I thought. But I don't think that way anymore because that is not what happened. You had Darius killed."

Again, the sultan said nothing. Silence hovered.

I dared not even breathe. I couldn't believe my teacher was speaking so bluntly right to the sultan's face. Perhaps after all we had been through, he was beyond caring for royal flatteries.

Mr. Ascham went on. "Until the other night, you did not know of Darius's affair with your wife, the queen. But you discovered it from the men you had stationed within the walls or ceiling of my quarters. For the day *after* Bess here informed me of Darius's liaison with your wife, the wrestler went missing. We found him today, weighted down in a cistern and drowned, a method I am told you use."

The sultan blinked once and slowly, but said nothing.

"And so we come to the final attempted murder," Mr. Ascham said, "the one here before us, that of Cardinal Cardoza himself, the cause of this chain of human destruction. This attempted killing was performed at the order of our fourth would-be murderer: your wife, Queen Rox-elana. It was purely an act of vengeance. For it was only yesterday, when I spoke with her, that your wife discovered Cardinal Cardoza was ex-tracting carnal favors from her lover in exchange for keeping her affair with Darius a secret from you.

"As I am sure you know, the queen commands the loyalty of a select group of guards, notably those in your dungeons. At her orders, they called the cardinal from the chess match, asking him to return to his embassy, presumably to meet with the queen, but they had released the insane fiend into the embassy. And here the cardinal met with the fiend and the sharp end of his blade. All the while, the queen's dungeon guards formed a circle around the embassy. They intended to catch the fiend afterward and re-imprison him after the cardinal had been flayed and killed. Then they could make up any story they wanted about his escaping for a short while."

Still the sultan said nothing.

"The boy Pietro still lives and I know his whereabouts," Mr. Ascham said. "However, it is my advice to you not to go in search of him. He alone acted nobly in all this, attempting to avenge his brother. Yes, he killed Cardinal Farnese, but the visiting cardinal also indulged in the abuse of boys, so his passing will not be mourned by right-minded folk. Besides, the boy is now burdened with the terrible knowledge that his reckless act brought about the deaths of his parents."

"What of the cardinal's manservant?" the sultan asked. "The one who killed the chef and his wife at the cardinal's command? Where is he?"

"He is dead. I killed him," Mr. Ascham said evenly. "His body is in a cistern underneath your palace."

The sultan raised an eyebrow, genuinely surprised. "*You* killed him? The humble schoolmaster from Cambridge? You may be more formidable than I gave you credit for. So there were *seven* murders, then?"

"It was not murder. He must have seen Elizabeth and me enter the cisterns and he waited at the entrance to kill us. I killed him in defense of myself and the young princess."

"I see."

The sultan fell silent for a time, deep in thought.

Then he spoke in a very icy tone. "You are a clever man, Mr. Roger Ascham. And a bold one, too, to level an accusation of murder against a sultan."

Now it was my teacher who said nothing.

He waited for the sultan to continue.

The sultan said, "For your information, sultans do not commit murder. Sultans do whatever they desire. If someone's continued existence causes me unhappiness then it is my prerogative to end that person's life. I am beholden to no one but Allah himself."

"You asked me to investigate a murder and I did," my teacher replied firmly. "The answers are the answers, however unpleasant they may be. I am merely the one who brought them to light."

"This is true. This is true," the sultan said.

But Mr. Ascham was not finished. "I also know a few other things, Your Majesty, about your tournament."

I froze. What in God's name was my teacher doing?

The sultan tilted his head calmly. "Oh, yes?"

"You doctored the draw. You sent one of your men to poison my player, Mr. Giles, on the way here and I suspect you sent someone to poison the Wallachian player, Dragan, too. You threatened players so that they would deliberately lose matches and you have a team of men giving assistance to your cousin Zaman to help him win. The world may not see it, Your Majesty, but I know that your tournament is a dirty ruse and a disgrace."

I almost fainted at my teacher's shocking words. This was impudence of the highest order. No one spoke like that to a king. No one, that is, except Roger Ascham.

The sultan stared at the floor in silence, digesting the accusations that had just been leveled at him. A thin smile appeared on his lips.

"Mr. Ascham," he said softly and menacingly. "Observe the cardinal over there." The sultan cocked his chin at the body of the still alive but mutilated Cardoza. The cardinal wheezed, a blood bubble forming over his fleshy mouth. "For causing all this trouble, the cardinal here will spend the rest of his days in my dungeons. Those days will be spent in excruciating pain as he is tortured every morning and every night. As for you, Roger Ascham"—the sultan leveled his gaze at my teacher—"not only do you know far too much about the intrigues within my palace and the workings of my tournament, you dare to insult a king. I have had men's tongues cut out for less than that. Your rudeness pains me more than the acts of the cardinal do, and look at the punishment that awaits *him*. What, pray then, do I do with you?"

My eyes widened. I did not like where this was going.

My teacher, however, simply stood his ground.

"But . . ." The sultan paused. "Through your investigations and at some danger to yourself, you have brought to light matters I would otherwise never have known about, and for that, I *do* owe you a debt. Consider that debt repaid, Mr. Ascham, by my sparing your life now."

The sultan abruptly turned on his heel and headed for the door. He did not look back as he spoke. "You will tell no one of this investigation or the secrets of my tournament. I suggest to you that it is in your interest to leave Constantinople by noon tomorrow, for by that time I may have decided that your continued existence causes me unhappiness. It has been a pleasure meeting you, Mr. Roger Ascham, and you, too, Princess Elizabeth. I thank you for your efforts. Peace be upon you."

And with those words, he was gone.

THE LAST NIGHT
IN CONSTANTINOPLE

IT WAS EARLY EVENING WHEN WE LEFT the cardinal's embassy, shaken, wet, bloodied and bruised.

"Mr. Ascham," I said as we crossed the lawn, "what madness prompted you to upbraid the sultan about his tournament? One does not scold kings like that. You could have got yourself killed."

My teacher seemed to ponder this for a moment. "Why did I do it? Because no matter how this tournament ends—and I imagine it will probably end with the result the sultan desires—in my humble opinion the sultan needed to be made aware that *someone* knew of his cheating. I suppose, more than anything, he offended my British sense of fairness."

"Your British sense of fairness?" I said, astonished.

"Bess, I have always felt that there is something very special about Britain and the men and women who inhabit it. We stand shoulder to shoulder in battle, we gird ourselves against the coldest winds and rain, and we only ask—we *only* ask—that any fight be fair."

I just shook my head and smiled.

———

Apparently, the match between Zaman and Brother Raul was still going, having entered a seventh and final game. Since the sun had set, it was reputedly being finished under the glow of a thousand candles.

After the terror of the confrontation with the fiend and our rather chilling conversation with the sultan, neither Mr. Ascham nor I felt like returning to watch the chess match.

"We already know who will win," my teacher said as we headed back to our quarters. "Zaman will emerge victorious."

And, of course, Zaman did emerge victorious, in almost exactly the same way as he had done against the Muscovite: after losing two early games, he miraculously figured out Brother Raul's attacking patterns and started to counter them almost before Brother Raul enacted them. Zaman soon led by three games to two.

Raul, however, was a strong and canny player and he adapted his tactics and managed to tie the match at three games apiece. But in that final, tense, candlelit game, Zaman would triumph, ultimately beating the Church's man four games to three. At the end of it, Brother Raul slumped against the table, completely exhausted. He later said it felt like he had been playing five men instead of one.

And so Zaman progressed to the final round, to the utter delight of the crowd. As far as they knew, the two local champions had conquered the best players in the world to make the final.

And as the people of Constantinople left the Hagia Sophia that evening, they murmured excitedly about the deciding match to be played the following day. They praised their god and their sultan, and all was right with their world.

———

But as evening became night and the moon and the stars rose over that ancient city, all was not right in my world.

For while my teacher had solved his riddle and we packed our trunks in anticipation of departing from Constantinople the next morning, one thing was amiss.

Elsie had not returned from her lunch with the crown prince.

Elsie had disappeared.

—VI—

KING

The object of chess is to checkmate the king. But curiously, while the king is the crux of the game, he is the most impotent piece on the board. Even pawns can become queens and every other piece can move more than one square.

And so the king in chess is like a king in life: his continued reign depends upon his keeping his castles intact and his subjects onside. He is hostage to his people's continued happiness.

But a warning: ignore the king at your peril. He can most certainly still take other pieces and in a tense endgame, he is to be watched carefully, for when threatened he is prone to attack.

From: *Chess in the Middle Ages,*
Tel Jackson (W. M. Lawry & Co., London, 1992)

I know I have the body of a weak and feeble woman,
but I have the heart and stomach of a king,
and of a king of England, too.

—QUEEN ELIZABETH I

THE LAST DAY

DAWN WOKE ME ON MY LAST DAY in Constantinople and no sooner were my eyes open than they darted to Elsie's bed, expecting to see her lying there, having returned from another long night of debauchery.

But her bed lay empty, untouched.

I found Mr. Ascham and Mr. Giles in their rooms, closing their trunks.

"Elsie is missing," I said.

"Missing?" my teacher said.

"I have not seen her since lunch yesterday, when she went off to dine with the crown prince and his friends in the city."

"Ah, yes, the crown prince . . ." Mr. Ascham said. "This is where she has been sneaking off to in the evenings. To *gatherings* hosted by Crown Prince Selim."

"Yes. But she has always been back by morning."

My teacher swapped a glance with Mr. Giles.

Mr. Giles said, "The crown prince is a notorious carouser."

"But why would she not return?" Mr. Ascham said.

"Perhaps he has asked Elsie to marry him," I suggested helpfully. "It is what she wanted more than anything else. Elsie told me they, well, consummated their relationship just the other night, so maybe he asked her to marry him and she went back to the harem to see her future home."

Mr. Ascham's face darkened.

"Wait a moment, Bess. Are you saying that Elsie had relations with the crown prince himself?"

My face reddened. "Well . . ."

"Please, tell me. It might be important."

"She did. She tried for several nights to attract his attention and on the final occasion, she ensnared him. Elsie thought pleasuring him might be a good way to impress him and thus become his queen—"

"*When* did she bed him?" my teacher asked with an exactness that surprised me.

"When?"

"Yes, *when*? Three nights ago? Two? When?"

I thought for a moment. "It was the night before last. The evening before he invited her to lunch with him in the city. She had flirted with him greatly before then, but it was only on that night that they actually consummated their desire."

"Did she dine with him in the city on any other occasion? Lunch, dinner?"

"No. This was the first time."

"So the day after he plucks her, he invites her to the city, and then she disappears. Oh, my God . . ." my teacher said. "Foolish, foolish girl."

He started moving quickly. He threw some final objects into his trunk and slammed the lid. "Bess, get your things. It's time for us to leave this accursed city."

"What about Elsie?"

"I have an idea where she has gone and we shall try to grab her on our way out, if that is indeed possible."

"If it is *possible*?" I said, shocked. "Why? What do you think has become of her? Where do you think she is?"

"She has most certainly not become a queen, of that I am certain," Mr. Ascham said. "If she is where I think she is, she is in a whole new world of horror."

———

When the three of us were ready to depart, we moved toward the outer door of our lodgings.

It was only then that Mr. Giles noticed that sometime during the night, someone had slipped an envelope under the door.

It was a scarlet envelope, just like the one we had brought with us to the tournament.

"It's addressed to Bess," Mr. Giles said, surprised.

He handed it to me. I turned it over in my hands.

It was indeed addressed to me: "For Princess Elizabeth Tudor." It was also sealed with fine red wax that was imprinted with the circular seal of the sultan himself.

"You can read it later, Bess," Mr. Ascham said. "It is time for us to leave."

————

And so we departed from our lodgings at Topkapi Palace, not in a blaze of pomp and ceremony, but in quiet, almost shameful, anonymity.

On our way out we stopped by the eunuchs' quarters, where we found Latif with his bald head heavily bandaged. Mr. Ascham wanted to return his ornate bow to him, but the eunuch would have none of it.

"Please, keep it." Latif handed Mr. Ascham the matching quiver. "I owe my life to you and your bright young student here." He nodded at me. "Keep my bow and its arrows as a gift from me and a reminder of your time here."

"Thank you," my teacher said.

"Oh, and, sir," Latif said as we made to leave. "The sultan's guards went down into the cisterns this morning in search of the boy. The other children were long gone, but the guards found Pietro's body. He had weighed down his pockets with heavy stones and drowned himself."

A great sadness came over me. Poor Pietro.

"You guessed he would do this . . ." I said to my teacher.

"He couldn't have known the trail of destruction he would set in motion," Mr. Ascham said. He took my hand and we left the eunuchs' quarters.

At the palace gates, Mr. Ascham, Mr. Giles and I put our trunks on the back of a wagon pulled by a donkey and left the palace for good, farewelled by no one, not by our host the sultan, his son the crown prince, or even by our friend Michelangelo.

We were leaving in stealth.

My teacher looked about us cautiously as we made our way down the wide boulevard that led away from the palace and past the mighty Hagia Sophia, as if searching for assassins behind every corner.

"We will meet the Ponsonbys and our English escorts at the Golden Gate," he said, "and only then will I feel something akin to safety."

We passed the Hagia Sophia. A colossal throng of spectators, larger than any we had seen previously, spilled out from every door of the massive cathedral, all of them trying to get in to see the all-Moslem final between Zaman and Ibrahim.

Not one of them noticed us passing by.

I was still very alarmed that we were leaving the palace without Elsie.

"She's not in the palace," Mr. Ascham said as he strode through the streets. "And if she's not where I think she is, then we have no hope of finding her in this sprawling city."

A few corners later, he turned suddenly and led us down a wide street. To my surprise, it was a street I had seen before.

It was the boulevard containing the establishment of Afridi, the gaudily dressed whoremonger, the one who had argued with Cardinal Cardoza about stealing his business; the one who owned several whore-houses in Constantinople of which this was the largest.

We stopped in front of the brothel with its Roman-era lower half and newer upper half.

"Here?" I asked. "What makes you think Elsie is here?"

"Just stay close to me," my teacher said. "Giles, do you have your sword?"

Mr. Giles revealed his sword beneath his cloak, and it was only then that I saw that Mr. Ascham carried Latif's bow underneath his oilskin coat with an arrow already nocked.

We were going into that place armed.

———

An oily bearded Arab greeted us at the street-side door. "Good sirs, hello! How are you? How may I help you? We have many girls available right now, as most of the city is out watching the chess match—"

Mr. Ascham just brushed past him, marched inside.

He strode across the main chamber of the brothel, heading straight for the room with the gold-painted door.

"Hey! Wait there!" the bearded Arab wailed, but my teacher arrived at the room and threw open its glittering door.

"Oh, Lord . . ." he said as I caught up with him. "Wait, Bess! No! Don't look . . ."

But it was too late. I had already caught a glimpse—a fleeting glimpse—of what lay beyond the golden doorway, and even though I saw it for only the briefest of moments, it was an image that would stay with me for the rest of my life.

What I saw sickened me.

Through the half-opened doorway I glimpsed Elsie: sweet Elsie; a silly girl, yes, reckless, too, but she didn't deserve this.

She lay spread-eagled on the gigantic bed in the center of the elaborately decorated bedchamber, on her back, her hands tied to the headboard, her feet tied to the foot posts but spread wide so that a customer could easily enter her. Her inner thighs were red raw.

She looked like a battered sexual plaything, a toy for the beastly men of Constantinople to occupy however roughly they liked.

The sign above her read:

شهزاده نك كنديسينك ده قوللاندغى كيبى

And suddenly I understood its awful meaning. Of course, my teacher had deciphered the foul phrase long before I had, which was why he had brought us here.

It was like the royal endorsements displayed by the silk sellers in the Grand Bazaar: "As used by the sultan!"

Only this was a more sinister endorsement.

Having grown a little more accustomed to the local script in recent days, I was able to translate the sign above Elsie's bed:

AS USED BY THE CROWN PRINCE!

My teacher hurried inside the bedchamber, closing the door behind him, mercifully cutting off my view. He emerged moments later carrying Elsie in his arms. She gazed at him in a daze. She was alive but she did not have her wits about her; she appeared drunk or drugged.

"Who would do this?" I asked as he marched past me.

"The crown prince," my teacher said. "The callous crown prince. I imagine he finds this humorous, bedding and then discarding a foreign beauty. Perhaps he and Afridi are friends; perhaps they have an arrangement. No sooner does he pluck Elsie than he hands her to the whoremonger who sells her at a premium price to other men because of the prince's endorsement. I wouldn't be surprised if the prince takes a cut from Afridi."

It was as if the mention of his name had summoned him forth: as we strode away from the golden bedchamber, we were confronted by Afridi, dressed in a shiny gold suit today and flanked by two very large bodyguards bearing scimitars. The three of them blocked the exit.

"Just where do you think you are going with my prize girl?" Afridi asked in a low voice.

"She is not yours to sell," Mr. Ascham retorted. "She is a subject of the King of England."

"We are not in England. The crown prince himself gave this girl to me. She is mine. And she turned over a tidy sum last night. The crown prince's recommendation is very lucrative in my trade. She was my most popular girl. Selim was right: English roses make for fine fucks."

"You will let us pass," my teacher said evenly.

"No."

My teacher handed Elsie to me. She slumped over my shoulder, barely able to stand.

"You will let us pass . . . now," my teacher said, extracting the bow from his cloak. Beside him, Mr. Giles drew his sword.

Mr. Ascham drew his arrow back and aimed it squarely at Afridi's head. "I am a fine shot and you will be dead before your thugs can even take a step toward us."

Afridi smiled quickly, stepping aside, raising his hands. "Of course, on the other hand, I might be open to some bargaining."

"No bargains," my teacher said as we moved slowly and cautiously around the whoremonger and his thugs. The whole time he kept his arrow trained on Afridi's nose, while Giles eyed the two thugs.

We stepped through the arched doorway and onto the street outside that awful establishment, emerging into welcome sunshine.

Afridi watched us from the door. "Leave this city quickly, Englishman. For I shall have my people on your tail within the hour."

My teacher paused, as if suddenly struck by a thought.

He jerked his chin at the whoremonger. "I am taking this girl whether you like it or not. But in exchange for you *not* sending anyone after us, I will offer you some information."

"What kind of information?" Afridi asked coolly.

"I imagine that the whoremongers and the gamblers are quite close in this town," my teacher said. "You have associates who take wagers? Perhaps on the chess match being played today?"

"I do, yes," Afridi said warily. "I myself have taken many bets."

"Who do most of the gamblers bet on?"

"The people *like* Ibrahim but they bet on Zaman. If Zaman wins, I will lose a substantial sum."

"Zaman will win," my teacher said. "Of that there is no doubt. The information I offer you is this: during the match, find a way to observe the sultan's private worshipping balcony inside the Hagia Sophia. There you will see Zaman's advantage."

Afridi's eyes narrowed.

He was a creature of the street and he seemed to realize that the information being offered him now was worthy of his attention.

"Go, Englishman. I may well investigate what you say, and if I find that you have lied to me, I will make sure that you are hunted down like a dog."

"I accept those terms," my teacher said, and with those words, we left.

———

By the time we arrived at the outer walls of the city an hour later, the rumors had already overtaken us, for while we had traveled on foot, they had traveled by voice from balcony to balcony, rooftop to rooftop.

There was great unrest at the Hagia Sophia.

Zaman had taken an early lead in his match against Ibrahim, but then—so the rumors said—the well-known whoremonger, Afridi, had arrived at the Great Hall and spotted Zaman receiving signals from a group of five men up in the sultan's private worshipping balcony. Afridi raised an indignant shout, pointing them out, and accused Zaman of cheating. The crowd started hissing and booing.

The *sadrazam* called for calm, but the crowd, angered that the sultan's man was cheating against their champion, rose up in anger and demanded that the men on the private balcony be brought down to the floor of the hall.

The sultan seemed taken aback. He did not know what to say. The crowd started throwing food and then shoes at Zaman. Some started yelling at the royal stage, calling for justice. The few royal guards in front of the sultan's stage drew their weapons and commanded the surging, angry crowd to stay back.

But it was too late. The mob was unleashed.

The furious crowd rushed the playing stage.

A melee ensued and the crowd invaded the stage, overcoming the four guards on it before grabbing Zaman and hurling him off the platform into the roiling mass of people. Punches were thrown and Zaman fell to the ground where he was trampled to death in the stampede. The chessboard was flung into the air, the priceless gold and silver pieces scattering among the crowd, and there was an ungodly rush as people scrambled to grab them.

Then another enraged group of spectators overturned the huge sign showing the draw for the tournament, while Afridi shouted, "It's a sham! The whole thing is a sham!" and with that the entire crowd began to riot.

The playing stage was upturned and smashed to splinters by the crowd. Fires were lit. The people rampaged.

Seeing the chaos, the sultan fled, dashing off his royal stage, heading for the safety of the palace. The last rumor had his palace guards storming the Hagia Sophia with swords and shields, trying to disperse the crowd and restore order.

Thus the Moslem sultan's invitational chess championship of 1546 ended: in ignominy, with allegations of subterfuge and favoritism, without a winner being declared. History would never know of it.

————

We rejoined Mr. and Mrs. Ponsonby and our English guards at the village outside the Golden Gate and immediately commenced the long journey home.

Mrs. Ponsonby had not wholly recovered from her poisoning, but she was looking much better. Upon seeing us, she was well enough to opine, "I do hope you protected the princess's morals while you were in that city, Mr. Ascham."

"I did my level best, madam," my teacher replied, and I think, like me, he was glad to see Mrs. Ponsonby behaving like her old self again.

Elsie lay curled in a tight ball in the back of one of our wagons, wrapped in a blanket, saying nothing. She would never be the same. Her coltish spirit had been broken, her reckless taste for the pleasures of the flesh destroyed. I don't know if she ever lay with a man again.

As I sat with her in that wagon, with her head in my lap, stroking her hair, I pulled out the scarlet envelope that had been pushed under our door during the previous night.

I cracked the sultan's wax seal and found a letter inside, written in English in the sultan's own hand:

Dear Elizabeth,

It was my great pleasure to meet you.

There is something I wish to tell you as you leave my lands. By now you will have heard that every delegation that came to my tournament had to bring me a chest of gold or face invasion.

Of all the delegations to send a player, only one did not send a chest. Yours.

Instead of a chest of gold, I received a note from your father, King Henry. In that note, he wrote: "Good sir, I do not pay blood money to anyone. There are kings in this world and there are kings of England. I am a king of England. If you wish to invade my lands, put on your armor and try your best.

"Henry VIII Rex"

I bid you good fortune, young Elizabeth, but I don't think you will need it. With your clever teacher at your side and your father showing you how a true king should act, I imagine that, if God wills it, you will become a most formidable queen.

Suleiman,
Caliph and Sultan of the Ottoman Lands

With a sad smile, I folded the letter, placed it in my luggage and settled in for the journey.

All the way home, my teacher, the great Roger Ascham, rode out in front on his mare with an arrow nocked in his bow.

EPILOGUE
1603

MY QUEEN FINISHED SPEAKING.

She would be dead a few weeks later.

But now I knew: knew of her secret journey to that faraway land, of the tournament held there, of why Elsie had come home a shadow of her former self, and how my friend Bessie had come home hardened, made of sterner stuff.

She was also different in other ways.

From the moment she returned, she treated me with greater kindness, constantly telling me what a valued friend I was, even when I did not feel I deserved such praise. Her kind words would continue for the rest of our lives, even after she became queen.

I had often wondered what had caused this profound change in my friend and now I knew. Sometimes we must go away to discover things about ourselves. Sometimes we go away with the wrong people. Sometimes we go away with the right teachers.

As Queen of England, she would look after Roger Ascham to the end of his days, granting him property and even a canonry, despite the fact that he was not a minister of religion. And she called on him for advice. I know of at least two occasions when she did so—I was even present when in 1559 she called him at short notice to St. Michael's Mount to settle a most grim and frightening matter, but that is another tale for another day.

I also recalled a time, much later in her life, when she dispatched a delegation of ambassadors to Constantinople to meet with the Sultan

Suleiman. She had done it quite suddenly and for no apparent reason. At the time, no one at court knew why.

But when her men returned, I overheard one of them report to her: "The sultan is a spent force, ma'am, broken and bitter. He is solitary and distrustful, even to members of his own family, and has become prone to long melancholy moods. The city, too, has fallen into disrepair."

Elizabeth asked about the palace and the Catholic embassy there. "It no longer exists. The sultan ordered the Church's embassy to be razed to the ground. Shortly after that, he expelled all representatives of the Holy See from his lands."

"So would I be correct in the opinion that Suleiman is no longer a threat to Europe?" my queen asked.

"He is not, ma'am."

The day after that conversation, I noticed a new ornament on the desk in her private study: a golden chess piece, inlaid with rubies and emeralds.

It was a pawn.

I now believe that Elizabeth sent that delegation to Constantinople not only to see what had become of the sultan and his empire but also to trawl its stalls and bazaars for any piece of the chess set that had been scattered during the riot.

For the rest of her life, that golden pawn carved by Michelangelo himself sat on her desk, a physical reminder of one of the great formative experiences of her life, an event that no one knew of till now: her secret journey to the lands of the Ottomans in the year 1546 to witness a great tournament that has forever been lost to history.

POSTSCRIPT

———

MANY OF THE CHARACTERS in this novel actually lived in 1546. Their fates were as follows:

SULEIMAN THE MAGNIFICENT would rule over the Ottoman Empire for the next twenty years. His reign would mark the high point of Islamic civilization. The Ottoman Empire would remain in steady decline for the next four hundred years until it was dismantled after the First World War.

In 1566, he would be succeeded as sultan by his son, **SELIM**, who was renowned for his decadent lifestyle and his indifference to matters of state. He became known as Selim the Drunkard. Later in his life, Selim's armies would face off against his northern neighbors, the Rus people. Under Ivan IV, the Russians completely outwitted and outmaneuvered Selim's army, forcing him into a humiliating treaty in 1570.

IVAN IV, at the age of seventeen, would crown himself the first "tsar" of Russia. Known to history as *Ivan Grozny* (variously translated as "Ivan the Terrible," "the Formidable" or "the Awesome"), he transformed Russia into a formidable nation-state. He would build many great monuments including the famous St. Basil's in Moscow and he would correspond with Queen Elizabeth I for a period of fifteen years (he even proposed marriage to her, but she declined). Ivan would ultimately be remembered for the cruelty of his later reign, during which time he organized the torture of some fifteen thousand people, variously boiling, impaling and beheading them. He died in 1584 having turned Russia into a virtual police state. And he died, apparently, while playing chess.

IGNATIUS OF LOYOLA founded the religious order known as the Society of Jesus, or the Jesuits. His Catholic missionaries would indeed do battle with Queen Elizabeth I for the hearts and souls of England's Christian population, with many of them being hanged, drawn and quartered at Tyburn during her reign. Ignatius died in 1556. There is a statue of him in St. Peter's Basilica.

In addition to his many other famous works, **MICHELANGELO** completed the magnificent dome of St. Peter's Basilica, having accepted the commission from Pope Paul III with some reluctance. He died in 1564.

The quote from **MARTIN LUTHER** about girls being "weeds" is real.

ELIZABETH I was Queen of England from 1558 to 1603. Known as "the Virgin Queen" or "Good Queen Bess," she is widely regarded as England's most successful monarch. She became queen at the age of twenty-five after her younger half brother, Edward, died of tuberculosis (in 1553) and her half sister, Mary, also died (in 1558). At one point during Mary's reign, Elizabeth was imprisoned for two months in the dreaded Tower of London.

She would rule over what has been described as a golden age of English life, one that saw the works of Shakespeare written and performed, the defeat of the Spanish armada, the establishment of diplomatic relations with the Ottoman Empire, and the exploration and exploitation of the American colonies. During her reign, Elizabeth employed and made great use of the brilliant master of spies Sir Francis Walsingham. She also opened up the animal collection in the Bulwark of the Tower of London to public view. Famously, she never married.

ROGER ASCHAM is regarded as one of history's finest teachers. He was an expert in Latin and Greek and a believer in "gentle" schooling techniques (his book *The Schoolmaster* was one of the first major works on teaching). From 1544, his protégé, William Grindal, was Elizabeth's primary tutor, although Ascham did actively participate in her education. When Grindal died in 1548, Ascham took over her teaching full-time. He was a lifelong advocate of the bow and argued that every Englishman should be proficient in its use. He died in 1568.

SELECTED SOURCES

WHILE RESEARCHING THIS NOVEL, I discovered several fine books on the topics of both chess and Queen Elizabeth's life that deserve special mention.

First, *The Immortal Game* by David Shenk (Random House, New York, 2006) is a marvelous history of chess throughout the centuries and is a most enjoyable read to boot.

As for Elizabeth, her early life is only loosely recorded. As Elizabeth was a child who was always at least one step removed from the line of succession and who was disinherited at an early age, historians of the time may have decided she was not worth following—until she was suddenly restored to the line of succession and became a legitimate player again. Her childhood is thus not as closely documented as her famed later rule, but some excellent works which do address her childhood are:

Elizabeth by David Starkey (Random House, London, 2000) is very comprehensive in its coverage of Elizabeth's childhood and early learning under William Grindal and Roger Ascham.

Elizabeth & Mary by Jane Dunn (HarperCollins, London, 2003) follows the parallel lives of Elizabeth and her rival, Mary Queen of Scots. I am indebted to both of these books.

For insights into everyday life in sixteenth-century England, *Elizabeth's London* by Liza Picard (Weidenfeld & Nicolson, London, 2003) was invaluable. It was this book that introduced me to the term "occupy" as a synonym for sexual intercourse. Needless to say, if you have gotten this far, you will have seen that I use several more terms to describe it in the novel.

I am also a huge fan of Robert Lacey's *Great Tales from English History* (volumes I–III; Little, Brown; London, 2003, 2004, 2006). It is a marvelous summation of myths, incidents and memorable moments over the last thousand years of English history. Elizabeth I and Henry VIII feature prominently and I owe the wonderful term "sportsman-king" as a description of Henry VIII to Lacey.

When it comes to Islam, I would direct the interested reader to *Nine Parts of Desire* by Geraldine Brooks. It was in this book that I discovered the notion that the modern veiling of Muslim women comes from ordinary Muslims imitating Muhammad's veiled wives.

I first learned about the Didache of A.D. 60 and those other historical instances of the Catholic Church's problem with pedophile priests in an episode of the excellent TV show, *Hungry Beast*, which aired on the Australian ABC network. This was a great show that, alas, is no longer around. I did my own further research to verify what I saw in that episode.

Finally, regarding chess and life, I would thoroughly recommend Joshua Waitzkin's *The Art of Learning*. Waitzkin was a chess prodigy as a child and the subject of the book (and film) *Searching for Bobby Fischer*. It was from his wonderful book, however, that I learned of the Tai Chi notion: "If aggression meets empty space it tends to defeat itself." (I also read about some of the distracting tactics employed by less scrupulous players in competitive chess!) It's a truly great book.

After all that, any errors in this novel are mine and mine alone. I have made every effort to ensure that all historical references, including the locations, the vocabularies used by the various characters, their dress and their weapons are accurate. I might have added a few languages to Elizabeth's and the sultan's abilities, but this is, ultimately, a story, and I felt it helped the tale along.

M.R.

ABOUT THE AUTHOR

———

MATTHEW REILLY is the *New York Times* and #1 international best-selling author of numerous novels, including *The Great Zoo of China*, *The Five Greatest Warriors*, *The Six Sacred Stones*, *Seven Deadly Wonders*, *Ice Station*, *Temple*, *Contest*, *Area 7*, *Scarecrow*, the children's book *Hover Car Racer*, and the novella, *Hell Island*. His books are published in more than twenty languages, in twenty countries, and he has sold over 7 million copies worldwide.

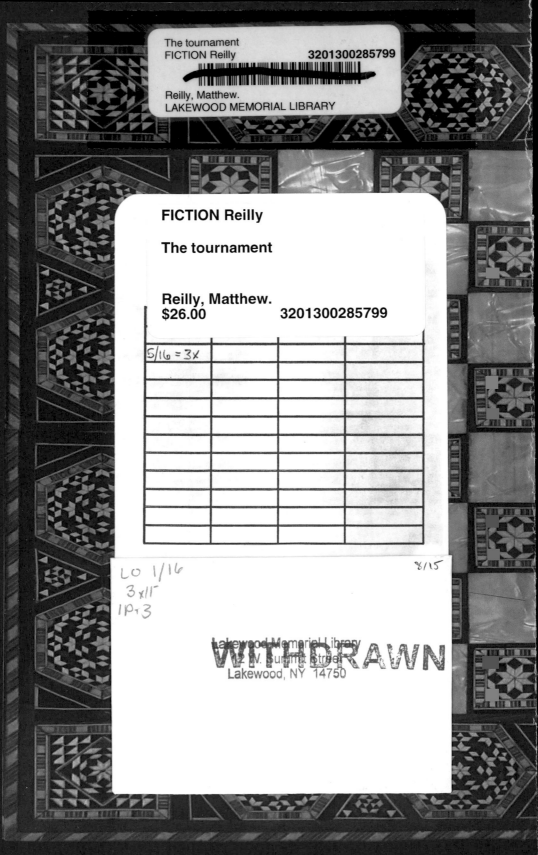

The tournament
FICTION Reilly   3201300285799

Reilly, Matthew.
LAKEWOOD MEMORIAL LIBRARY

FICTION Reilly

The tournament

Reilly, Matthew.
$26.00   3201300285799

5/16 = 3x			

LO 1/16   8/15
  3 x 15
1 Pt 3

Lakewood Memorial Library
12 W. Summit Street
Lakewood, NY 14750

WITHDRAWN